THE MANIPULATOR

BOOK ONE: A PRIVATE LIFE
IN PUBLIC RELATIONS

BY

STEVE LUNDIN

Illustrations by Sam Booker, Jay Lynch,
Mitch O'Connell and Skip Williamson

BIGfrontier Books

A BIGfrontier Book

This is a work of fiction.

ISBN: 0615964559

Printed in the United States of America

For all the friends, family and pets who left me
alone long enough to get this book done, thank you.

Ligner's Marketing Ethics

When facts and fictions are interpreted together a hybrid concept becomes the new reality: some truths will live and some will die.

PART ONE
LIGHT THE FUSE

CHAPTER ONE
Uncrossed legs

Chicago, IL: the offices of Mobile Vision Network (MVN)
Monday, December 18, 2017 9:00 AM

"*This is a joke*, right Vance? Where's the real presentation?" asked Sidney Brill, the only man in the corporate boardroom whose opinion really mattered. Brill, CEO of a startup that just received three billion dollars in venture funding to launch the world's first 24/7 mobile content network stroked his stylishly-stubbled chin with newly manicured fingers. Jack Vance had been in this unwelcome dog and pony audition so many times he could play out the rest of the meeting in his head. Explanations of strategies and executions were a complete waste of billable time. Why the companies that hired his agency didn't just sign checks and let him do his job baffled him. Everything he did worked, period. That's all they really needed to know. And in the end the prettiest clients took off their panties anyway. He always delivered, and how he did it was his own *God Damned business.* It wasn't out of fondness, but a grudging respect for an unmatched ability to sell and deliver the impossible that the marketing industry had nicknamed Vance "*the Manipulator.*"

"We're delivering an entire television network through mobile devices...the investors expect people to subscribe, Vance...to watch our programming, *not just one show.*"

"Really? You need more than a spoonful of fried rice to know you're at a Chinese restaurant, Sidney?"

"We've got dramas and news and comedies, remember? How long you think our money will last? When it's gone, it's gone and we've either got subscribers and ads or we're out of business. We can't gamble the whole thing on your idea Vance, what else you got?"

"Number one, I'm not joking Sidney. When I joke people laugh. Number two, why are you still calling this beast a *television* network! You think people are going to watch your shows in their living rooms?"

Brill stopped to catch his breath. He didn't expect to have this conversation in front of his board. He had worked too hard, come too far. This should be a smooth and orderly validation of why he was about to engage Vance's Blowfish Communications, not a blasted pissing match over an insane launch program. Brill sat down in his chair, exhaling loudly.

Despite having recently acquired a personal brand manager, Brill still looked every second of his 62 years. His venture-purchased silk Zegna suit and whitened teeth didn't emit enough of a glow to lop even a day off his appearance. He was getting too old for these boardroom smack downs and was about as capable of running a network as he was of running a thousand mile marathon. He needed Vance and his stable of marketing fire eaters to do this job for him. *So why the fuck was the man making it so God damned hard!*

"I'm listening," Brill said.

"You asked me for three things when you came into my office." Vance felt a soliloquy coming on.

"I asked for one."

"You asked for three and didn't know it."

"So what do I want?

"You want a program to spearhead the network launch, you want ads and subscribers and you want to change people's lives. *Some Will Die* does all that."

"That's four."

"Wait six months and the dinosaur networks will figure this out. You can always live off your TNT shares."

Jack Vance never hid his world view from clients; he had built two marketing firms around the philosophy of "buy in or fuck off." He wasn't being paid to agree or say yes unless someone in the room besides himself said anything of value. He had made companies with nothing into hot acquisition targets only to be kicked out of the celebration party for groping the wrong someone during a blackout drunk.

Today was a little different. There was a scale to be balanced with blood on both sides. Vance was Brill's curse and savior. He was the man who had proposed the series that resulted in Brill's recent termination from TNT and was also the man who ultimately got him the job of running the newly funded Mobile Vision Network (MVN).

Sidney Brill had been fired a month before his retirement for producing *"Cop Swap,"* a live reality show that followed city and country police officers who traded beats and patrol cars. On paper the appeal was clear: take big city cops, dump them in the 'burbs and watch what happens, live. Three innocent citizens were gunned down in a Schererville, Indiana mall by a Chicago cop during the first and only episode. Jack Vance had sold Brill on the idea. Vance was representing the maker of the famous "Jackhole" dual wield concealed shoulder holster system and correctly surmised that seeing a cop use the rig in action would do for the company what *Miami Vice* had done for Ray Ban Wayfarers. He was correct. Sales for the Jackhole went through the roof as quickly as Brill's career went down the toilet.

Following his firing Brill was looking down the loaded barrel of a late middle aged, virtually unemployable "life" of watching his savings diminish, houses get smaller and cars get older. Vance reemerged with an unlikely opportunity: the CEOship of a full-on mobile network play about to receive a pile of venture money. He helped Brill embellish his resume, dye his hair, get a tan, lose some weight and purchase "look at me" suits. He then connected him to the right people. The agreement didn't need to be verbalized: if Brill got the job Vance's marketing firm would be awarded the launch contract. Somehow Brill pulled off the best second act of anyone's life. MVN would be his swan song and his revenge. He just had to make it through the launch and one season.

"*Killing people* is changing lives, Vance?" Brill asked.

"It's voluntary. Someone can either lose weight or die trying. Consider the payoff. Remember *Biggest Loser, Survivor*? Stellar ratings with a sliver of the dramatic potential of *Some Will Die*. I'm giving you something that makes more than ratings Sidney, it makes history. And your name is all over it."

"Give us a couple of days..."

"I don't think so," Vance dramatically checked the time on his vintage stainless steel Blainpain Fifty Fathoms dive watch. "I'll give you until right now. Then it's off the table."

"You're asking for a lot of cash, Vance."

"Don't be a pussy Sidney. You're playing with other people's money."

Vance stood up and ran his eyes over MVN's Board of Directors, not that a roomful of obsequious toadies really mattered to him. He knew the only real influencer in a man's life was the woman who kept her legs crossed or the bank that said "no." And uncrossing legs was his métier.

Like all newly minted CEO's about to spend money, Brill had to prove himself to his board. They were more than just window dressing to appease the investors; they were embedded corporate reporters who would gleefully document his failures. The six men and women looked generally unsupportive. It was always safer to turn down a potentially successful controversial campaign in favor of a safe, mediocre one. He gave them the "I'd like your opinion look," as part of the game he felt pressured to play. MVN's CFO Marvin Scrum finally cracked under the pressure of the silence.

"The Fishman, Unicorn, Cooper and Kamen program guaranteed us at least a 3% market share or they'd return 10% of the first month's retainer. Will Blowfish give us any kind of assurance like that?" Scrum directed the comment at both Vance and Brill to document his concern for the company's interests on the room's built-in recording system. He knew that there was a connection between the two men and that Brill was going to hire Vance no matter how many other proposals were solicited. The whole brinksmanship charade was just a boardroom circle jerk, and only Vance and Brill were allowed to come.

Vance slithered across the spare conference room and looked down over Chicago. The city always appeared so much nicer from any elevation over 30 stories. He cracked a small vent, opened his silver cigar holder, extracted the remainder of a Cuban cigarillo that he had rolled in hash oil and puffed it to life with an Art Deco enameled DuPont lighter. One of the board members, probably the "communications expert" because he was wearing Gucci jeans and a fitted Michael Kors shirt, politely attempted to dissuade Vance from smoking.

"I'm not smoking, I'm giving you guys another five minutes," he said loudly, exhaling as much of the drug infused smoke into the room as he could. His only regret was that he hadn't soaked it in LSD 25.

Ten minutes later Vance was riding down the building's elevator with a $250,000 retainer check in his pocket. He always insisted on paper checks because he could hold them, show them off or post them everywhere if they were dishonored. He checked himself in the elevator's mirror. In the right dim light, at the well-worn age of 45, he still looked better than most guys of his vintage. His dark hair was thick enough to blow the right way in a convertible. He could bench press his own weight. His profile still retained enough sharp edges to offset the saggy pull of gravity on flesh. Vance knew a soft body reflected a soft head. In his game a tight look was an edge and the right mixture of truth and "reputational enhancement," opened doors and made deals.

He hit the building's lobby and pulled his North Face Kevlar weave overcoat tight, passing a large glossy metal MVN plaque, probably installed the night before. It was located right under the large *"Keep your phone on: it's the law"* signs that were everywhere these days. He stopped, put a visible thumbprint in the middle of the plaque and whispered "douche bags" as he exited the lobby to the street. The launch campaign was brilliant and everyone knew it, they just didn't want to admit that risky and scary paid better than safe and steady. This plan had been sitting in his pocket for seven years, waiting for the right home, and thanks to his relationship with Sidney Brill, it would finally see the outside of a desk drawer.

Vance had a system for developing campaigns quickly. No matter how drunk or stoned he was, or how outlandish a scheme seemed, he wrote it down. Over the years he had compiled hundreds of plans and programs that could be applied to market everything from fertilizer brownies to kelp loaf. Sidney Brill had just purchased a gambit scrawled on the back of a gin soaked napkin way back in 2010.

Vance's technique allowed him to measure his progress in consumption, not dreary conventional development meetings. Technically his investment in this piece of business consisted of one bottle of Boodles Gin, three phone calls and 90 minutes of acting. He looked down at the check confirming his belief that ideas were valueless until somebody else bought them.

CHAPTER TWO
A Pastry Chef in the Land of Swine

Chicago, IL, The Loop
Monday, December 18, 2017 9:45 AM

Vance walked east on Madison Street, towards his office in the Hancock Building, the best location that he could find after being marooned in Chicago. If he cut through the right streets in the Chicago Loop during one of his semi-blind drunk stupors it almost felt like being back in Manhattan. That is until he heard that unmistakable Chicago accent: a shrilly high pitched sputter that bumbled carelessly over every vowel like a 350 pound plumber working his ass to a middle seat at a ball game. There was nothing lyrical about it. That's why most home brewed actors, except those specializing in playing Chicago cops, worked slavishly to hide the true tenor of their vocal delivery.

He was still in shock over the whole New York debacle that had sent him to purgatory in this *Land of Swine.* Did he really deserve banishment from Manhattan for hiring a group of fighter jets for a promotional low pass over the Macy's Day Parade? *He was doing his job!* That God-damned thin-skinned New York Mayor Marjorie Stetson had permanently banned him from ever having a business or address in *his* city right after the stunt. It had come down to a personal deal: relocate to Chicago, Cleveland or Milwaukee and she wouldn't put him in jail. Vance knew she had been advised by his direct competitor, Roger Drab, of Drab and Associates. Getting Blowfish out of the way left the field open for Drab, not that it would improve their creative product. Drab and Associates still maintained an industry record for most Honorable Mentions and Bronzes.

That was three years ago, and the dust up over the incident had forced him to rebuild his marketing agency from scratch. He picked the best he could from amongst the high pitched sausage eaters of the Midwest and he felt like he had succeeded in building a team that could pry business away from either coast...one of these days.

His right ear vibrated and his groin muscles tightened for a second until he saw the words "Blowfish: Stanley Best" race across the field of view on his Oliver Peoples HUD glasses. Why couldn't it be Naomi? She was the one wet dream companion who would probably never join him while he was conscious. Naomi Stiles was *strictly business* and had been since the day he hired her.

The call was coming through his unregistered cochlear device, a multi-band cellular chip that he had implanted in his head by a lab in Cuba. The device could be utilized multiple ways: through a wireless phone or earpiece connection, or by using his skull as a sounding board with a signal piped directly into his ear. It wasn't legal in the United States. It was a cloaked, Off The Grid technology. Exactly five people in the world knew this most personal of numbers. He kept a traditional always-on, registered Smart Phone wrapped around his right wrist for incoming calls, because it was illegal to leave a phone at home or turn it off. How else would the NSA be able to maintain every citizen's exact location, at all times, for their own safety, of course.

Vance made most of his outgoing calls on one of the many disposable pre-ban burner phones he kept in his pocket. He had purchased 50 of the burners just days before the ban on owning anonymous numbers was enacted. His were all registered to King

Kong, Popeye, Hercules, Mary Poppins and John Doe. He answered the cochlear call by yanking on his right earlobe.

"Well?" Said Stanley Best, Blowfish COO.

"I've got a check for $250,000 in my pocket; down payment on the first month of the project."

"A paper check? Better cash it on the way over."

"I scanned it in the elevator. It's already in the account. I'll wipe my ass with the hard copy."

"And they bought the whole idea, even that *Some Will Die* death thing?"

"That's what we're selling Stanley. Without death, it's just another show on another content mill. Assemble the team in the War Room, I'll tell everybody myself." Vance shook his wrist, ending the call, and realized that he hadn't properly celebrated.

The Smart Phone on his wrist started vibrating as he passed restaurants and stores, his profile was being accessed by Near Field marketing devices that were triggered and sent local offers his way. He hated the way marketing had come to dominate the world and he responded to the always on, radio wave culture by remaining one technological step ahead of it.

He carried a small illegal jammer that would effectively shroud him. It was a $20,000 handmade lab unit, not one of the cheap models that the government routinely issued on the Black Market, designed to send out a notification signal when activated. He used his jammer with caution; going Off The Grid sent out a red flag. His device rendered a fuzzy signal, just enough to obscure him but not enough to create a warning. It also blocked all incoming calls. He turned it on, looking forward to a few drinks in private.

The Hard Rock Hotel on the corner of Michigan and Wacker Place lie just ahead of him. He pushed through the Hotel's revolving street door, turned sharply on the ancient marble floor and entered the bar area. He always found a full wall of alcohol a comforting feeling, knowing that its gallons of liquid magic could do everything from assuage guilt to turbo-charge brainstorming sessions.

A middle aged bartender swabbed the bar. His attempt at a pompadour and pork chop sideburns was more dark paint than hair. Vance idled up, slipped into a stool and asked for a triple Belvedere with a splash of absinthe. Hair Club Elvis checked his watch then looked back at his sole customer.

"Come back in two, we open at lunch."

"How about a drink now, Mr. Presley?" Vance pulled a 100 euro note out of his pocket and slid it over. "And keep the change." The bartender looked at it.

"That's about $15 U.S., right? Think I'll keep my job instead." Vance had the inimitable quality of being able to instantly size up someone's weakest point and exploit it in a manner guaranteed to beg, if not elicit a violent response.

"Keep it...for the real hairline fund." He left, pulled his flask out of his pocket and exited the Hotel, turning right, then North on Michigan Avenue.

Vance unscrewed the cap on a flask that bore the worn badge of the French Union Forces. It had belonged to his father who carried it during the early days of the First Indochina War. His dad, Benjamin Vance, had served as a U.S. technical advisor during the conflict. This flask saw combat from the jungles to the boardroom. Today it contained the last of Vance's home brew: a base of Balkan 176 vodka, La Fée Absinthe and Ritalin. He had switched from a gram of cocaine per flask to 100 mg of Ritalin when he turned 40, to keep his health in check.

Vance grew up in a household with parents whose professions were not dinner conversation. He pieced together a patchwork concept of what they did from the stories they related whenever they happened to be in the same country, at the same time and wound up under the same roof. His father travelled with weapons and was often away for months at a time, occasionally returning with a severe tan that ended at his beard line. They were either government agents or private security, up to sneaky stuff in other parts of the world. He told his classmates his father was a travelling salesman, hawking technology, and his mother an airline employee. It seemed to stick and was the first test of his ability to twist little facts into new truths that served his purposes.

His house was always full of the latest electronic gear, things that he read about in magazines or saw in movies. Some of the items weren't supposed to exist yet. He was the only kid in school who called friends on a satellite phone and watched the neighbor girl disrobe through second generation night vision binoculars. The situation allowed him to understand how technology could be both a key and a lock.

He was raised by a series of Eastern European housekeepers and spent most of his youth in the Washington DC area, save for summers when he was sent off to the Hargrave Military Academy in Chatham, Virginia. Vance entered the School of Media and Public Affairs at George Washington University to equip himself with the investigative tools to research and understand the difference between truth and perception. He grew fascinated with prevarication: both private and professional. As a student he was disciplined and exceptional for his first three years, until he became publicity manager of the *GW Hatchet* and discovered his voice.

The paper gave him something that was in diametric opposition to the cloistered secrecy of his childhood: public exposure. And he loved every second of it. He engineered publicity campaigns to boost the paper's circulation and organized protests that gained national press. The nature of the protests were irrelevant to him, the fact that he could make them happen was all that he found interesting. He was message agnostic. The job became his life and his grades suffered, moving his GPA from the top 1% of his class to a watery 93%. Respectable, but not what gets you a W2 from the *Washington Post.*

After graduation Vance took the best job he could find that allowed him to continue living in DC: he worked as a research assistant to the technology editor of the *Washington Times.* To his delight Vance found that he was the column's gatekeeper and was suddenly receiving everything from free laptops to private flights to the annual Consumer Electronics Show. As a lifelong technology freak and byte snob, he was in heaven.

While he may have only made $35,000 a year and didn't have the exposure of a byline, he enjoyed the spoils and access of a real "playa," courtesy of the wide open expense budgets of 1996's web 1.0 marketing firms. After attending enough private trade show parties and seeing his hosts enter the little rooms with the cocaine and the super-model hookers, Vance realized that while a press pass got him to the table, it didn't get him a plate of caviar. The newly minted Internet CEO's wanted exposure for their software, not their private lives.

Making the jump from press to marketing was easy. He found his guide in Johnny Shadow, a self-destructive PR boozer who worked for a New York firm and represented a handful of technology accounts. Shadow worked the press the old fashioned way, with drugs and bribes, sweetened with hints of access and sex. He had a mouth, guts and just enough of a sense of the dramatic to sell a story. What he didn't have was Vance's education, encyclopedic love of technology and innate promotional capabilities. Vance could instantly see a campaign where Shadow saw a press release. Shadow, thug-like in a peculiar American-Irish sort of way, was just smart enough to know that with the right tweaking, Vance would make one hell of an Agency lead account man. He was just the corporate comet Shadow needed as a companion for his own rise.

After a night of Red Bull and vodka shots with a 17 year old and his team of 14 year old drop outs celebrating the sale of their game company to LucasArts, Shadow was able to convince Vance to send the email that changed his life. At 4:45 AM, from an Aria Hotel room in Las Vegas located next to the E3 show, he sent a message to the *Washington Times* HR department:

"I resign effective immediately."

Within 24 hours Vance was sitting in a cube next to Shadow's at Rocket Trail PR in New York City, with the title of "Assistant Account Manager" scrolling across the screensaver on his 21 inch Trinitron monitor, and an extra $4,000 a month in his bank account. He was now a flack. Under Shadow's wing learned to tell women what they wanted to hear, out drink and out drug just about everyone in a room and make clients believe in miracles. It would be another 14 years before he opened his own firm and realized that employees like Johnny Shadow came with a price tag he'd never be willing to pay.

By the time Vance covered the ¾ of a mile walk from the Wrigley Building to the Hancock Building, the flask was empty and he was ready to issue orders to his staff. After all, there was a lot of work to be done and someone had to do it. God knows he had done the heavy lifting when he closed the deal this morning.

Vance entered his headquarters through the 175 East Delaware side. He tried to vary the routine as much as possible, sometimes even going in through one of the ground floor retail spaces and slipping through the back and out a service door. He had built his career on designing the most over the top, controversial marketing campaigns in the world and had no qualms on alienating certain demographics to capture others. His success had yielded death threats that seemed to persist after the last retainer check had cleared.

His campaign for PETA, declaring open paintball hunting season on anyone wearing a fur coat, had sparked protests outside his old Hudson Street offices in New York. Several hundred men and women wore their paint splattered furs in protest of the violence that his campaign created. The exposure helped him score sporting goods retailer Cabela's as a client. He didn't really take any of the threats seriously until his beloved Maserati Coupe exploded just minutes after he parked it.

That evening he told CNN's Nightfall host Gordon Basri, "People who wear fur should be able to afford better bomb-makers." The comment became the basis for a failed defamation suit against him by the National Fur Association. Shortly afterwards he picked up the North Face account and proceeded to promote goose down over fur as the ethical option to staying warm. When he found the tires on his replacement Maserati melted he ultimately gave up on the brand, switching to British cars. Driving Italian was just plain bad luck.

Blowfish Chicago, located in suite 2130, filled 11,000 square feet of the city's skyline. There were 11 offices, 14 cubes, a lunch room and a War Room. Vance didn't keep a personal office because he wouldn't acknowledge the fact that he was actually working in Chicago. He had a small leather chair, crafted for him by the good people at Herman Miller, which he rolled from room to room, parking himself on the corner of anyone's desk for a few hours to work.

Vance thought nothing of interrupting calls, conducting impromptu video conferences or spreading out over an employee's work space. After all, what could be more important than what he was doing? If the employees weren't an extension of his arms and legs, fingers and toes, there to amplify and execute his ideas, then what were they? He had attained success by hiring smart fists, not weak wrists.

The office lobby door flew open before Vance could put a hand on it and Stanley Best pushed him back into the hallway. Vance had hired Stanley as his VP/Director of Operations for three reasons: His bald head glistened nicely when tanned, he was very good at understanding people and Jack owed him under the 'get out of jail free' payback clause.

Best had been the New Jersey State Trooper who pulled Vance over on "suspicion" of vehicular manslaughter back in 2013. Both men knew that Vance, although under the influence of psychoactive mushrooms, had not caused the 96 year old woman in the car ahead of him to slide off an icy country highway and into a creek. She had slammed on her brakes, explaining why the rear bumper of her 1998 Tercel was embedded in the plastic front end of Vance's 2012 Aston Martin. They came to an understanding on the spot: Best would join Blowfish as the new VP at a salary four times what he made as a trooper with the Aston Martin as his company car, and Vance would take a cab back to Manhattan.

Best sniffed dramatically. "Hell of a time for a drink, Jack."

"Am I driving, officer? Fuck you, Stan. I just made our numbers for the year. Where are the balloons and the music?"

"Not today Jack. The Western Air account just went south because of that stunt you pulled flour bombing the Panama Canal."

"*Ungrateful fucktards*. It was international news! In ten seconds, everyone knew they were opening new Latin American routes."

"The Panamanians are suing Western and barring them from landing at any airports."

Vance pondered the question for a second.

"Fuck them too. We'll pitch Panama Air on a campaign to keep the Gringos from monopolizing Latin American travel and open some gates for them in the U.S. Now where the hell is everybody?"

"In the War Room, wondering if you're going to have enough money to pay their salaries."

"*The money thing again?* This place is starting to feel like a marriage! Let's go Stan. In two weeks you chickens will be shooting yourselves for not taking Blowfish stock options instead of salaries when you had the chance." Vance pushed past Best into his offices; it was time to start earning that retainer.

CHAPTER THREE
Team Playas

Chicago, IL, Blowfish Offices in the Hancock Building
Monday, December 18, 2017 10:30 AM

Missy Slats tried her hardest to get Vance's attention as he blew past her receptionist's desk into the Blowfish offices. Every single day she piled a neat stack of handwritten messages, complaints and issues that needed to be resolved, and made sure that he knew they were in her possession, waiting for his response. She sometimes wondered, when she rode back on the CTA bus, how many of these missives were deleted or shredded. No one told her when one client was added and another deleted or who the hush-hush people were when they slipped by her desk into private conference rooms. It was supposed to be her job to know everything in an office, but she felt like she knew nothing about Blowfish or the flashy, outrageous Jack Vance. And that wasn't right.

There he is again, she thought, covering his boozy stench with a whore's bath of cologne and hand sanitizer. Today is going to be different. Today, he is going to read his messages in front of her and she will watch his eyes and study his reactions and then she will know something that no one else does. She'll discern secrets, because that's what a receptionist is supposed to do. According to the week's scuttlebutt if he didn't bring home a winner, her paycheck would bounce. His eyes would tell if that was going to happen when he read those messages. If they were going under she'd walk away with no regrets, save for the fact that she'd be the only woman in the office without grounds for a sexual harassment suit. Sometimes she felt like she'd been panning for lead during a gold rush.

Vance glanced over at Missy the Receptionist as he entered the office. She was a valuable 300 pound manatee that he hired solely to get an SBA minority business development loan when he was "relocated" to Chicago. He silently thanked her fat ass every time he walked past her desk. She qualified Blowfish for minority, female and disabled status in one fell swoop. On paper he was running a noble business with an open door hiring policy. He couldn't tell if today's agitated waving was any more significant than any other day, but the flask had made him feel all warm and charitable, so he stopped on his way to the team meeting.

"Missy, you look..."

"Lovely today? Pretty? Almost like someone you'd like to kiss?"

"Concerned. Very concerned. What's the message?"

"Mr. Bozoz has been calling. Athena's merchandise delivery drones were hacked and started crashing into people in Seattle. He says the press is calling him a *death from above book terrorist* and wants some crisis help." She handed him a stack of notes. He accepted them and immediately slid them all into the shredder installed in the front of her desk, just for such occasions. Disguised as a locked mail chute, it was situated right below the Blowfish tagline: *Truth is overrated.*

Vance wasn't going to let his freight train ride through the morning be shunted to a side track for something like a stack of paperwork. If he didn't keep one step ahead of the drugs and alcohol, he was lost. He put on his nicest, not-too-nice face. He didn't need this fatty attempting to file some kind of trumped up harassment suit against him like the rest of the gold diggers in the office.

"Call Mr. Bozoz back and let him know that Blowfish thinks he is a *book terrorist* and we'll provide free marketing services to any public library that asks for it. Have someone put a release out on that. He thinks he's got a crisis now, just wait until we throw a little napalm on his marshmallow roast." He continued to the War Room with Stanley Best.

Vance had poured a half million dollars of Blowfish profits into his tech playground conference center, officially known as the War Room. It could impress the ghost of Steve Jobs. He approached its large double glass doors and placed his hand onto a biometric pad. The doors slid open with a swoosh sound lifted from the audio files of the first season of the original "Star Trek." A hailing whistle from the same show announced his presence.

The War Room ate up 1500 square feet of his offices. He had purchased the suite on the floor above, knocked out the ceiling and added its space to accommodate the Room's technology. The Room had been designed by a Hollywood set artist to look like a cross between a CIA drone control center and the bridge of the Death Star. It was ringed with projectors that tracked news and Blowfish initiatives, providing a real time global base of operations for all campaigns.

The images appeared on a shimmering translucent cloud that filled the top of the room with a dynamic media hive of information. The cloud itself was formed by multiple streams of gas that could be colored, heated, stirred up, scented or instantly evacuated. As a test Vance had once superheated, then immediately cooled it, sending red waves of drizzle and hail down on his employees. Several 3D printers were situated around the room because Vance felt that sometimes you had to actually hold an idea to fully understand and help it evolve.

The central conference table was an interactive white board with an algorithm that had been programmed to reflect Vance's thinking. It responded to conversations in the room. "Good" ideas, those that Vance himself might have thought of, were automatically stored and the creator received an additional day of pay. Conversely, "bad" ideas were deleted and the author's pay was docked a day. Enough bad ideas could cost a job, with the newly unemployed technically owing Blowfish money. Most approached the white board with trepidation. However, participation at least once during every meeting was mandatory. Vance knew his staff could handle the pressure, or they wouldn't have Blowfish sigs.

Vance crossed the room to his control chair at the head of the table. It was loosely modeled after Number Two's chair from the 1960's BBC television program *The Prisoner*. The table held eight other chairs and represented all the key elements of his agency. His executive staff was known as the Group of Eight: Naomi Stiles, Psy Ops, Stanley Best, COO, Tom Agness, Associate Strategist, Bill Neville, Public Relations Director, Jimmy Welles, Account Group Supervisor, Peggy Bump, CFO, Jason Mayhew, Content Coordinator and himself, of course. He knew the Big Questions racing through the collective intelligence of his executive staff: What happened with the pitch? How large was the contract? What did they buy? And everyone's favorite: Are we getting paid this week?

"Don't everyone talk at once," Vance chided the group.

He looked to his right at the only staffer who wasn't waiting like a twitchy pug dog on a blue cheese burger: Jason Mayhew. The former *Chicago Sun-Tribune* reporter had won a Pulitzer Prize for breaking the Ari Elohim Chicago mayoral scandal case and immediately refused to write another sentence for any publication, ever. He explained obtusely to anyone who asked about it, "what's the point of getting another boner when you've already slept with the prettiest girl in the world?" As Blowfish's Content Coordinator his one responsibility lie in making sure that every word leaving the agency sounded right, true or not. Diabetic, overweight, pushing 60 and wearing a shirt that doubled as a napkin for pig outs at KFC, he slavishly poured over his daily obsession: reviewing the *Sun-Tribune* for errors.

"You will be paid Friday and..." Before Vance could finish, the room burst into conversation, his Group of Eight collectively returned to life.

"And we have a new client." Vance touched his Smart Phone and a scan of the $250,000 check filled the Cloud. "This is just for the remainder of the month."

Vance was convinced that Naomi Stiles had come all the way from her birthplace in Liverpool, England for one reason, to be his personal carrot, so near yet so incredibly far out of reach. In his eyes she was a black haired, tanned, flawless living definition of his life mate: smart, somewhat funny and just ruthless enough to scare the hell out of anyone who got in her way. He knew that under his tutelage he could break down her stubbornness to the two things that stood between them: himself and her bothersome concept of high personal ethics. She was just too damned much of a good guy for Vance. But he had faith in his ability to corrupt absolutely. There was a Natasha inside her just waiting to join his Boris.

Stiles was Blowfish Chicago employee number three and believed Vance's business chatter when it was backed up with one thing: money. The only reason that she had put up with his bullshit, from drunken gropings to hiding a spy cam under her desk, was his uncanny ability to talk clients into campaigns and then paying her to execute them. She was the former Regional Director of Psy Ops for Google. Vance liked her title so much that he allowed her to keep it when he seduced her into resigning from being a corporate spook to working at Blowfish. She was the only member of the Blowfish G8 privy to the MVN campaign pitch and knew at least two people in the agency would resign upon hearing the plan. It was her job to keep Stu Gould, corporate counsel, on speed dial. She depressed a small button on the arm of her chair. A big question mark appeared on the table in front of her. She knew her part.

"What campaign will we be conducting for our new client?"

Vance stood up and waved his right arm. The cloud floating above the room turned all angry and red and three black words slowly dissolved onto its soft, ethereal form: *SOME WILL DIE.*

CHAPTER FOUR
Scorned and Scorched

Chicago, IL, Blowfish Offices in the Hancock Building
Monday, December 18, 2017 10:50 AM

Vance enjoyed any opportunity to tease his little crowd into an intellectual orgasm. A fire hose of adrenaline blasting through his body was the only thing keeping his booze and alcohol jellied spine from collapsing when he stood at the head of the War Room table. He was in his element as the tightrope walker, and this campaign was a high wire act that would either make Blowfish the hottest property in the county or a valueless home business, staffed with Craigslist part timers. This was going to be his second sale of the day.

"*Some Will Die* is a reality game show and the critical centerpiece of the launch strategy for MVN Online. It will be a controversial gaper's delay. It will be polarizing. It will cause pain and suffering and debates. We're going to turn obesity into the life or death lifestyle decision that it really is. And we're going to offer our new viewers something they've never seen before. People... dying... to lose weight."

Vance let his words percolate around the room. As he spoke, the War Room's custom software algorithm ran images that reflected what he was saying: people stuffing their faces with food, lying in the hospital on heart monitors and everyone's favorite, funerals.

One of the 3D printers spat out a blob of fat based on a photo from a medical website.

"Is that it? We're launching a whole network around one show?" asked Mayhew.

"It's *how* we're launching that will make the entire network a must-watch. This *one show* is the major teaser."

Tom Agness, Blowfish Associate Strategist, employee number nineteen, and a recent member of the Group of Eight by virtue of a firing, had heard this puffery before. Vance up-sells a client on some wild scheme then delivers a stunning two months of work before his ADHD kicks in and turns his head in a different direction. Agness had been dragged through more "world upending" campaigns than anyone deserved. Most worked, but the toll they exacted on everyone was hardly worth the salary. His boss was the only one in the room driving a new Bentley.

Despite his misgivings, Agness felt that he was being groomed for second in command, even if Vance hadn't admitted it. He carried Vance's same penchant for self destruction and occasionally showed flashes of true strategic insight. He even looked uncannily like a 35 year old version of a 45 year old Vance. But Agness saw one big obstacle lying (with open legs he assumed) across his career superhighway: Naomi Stiles. For every "good idea, here's a bottle of single malt" that Agness was awarded, she received a bonus. And not just any bonus. *The bitch* had taken trips around the world, drove a two year old Mercedes CLK, and lived in a condo without a mortgage. Agness *goddamn* well knew her trappings were courtesy of Blowfish.

He was counting on Vance closing the MVN deal, paying out a big Christmas bonus and knighting him with the title of Senior Strategist. Now it was happening. He could make his move out of Blowfish the second week of the New Year when agencies started hiring again. No one at any other shop in the city would question why Agness wanted to beam out of Vance's loopy starship. Three years and five different business cards would pay off as soon as he had a little walking around money and the moniker "Senior" in front of his name. That title was his ticket out the door, without it he was just another churn-and-burn mid level grunt. Vance would expect his comments now, to prove that he was engaged and was a "team playa." He knew the part well.

"Let's look beyond the death issue Jack...aren't reality shows a little dated? Kind of 2002? If we're pegged as '*Biggest Loser* meets the *Island of Dr. Moreau*' the only thing people will be dying of is laughter." He leaned back in his chair, arms folded in the healthy skepticism a "Senior Strategist" should exhibit. The cloud filled with images of Marlon Brando and Val Kilmer from the most recent *Dr. Moreau* film.

Vance knew Agness was in it for the money, treading water until a better job or a bigger bonus came along. The aggressive little smart ass he hired from the Lee Burnout agency three years ago had turned from a potential star into a toadying "maybe" man. Vance didn't like to see his employees compete for anything but business, especially one who looked like his twin brother. He hated crack kissers or those who made a career out of ladder climbing.

Vance had tried to wring the cancer of Big Agency brainwashing out of Agness but the experiment had failed. The man-boy's zeal for corporate ascension landed him at the big table, but it was the title he was looking for to make his resume float upstream. Jumping from mid-level at Burnout to Senior Strategist at Blowfish made him look like one hell of a shooting star, at least on paper. Vance looked at him for a cool second, sat back down in his chair and handed his employee the rope.

"You don't like it, Tom? What's your solution? Run with it. We'll toss out the whole program. Give us a better one. Wrap it around a new strategy." Vance knitted his fingers, something he did exactly once a year, usually around Christmas. It meant only one thing.

"A better one? I don't know your strategy yet. I'd have to do some...market analysis, some research..."

"If my program sucks my whole plan probably sucks too. Toss it all. Ohhh...but wait! The client paid for an answer today Tom. TO-DAY. We don't have time for any research. The network is launching early next year. You're a strategist. Give me what I hired you to deliver. *Give me a strategy.*"

Agness looked at Vance and suddenly felt very transparent. *Did he fucking know?* This couldn't be happening now. The timing was all wrong. Besides that he had a date tonight and wanted to borrow Vance's Bentley. Vance snapped his fingers.

"We sold a program wrapped around *Some Will Die*, Tom. Give me a better play or you're the first victim."

"I don't know the play...what is it?"

"You don't need to know it. I want your ideas. Spit it out or leave."

"Leave? Leave where?"

"Home, a bar, your next office. Wherever. Anywhere that doesn't involve staying here."

"And if I have a better idea I can stay?"

"Ten seconds Tom."

"So you're firing me?"

"That the best you got? *Another question?*"

"It's almost Christmas and you're firing me?"

"What does a Jew care about Christmas?"

"What the hell does that mean Jack? You're Jewish now? We're pitching a matzo company next?"

"Answers not questions Tom."

The room went quiet the moment Vance started "knitting." There had been a blood-letting every year around Christmas since Blowfish Chicago opened, but no one could ever prepare for it. The moment of flinching had passed. The needle was entering the skin.

"Give me a little time and I'll get it."

For the second time in the same morning Vance consulted his watch for dramatic emphasis.

"You have until right now. Give me an answer or give me your key card." Vance pressed a button on the arm of his chair, signaling Chuck Giletti, Vance's bodyguard/security guard/chauffer, to enter the room. Agness stood when he saw Giletti march in, Taser at the ready. Vance pulled a $100 euro note from his pocket.

"Here's your severance. Get your suit cleaned for that interview with Edelberg next week."

"Who told you about *Edelberg*?" Giletti took Agness' arm. Vance pulled his flask from his pocket, remembered it was empty and slid it back.

"You did, when you started worrying more about being a shill than a star. With an attitude like yours you'll fit in at any big agency in the city."

Agness felt flushed and dizzy and nauseous as he made his way towards the door, knowing that Giletti would Taser him at any given opportunity. He had seen it happen before. This was not good. He turned, feeling compelled to throw the obligatory "fuck you asshole, take a napalm bath" epitaph into the room and saw Vance, arms folded, waiting impatiently for the predictable. Agness straightened and looked directly at his about-to-be former boss.

"Keep the keys to this Monkey House, Jack. I'll own your mortgage before we're through."

This wasn't the first "I'll be back" Vance had received from a terminated employee. He had absolute faith that Agness would slip back into the corporate urinal and wind up just another deodorant cake, waiting to be pissed on. But as a concession to his avuncular instincts he felt compelled to leave Agness with some advice that might serve him in his journey through life.

"Go find your O.J., Kato."

Agness turned and left the room, his mind ticking away on a retort that didn't beat his journey to the door.

Mayhew looked up from his paper.

"Vance is kind of an unusual Jewish name."

"I didn't say I was Jewish. I asked him what a Jew cares about Christmas. If he listened to the question and answered it I might have let him stay through the New Year."

"So a riddle then."

"Like everything around here Mayhew. Now, what's your take on *Some Will Die*? I'm just getting warmed up."

CHAPTER FIVE
Some Will Die

Chicago, IL, Blowfish Offices in the Hancock Building
Monday, December 18, 2017 11:00 AM

Vance let the room settle for a silent 60 second "fired employee wake" before resuming his presentation. The good alcohol and drugs in his system did their calming work. He pulled a bottle of twelve year old Laphroig single malt scotch from a compartment next to his knee, twisted the cap, took a slow pull and passed it to Mayhew on his right.

"I'm not going to start drinking over Tom Agness. Let's get on with the program."

Mayhew passed to bottle to CFO Peggy Bump, who promptly passed it along to Jimmy Welles. Bump wanted answers, not alcohol.

Peggy Bump was comfortable with her 2017 investment strategies. What Vance squandered on RFP's and expense overages she had made up in the market. But she didn't need the fringe benefits and adoration like that little Brit tart Naomi Stiles. Oh, Bump could play that game if she wanted to, dress all leggy and breasty, but that wasn't the job of a CFO. She'd continue to wear her concealing business suits in the summer and high collared sweaters in the fall as long as Blowfish remained profitable and she kept her piece of the black ink. The $250,000 that Vance just delivered into her corporate chest guaranteed she'd stick around for at least the first quarter of 2018.

"Now Mr. Vance, what specifically are we delivering, how much time do we have and who are we assigning to this account?" Bump asked, staring owlishly.

Trust it to his matronly CFO to ruin the mood. Vance thanked God the doughy, dowdy spreadsheet queen kept her ever-widening girth properly covered, unlike that unbuttoned Missy Slats woman parked at the front desk. He pushed his business brain ahead of the reptile to respond to her questions. It was time to play CEO again.

"We have 48 days, a little over six weeks. And everyone's involved."

"Six weeks to launch a whole network? Why six weeks? This is a six month job with a staff three times what we've got," Mayhew commented, returning to his paper.

"We won't need the staff and we won't need more time. The date is the key. We've got the element of surprise, that's all we'll need. *Some Will Die* will make MVN the biggest thing in the history of communication."

Naomi Stiles felt uncomfortable being quiet during this morning "meeting." She knew that Vance was a gambler, but this program had the hallmarks of a do-or-die scenario. "All the personnel" meant that other accounts would be shorthanded and jeopardized. Vance was the kind of guy who would dump steady income like an out-of-date suit to focus on something that he thought would bring in even bigger fish. She nursed this agency through too many bad decisions to see it happen again.

"Everybody's asking the same question, Jack. What's the whole program?"

Vance stood, unsteadily. He picked up his bottle of scotch from the middle of the table, took another sip then sat back down, forgetting why he had stood up in the first place. The adrenaline rush of firing Agness had worn off.

"Let's start with the show, and then we'll discuss the launch. We're taking all the elements that have ever worked and amping them up a notch. Our show begins with a group of morbidly obese contestants..."

"Visually attractive morbidly obese contestants, right?" Jimmy Welles, the youngest member of the Blowfish G8, itched to add some value to the conversation. Welles was from Cleveland and felt that moving to Chicago was *making it*. He was probably the only person in the entire agency who paid for his own education, at Ohio State no less, working short cons and cards. In his mind his Asian/African-American heritage made him a natural Ninja Brother.

He kept a running tab on the number of actionable contributions that he made to the Agency and used his spreadsheet to solicit on-the-spot bonuses from both Vance and Peggy Bump. He was a ladder crawler like Agness, but wasn't afraid to get his hands dirty and demand quid pro quo results. He knew Vance would take an honest crook over a dishonest "saint" any day of the week. Welles was officially a Group Account Supervisor and unofficially Vance's hatchet man. Vance handed Jimmy the bottle knowing that he'd drink it to maintain solidarity.

"Attractive and obese only works when you throw in pregnancy. How about we just say we're looking for the bright shiny Twinkie buried under all that ugly Crisco?" Vance responded.

"Okay, we get the part about the fat people, how about the dying?" Stiles demanded, goosing the process along.

"We start with hyper-local auditions for entrants. The ticket for admission is simple: high weight and low self-esteem. Contestants have to be at least 300 pounds overweight and need to lose half their fat...in six weeks."

"Six weeks?" Stiles hissed in a nasty tone no one could miss.

"It's not called *Some Will Live* now is it? The contestants will sign a waiver indicating that they're willing to die trying to lose that weight. Here's the kicker: *we're going to try and kill most of them.* We just need the right drill sergeant/sadist type to keep the activities rolling. Josef Mengele meets Jillian Michaels."

Bill Neville, a 6'2" suburban shaved head ultra marathoner was used to Vance's hyperbole. The man at the head of the table would talk about causing a train wreck but deliver a fender bender. After two years at Blowfish he learned to look past the cover and read the fine print. As the Public Relations Director, Neville was concerned with the actual delivery of a product. Vance could razzle-dazzle a boardroom, but the general public was another story.

"So Jack, from a PR standpoint, what's the message, what's the motivation, what's the emotional connection with the brand?"

"Ask me a question worth answering Bill. We don't have time for your marketing mish-mosh talk this morning."

"What's in it for anyone who manages to survive this... public bloodbath?"

"Paradise! Five million bucks! The American dream, right? *No imagination needed.* Complete our rigorous, nationally televised, 24/7 total public humiliation contest and live like a rock star for six months in Hawaii, Fire island, Vietnam. Hell, whatever your flavor, sky's the limit. We feed every need, indulge every whim. Fast cars, boats, want to date an actress? Sleep with..."

"We get it." Stiles stood up now, bugged by something. Vance continued, ignoring her.

"We *Truman Show* that program as well. If they manage to survive it they keep the lifestyle for two whole years."

"And you'll be throwing every temptation under the sun at them" Jimmy Welles offered, seeing the program taking shape.

"Every day of that six months. I expect to lose the winners to drug addiction, alcoholism, STDs, dangerous lifestyles, you name it." He looked at Stiles, "That's where the screening for low self-esteem comes in. We'll have a nice betting site on every aspect of this program and make some tidy offshore money." Vance paused, he had this.

"And the follow up show is called *Some More Will Die.*" He was ready to let his brain trust do a little work. Between the excitement of closing this morning's deal followed by a constant stream of drugs and alcohol, the firing of Tom Agness and the presentation to his Group of Eight, now seven, his middle aged body was ready to listen for a few minutes. On top of that, the room was starting to spin.

"Any questions?" he asked before sliding down into the cool, climate controlled, leather cushioned embrace of his chair. Bill Neville raised his hand.

"Not a question, a comment. I have been through a lot of campaigns with this Agency, several coming close to what I would call ethical breaches. But this..."

"This what, Bill? You don't like the *message?*"

"No. I hate it. I can't work on it."

"So my Director of PR doesn't want to PR our biggest account?"

Vance saw an annoying faux-priest-like look of un-approval cross Neville's bony face and wondered if that was something they taught in PR school or he learned at church. That's what he got for hiring a guy who coached soccer for Special Olympics on the weekends. Blowfish wasn't the kind of place you worked at if you believed in things like higher powers or finding absolute truth, or ethics.

"It's a career killer, Jack. I can't touch this."

"Ethics are just an excuse for a *lack of creativity* Bill."

"You calling me uncreative now Jack? Because I don't want to frigging march desperate gullibles into the grave?"

"Save the press conference for your Priest, Bill. If you're too good to work on our BIGGEST DAMN ACCOUNT EVER then go work for God. Maybe he'll give you a *Christ*-mas bonus for being such an ethical guy. I'll have Peggy give you a month's pay and you can keep your stock. It's the ethical thing to do."

"So I'm fired over this?"

"Leave your key card with HR on the way out and follow that higher calling. *Vaya con dios.*"

Bill Neville had been waiting for the moment to give his farewell speech for months now. It was just like Vance to pour Jello on his campfire. Leaving this place would feel like walking from a urine shower into a rainforest. At least he wasn't being Tasered out like Agness. He stood up, looked around the room for any moist eyes and realized that he probably wasn't going to be missed. Neville felt no words within himself. Giletti appeared at the door, this time holding it open. Neville turned and walked quietly out of the room. Vance shouted at him as he left:

"And don't forget that NDA you signed. A peep of this goes any- where and our attorney, *Mr. Gould*, will be giving your attorney, Mr. *I'll-have-to-Google-somebody*, a call."

Vance knew that Neville lacked the killer instinct that would take Blowfish to the next level; it was just a matter of time before he walked. Next round, he'd get a psychoanalyst to screen his ap- plicants more closely. True public relations is an art form that re- quires a disposition to socio-pathological behavior and Neville just never had that gene. He'd handle the press himself on this one. It was good that this happened now, today, before they got started. Better to let the weak get run over on the country roads before jumping on the Autobahn.

Vance took stock of the remnants of his team: Stiles, Jimmy Welles, Peggy Bump, Mayhew, Stanley Best and himself. It was a group of six now and it time to execute. He looked at Mayhew.

"I need the right face in front of this. Someone who represents toughness, fitness, bad assed-ness. Someone with no problem working people to death. Suggestions?"

The War Room cloud slowly populated with images from Rance Livestrong to Ronald Albany, reflecting the question that Vance had posed. Jimmy Welles raised his hand.

"Phil Schlongberg." An image popped up and the program created a list of professional wrestlers. Schlongber's bio populated the screen.

"Jose Bravura," offered Bill Mayhew. Vance looked over at him.

"Do I see a theme here? These guys are about as controversial as gummy worms."

Vance's view of the room was getting blurry; a combination of his recreational ingestions and the actual work that had to be conducted on the candidate had extinguished what was left of his waning adrenaline flow. His head was heavy, so he let it rest in his hands. Then his hands became heavy so he placed the side of his face on the cool surface in front of him. The level of conversation rose in the room and he closed his eyes, just for a second.

Vance awoke and was able to work one eye open. The room was murky and he was looking down on himself. There he was, in full living color, barking out orders at his War Room desk, drunkenly weaving back and forth. He focused on what he was saying, rather belching, and couldn't believe what a douche bag he looked like. He saw the gravity of life pulling down at his face; the development of a slight stoop and paunch. *He was getting old and he was only 45!* Now it made sense: he was dead! If this is how he was going through life, drunken and idiotic, maybe it was better that he was gone.

He was about to close his eyes and surrender to eternity when a thunderclap of laughter slapped him in the side of the face. He opened his other eye and raised his head. He was in the War Room and his staff was watching their secret Jack Vance blooper reel. He cleared his throat. The laughing ceased and the cloud cleared, only to be re-populated with visual acres of charts, psychographic information and lists of candidates with bios and photos.

He offered a weak, "having fun?"

"Working for you is always a hoot," Stiles responded.

"We have our candidate," Mayhew said.

"Based on the criteria of overall appeal, ratings, proximate age..."

"I don't care how you got there. Who?"

"Vladimir Berber."

"Who?'

Naomi Stiles touched the table and the cloud filled with an image of a roguish mid 30's tough guy who could have been peeled from the cover of any Executioner pocketbook cover.

"You don't watch much TV for a *Public Relations Director*. Maybe you hired the wrong guy. He is the ex-Soviet army drill instructor who accidentally killed a fellow contestant on Survivor Chernobyl a couple years ago. Ring a bell?" Vance was waking up.

"That I remember." An unusual wave of natural euphoria washed over him. It was strangely pleasant, invigorating. He was suddenly more awake than he had been all month. They got it. *They really got it.* They bought the concept and amplified it. What was left of his executive team had coalesced, like a well concocted beaker of poison, into the essence of what Blowfish represented: unbridled ideas.

"I fucking love it. You all get a raise... if this pans out." Vance pulled himself up, tried to stand, and then decided to conduct business from a prone position for a few more minutes. He looked at his watch: 2:30 PM. He had been out for over three hours and felt like he had been turned inside out and run over by a truck. He needed some Oxy.

"There's only one hitch, Jack," Stiles added, the cloud populating with news stories. "He's in jail in Mexico on a manslaughter charge."

Vance's head filled with the opportunities that this new twist offered.

"Even better! We're going to very publicly get him out for the show. This isn't a setback, it's a ratings boost. We'll turn this fire-fly into a Roman Candle in 24 hours."

Mayhew ruffled his bowtie, a habit as annoying as the neckwear itself.

"And who is going to do that?"

"Our lawyer, Giletti, and the PR guy."

"You?" Stiles wrinkled her nose.

"Lawyers, guns and media. Get me a charter to Mexico and that Panasonic Lumix with the FX sensor and the good mic. We take off this afternoon."

"What about the rest of the launch program, Jack?" asked Mayhew.

"We'll go over it when I get back. Trust me, if you don't like what you hear I'll give you permission to quit."

Vance ended the meeting and exited to his private bath where he spent the next fifteen minutes alternating between drinking water out of the tap and vomiting.

CHAPTER SIX
Living the Life

Chicago, IL, Westin Hotel Bar on Michigan Avenue
Monday, December 18, 2017 3:00 PM

Tom Agness would have been happy with just a single returned call or acknowledgment from any one of the countless agencies, headhunters and industry associates he had spent the afternoon attempting to contact. He sat in the window of the Westin bar across the street from the Blowfish offices waiting for Vance to emerge, drinking what was left of his Blowfish corporate Amex card before it was shut off. Let that picky little dowager Peggy Bump classify this under the *'fuck you Jack'* expense category when she got the bill. Agness was sure she had one.

He unwrapped his flexible Smart Phone from his arm and stretched it out over the counter, summoning up a listing of his accounts. His live-for-the moment lifestyle played out in numbers. He had less than 10 grand in credit, a couple more in the bank and was looking at a $7K nut due over the next seven days. Between his condo payment, Certified Pre-Owned BMW payment, Harley payment, student loans, credit card payments and the $30 a month he put towards savings, Agness needed a new income stream fast. The firing had come at a completely inopportune time. No one was hiring associate *anything* over the holidays. He came to the conclusion several drinks ago that at this point his only real chance lay in finding a buyer for Blowfish intel and that meant one agency: the loathed *Drab and Associates*. He tapped out a number on the pad of his unrolled phone.

"Drab and Associates," a chirpy woman answered.

"This is Tom Agness again, is Mr. Drab free yet?"

"I gave Mr. Drab your earlier messages, Mr. Agness, is there someone else you'd like to speak with?"

"No, just tell him..."

At that moment Agness spied Vance and Giletti leaving the Hancock Building like a pair of hermit crabs exiting their shells. He ended the call, flagged down his waitress and pulled out the fancy Dunhill slim folding wallet that Vance had given everyone, including himself, as a Christmas present last year. The wallet was 1mm thick and held exactly four micro credit chips and a driver's license. Agness swiped the Amex chip and signed for a $1200 bar bill, adding a $500 tip. He slipped the chip into her hand.

"Go buy yourself something nice across the street," he nodded in the direction of Neiman Marcus, winked, watched her eyes widen, then grabbed her and gave her a deep kiss. She didn't resist. A little more time and privacy and that tip might turn into...but he had business to do. He hailed a cab just as Vance and Giletti entered one, confident that this pursuit would add to his small pile of intellectual currency.

Vance blew his directions at the driver as he slid into the cab.

"We need to pick someone up at 200 south LaSalle, and then out to O'Hare. And turn down that music, please. See the sign?" Vance pointed at the "passenger rights" sticker while the man punched the destination into his GPS. A cabbie who couldn't navigate an address less than a mile away was probably part of former Chicago Mayor Ari Elohim's *Right to Drive* program.

The doomed initiative allowed anyone from any country with a foreign cab driver's license to become a US citizen by driving for the City of Chicago's new fixed rate city taxi service for a year. Elohim lost the next election by a landslide, thanks to the investigative work of Vance's own Jason Mayhew, who found a clear trail of payoffs leading to a French taxi company and a sweetheart deal with the immigration and naturalization service. Elohim had been attempting to reshape the city in his own version of Paris, for reasons known only to him. The cab program was one jeté over the line. Chicago's sausage eating Grabowski population didn't take kindly to the loathed "Surrender Frog" service driven by a sudden influx of Frenchman. Elohim had since relocated to Cleveland where he ran a successful ballet school for boys.

Vance tapped his Smart Phone and rang up Stu Gould, his longtime pub slithering partner and the Blowfish corporate attorney. Gould was another of the five people Vance trusted with his cochlear personal number.

"Got anything cooking this afternoon, counselor?"

"Heeey, Buddy. Testing a new Jag over at Continental then heading out on Joel's boat. He's got a hottie lined up. 42 year with great tits, looks 38..."

"Be downstairs to pick you up in five. Got a job, double time for you."

"Double standard hourly?"

"Yeah. As of now, start the clock."

"How long? Joel's launching at 5:00. I just picked up the Belvedere."

"Bring it along. We'll need it. Wear a suit, tropical. And your passport, grab it."

"Suit? We're doing business? Love me some *biness!*"

Jack hung up and called Naomi Stiles. She had already secured a charter to Mexico. The trip, with a jet standing by to take them back, would eat $50,000 of the check that he received earlier that morning. He would have to pay Gould another ten grand for his time. The expenses were eating into profits, and that was something no Agency Man could tolerate. Vance rang Sidney Brill at MVN.

"Sidney? It's Vance. Listen, the program is coming along and we've found our host. Only thing is he needs an advance. And we have some expenses. That's right, already. We move fast. I need 70 K transferred to my account. I'll have Naomi Stiles send the numbers over." Pause. "The 250 was for the idea Sidney, and moving the ball to this point; for the intellectual property that you will own. The additional 70 is for making it happen." Pause. "Steep? We're just getting started. I can always return the money and we'll sell the idea to someone else, like NBC." Pause. "Okay. Yes we need the cash today. Yes I will keep you posted. Yeah, bye."

Every client played the little 'oh, I didn't know that wasn't part of the retainer' game when it came to expenses. God, Vance was sick of it. Did they think the ideas were free? He wasn't being paid to deliver the same kind of meat and potatoes tripe that was the bread and butter of most agencies. As far as Vance was concerned he was going to make MVN into a household name and that was worth almost every penny of the venture money his client had just received. Balking at expenses? He just threw the flag up on the meter and they were about to drive from New York to LA. *Get ready to spend...muthafucka.*

Gould was predictably late, emerging from his office ten minutes after scheduled. As usual, he wore the 'awe shucks' smile that served to cover everything from marital infidelities to debt welching. Somehow he made it work. Gould was around Jack's age but obsessed with balancing vice with health. He truly felt that he could offset his daily consumption of a fifth of alcohol and a handful of prescription painkillers with a discipline of kelp enemas, Metamucil, vitamins, free range chicken and wild caught fish. He piled into the back of the taxi with Vance and Chuck.

"Where we going, Bud?"

"Mexico."

"Fuck, they have some great weed down there. And hookers. I should be paying you. We got business, too?"

"Yeah, we got lots of business."

"I can't practice there."

"Don't let the Mexicans know."

"What's the gig?"

"Tell you on the plane. Snort?" Vance pulled his flask from his packet, remembered that it was empty and instructed the driver to make a stop at Binny's Beverage Depot on Grand Avenue. The driver stopped to punch in the address.

"Enough already! Just go west on Wacker, north on Wells and east on Grand. *You French?*" Vance directed in exasperation. The driver looked back at him with a face that mirrored his passenger's frustration.

"Où est l'ouest?

CHAPTER SEVEN
Directionless Destinations

Chicago, IL, O'Hare Airport
Monday, December 18, 2017 4:00 PM

Agness hated paying for his own expenses. It just wasn't natural for an Agency Man to pick up a bill that he couldn't charge to someone else. He had trailed Vance and company for over an hour only to arrive at O'Hare airport and have his quarry disappear into the Flight Charter Center private jet terminal. It would be hard to blend in with the limited traffic in the facility. He entered the bright lobby three minutes after Vance and watched as the Blowfish team exited the building and crossed the tarmac to a waiting Learjet 40.

Agness had been here before. Blowfish had used one of the operators, Stratos Jet Services, in the past. They were pricey, but had the best pilots, newest planes and were "negotiable" in the air; which meant their pilots would make unplanned stops and turn off tracking devices, for a price. It had to be them. Agness found their offices. A matter-of-fact guy in an official-looking blue utility shirt manned the Stratos desk. Agness nodded at Vance's jet, visible through the window behind the man.

"I'm interested in chartering that jet."

"*Outstanding.* Where you going, when and how many?"

"Where that jet's going now, maybe a week. Just me and my girl."

"And where is that?"

"Where that jet is going...I think I just said that."

"Okay, so where do *you* want to go?"

"Where they're going...how much is that?"

"I'm sorry sir, but their destination is confidential. Where would *you* like to go?"

"It's Okay. I'm with the party."

The alcohol that had powered Agness through breakfast and lunch was playing with his critical ability to lie effectively. The conversation became matter of fact and Blue Shirt looked down at the screen mounted under his counter.

"Manifest says flight of three. What's your name?"

"I'm not going on the trip. I'm just with the party."

"I don't see a fourth name here, sir. You'll have to give me the details of your destination or I just won't be able to help you."

"I need to...book another charter. Where my party is going."

Blue shirt paused.

"You want to go out and ask your party where they're headed or do you want me to call TSA and you can sort this out with them?"

Agness hated these moments. This guy was a firewall to information that he needed and the interview was in a tailspin. Agness picked a brochure off the table and slid to the side of the counter.

"I'll just let you know. Thanks."

Agness watched Vance's jet taxi off into the distance. He turned and left the building. Wherever Vance was headed it had to have something to do with his big gambit. Agness walked out to the parking lot and waited until the jet took off, watched it vector over the field and then head southwest. It wasn't much to go on, but with a little spit and snot he'd have just enough glue to string his crumbs of information into a Hail Mary play. It was time to make his move.

He headed for the commercial buildings to the Jet Blue counter in Terminal 3. An on-the-spot ticket was the most expensive way to fly but he had no choice. The first station was open. He approached a blue-clad desk attendant who appeared to have captured every shade of blond available in her streaked, shoulder length hair.

"I'd like a one way ticket to JFK. Next flight."

"I have seats left on our 7:30 nonstop to JFK arriving at 10:46. I can give you an exit seat for $700. Can I interest you in a cash back offer now? Just let us access the contact list on any device you're wearing and I can take $150 off your ticket today."

"That's my program you know."

"Excuse me, sir?"

"I thought of that $150 program when I worked at the Lee Burnout. You know, the big breakfast cereal ad agency in the city? My plan makes the consumer look like an asshole to his friends and gives the airline a list of contacts. Pretty clever, huh?"

"So that means you'd like the offer and the seat, sit?"

"Yeah. I'll feel like being an asshole today." Agness fished the burner phone that he used for Craigslist calls out of his pocket and slapped it on the desk. The woman found an appropriate adapter, slid it into the phone's port and began downloading its data.

"Window or aisle?"

"Aisle."

"Luggage?"

"Just carry on."

Agness burned through what was left on one of his Visa cards. At least he earned some miles for the effort. He pocketed his ticket and his boarding pass.

"And where's the nearest bar?'

She nodded at the gates.

"You'll find a selection of bars and restaurants right through security, Mr. Agness."

Agness was nursing his fifth Oban single malt scotch when his Smart Phone came to life. He had stretched it out to its full size of 8 X 14 inches and found himself staring down at Roger Drab. Drab was CEO of Drab and Associates and former communications consultant to New York Mayor Marjorie Stetson. He had personally engineered her response to Blowfish NY's ill fated promotional jet fighter strafing of the Macy's Day Parade, which resulted in Vance being booted out of Manhattan, permanently.

"Mr. Agness? This is Roger Drab. Can you please take your drink off the screen?"

Agness shoved his drink aside and wiped the screen with his napkin. This was it.

Drab looked much balder than his Linkedin profile; he had grown a thin goatee to offset the almost transparent fringe of hair that crested over his ears. One thing remained constant: his trademark round black glasses. Drab had purchased 100 pairs of the frames from the original manufacturer to maintain his "brand" for life.

"I'm the former Senior Strategist for Blowfish, Mr. Drab. I'd like to bring my skill-set to your agency."

"Then you should be calling HR, Mr. Agness. To the best of my knowledge we're full up on strategists. Shoot your resume over after the New Year and we'll take a look at it."

"I'm more than a strategist, Mr. Drab... I can help you acquire new clients."

"So you're biz dev? New Year is best, Mr. Agness, when you figure out what bucket you're in."

"I mean, I've got business now. Special business. Business that Blowfish can't afford to lose."

"I'm not hearing anything that can't wait, Mr. Agness."

"I can help you put Jack Vance out of business. Right now, Mr. Drab."

Agness felt Drab studying his sweaty face through the monitor. *Fucking video calls.* His heart beat twenty times in the three seconds it took Roger Drab to respond.

"Alright, Mr. Agness, we can discuss something like that. When can you be in my office?"

"I'm getting on a plane. Be there in the morning."

"I start the day at 7:00 AM, Mr. Agness. You'll have 20 minutes and no promises." Drab ended the call. Agness tapped the screen and the phone snapped down to its original size of 2 X 4 inches. He slapped its rubbery case over his wrist, where it lived. He ordered another scotch and tried not to dwell on what it would be like to kill the rest of the evening riding the New York subways until his morning meeting with Drab.

CHAPTER EIGHT
Love Disconnection

Somewhere over the Southwestern United States, 25,000 feet
Monday, December 18, 2017 6:00 PM

Vance reclined in his seat on the jet and smiled. A good personnel purge was like a needle shower, it only stung for the first second then it felt like a Quaalude rush. His bracelet vibrated and he tapped the temple on his Oliver People's glasses. A tiny message blinked into his right eye's field of view on the head's up display projected on the inside of the lens. It was a response from one of the women that he had been following on DNADate.com, a site that only allowed you to communicate with people who shared the same genetic profile. The chat was initiated by a 30-whatever, sandy blond with a vague background that sent her all over the world. She could be anything from travel agent to a drug mule; both attractive potentials to Vance. After a month of random back-and-forths was she finally ready to engage in a real conversation? The text appeared on his display:

You said cocktails not coffee. Where do you want to meet?

Vance mulled his response while he rummaged through his pockets and dumped a pile of burner phones, each the size of a credit card, on the tray table in front of him. He sorted through, found a small, flexible Smart Screen device and whispered into its flat speaker. The device converted his talk to text.

Not Milwaukee or Cleveland

It took nearly a minute for her response to appear. It was a tell. She was probably messaging a few guys at once to see who would jump through the highest hoop.

What's the diff? Paris - that measure up?

Home turf? Show me around?

2morrow nite?

On ASSignment. TB in a couple? Vance suddenly regretted using that term.

TB? Touch Base?

Y

This a biz lunch or a date?

It can be whtevr U wnt

A date. Give U a rain check. We can TB end of week if UR calendar opens up.

The chat ended and Vance wondered if he'd ever hear from her again. He was in mission mode and could honestly give a shit about his personal life. He abandoned most of his friends, family and romantic interests years ago, preferring the company of a good bottle of scotch, exotic drugs and a healthy balance sheet. When he was horny he used a service. Time was his life's currency and love wasn't in the budget.

CHAPTER NINE
Jailbreak

Reynosa, Mexico, 7,000 feet
Monday, December 18, 2017 8:00 PM

Vlad Berber couldn't have picked a more dreadful jail to call home. Reynosa had the ugly little reputation of being one of the ten most dangerous cities in Mexico, a chronic entry on the Lonely Planet's annual "must avoid" list. It lives on the northern Mexican border, directly across from Texas and is run by drug cartels with a hand from the government, because someone has to staff the prisons and make sure the inmates get their mail.

The pilot steering Vance's jet felt, legitimately, that his head might become the temporary hood ornament on a stolen Escalade. He banked the Learjet over General Lucio Blanco (REX) airport and took a tower command to enter on Runway 13, slowing his airspeed while he felt around under his seat. His Beretta M9 hung in its holster, kept company by a couple of magazines loaded with staggered .40mm hollow point and incendiary rounds. It was the same gun he had carried when he flew for the Marines. He prayed that the weapon would remain holstered during this trip.

Gould peered out the window at the patchy scrubland surrounding the airport. This wasn't the Mexico of topless women and warm beers that he was expecting. He ran through Vance's plan one more time.

"Okay, so we buy Vlad's freedom, then you conduct a jail cell interview with him that CNN streams to build some, whatever, buzz, around him. That's it? No downtime to check out the local color?"

Vance napped on the flight and was, at the moment, somewhat clear and sober.

"Right. Providing they go along with the deal. You throw a little legal mumbo on them to goose the process and we grease them with cash. Look around. This kind of place turns down Benjamin's?"

As they descended, remains of old cars decorated with bleached corpses became visible outside the airport's steel fenced runway. At some point there had been a gun battle; the winners leaving corpses, vehicles and bullet casings to mark their victory. Chuck Giletti pulled off his jacket, revealing twin Glock 18's in a gleaming russet Don Hume custom shoulder holster. He acquired the pair from an old friend in the Mossad. They were some of the rare factory fully auto models and the pride of his collection. He carried 10 spare magazines, five on each side of his leather braces, and two loaded weapons, providing him with a total of 202 rounds. 204 if you counted the ones in the chambers. He was looking forward to putting the automatics to use. Maybe this trip they could come out and play.

"And if the greenbacks don't work?" asked Gould. Vance patted Chuck on the back.

"Then we Wild Bunch it. And we don't turn on the cameras." Gould rolled his eyes.

"Kidding! We get them drunk and you make them love us."

Chuck opened his briefcase and handed Gould a .357 Colt Python revolver with a four inch barrel. The weapon was an idiot proof collector's item.

"I know you know how to use this, counselor. Pull and go bang." Gould accepted it, marveling at this gift from a professional. He had lusted after this particular weapon since he started playing Call of Duty Ten: Blacker Ops.

"OK. I'm in."

Chuck handed Vance a Sig Sauer .357, the preferred weapon of the US Air Marshall's service. Vance understood guns; they were one of the few things that he respected, being absolute and pure in their function. He grew up with weapons in his house and realized their importance in today's world. He dropped the magazine, slid back the slide and watched a round pop out of the chamber and into his lap. He placed it back in the chamber and let the slide close, reinserting the magazine. Chuck handed each man a shiny badge in a black leather flip case. He spoke for the first time during the trip.

"Just in case this becomes my show, I want backup. I know you both know how to shoot," he looked over at Gould, "or think you do. If the situation becomes a situation, follow my lead." Vance slid the weapon into his front jacket pocket. Gould placed the Python in the rear of his trousers, Mexican style. They touched down and the pilot looked back.

"Here comes your car. Call me the minute you are done. I'm keeping the engines on."

Jack and his party exited the plane as an armored Hummer H2 pulled up. If this didn't call attention to their activities, nothing did. He suddenly felt glad that Chuck had given him the Sig. The driver nodded his head silently as they entered the vehicle. He drove them to a private security gate where they all presented their passports, citing their visit as "pleasure."

The driver turned to speak with them as they exited the airport and entered the Reynosa Matomoros highway. Their destination, the Reynosa jail, was known for its history of escapes, disappearances, beatings and murder. The road there was equally dangerous.

"You got pleasure business at the jail?" the driver asked, turning to reveal a gold mine of metal in his mouth with M-E-X-I-C-O embossed across his front uppers.

"Yeah. And you gonna stay there while we work it out," Vance responded.

"You know a vehicle like this is very attractive to many here. Drug lords, gangs. They not bother with bullets. They drive us off road and use machetes. Keep the vehicle in better shape."

"So drive careful."

"There two routes. The main route which I paid to take, not so safe. Safe route I got keeps you alive. What you want me to do, Senor?"

Giletti knew where this was going. He hadn't spent years doing wetwork in Nicaragua to miss the scent of a fleece. He let his jacket open and made sure that the driver saw his .40 caliber fashion show then turned to Vance, hand open. It was the unspoken language of "I need money now." Vance handed him $100. Giletti shook his head. Vance added four more to the pile. Giletti reached over and slid two behind the driver's ear.

"There's another three when we get back. Take the safe route."

"It's more scenic. We have a chat. You post good Yelp review right?"

The Reynosa jail had exceeded its 1400 inmate capacity years ago. It currently held 2000 prisoners with internal control ebbing and shifting between rival Zeta and Gulf cartel gangsters. Gould and Vance had been the guests of several US jails during their decades-long nocturnal travels across the vice highway, but nothing like this. It was big, bricked, nasty and ringed with more barbed wire than all the bails in Farm and Fleet warehouses between Illinois and Iowa. Vance reached for his flask, reconsidered, and popped a couple Adderalls.

It took 30 minutes and another $1000 to travel from the front gate of the jail to the Commandant's office. $200 of it had assured that they weren't frisked. They arrived armed and lawyered up, just in time to wait an additional ten minutes outside the barred office door of Commandant Carlos Regus, the jail's decider-er in chief.

Regus was not the bushy mustached, easily snowed, roly-poly uniformed Mexican official from some xenophobic 70's biker movie that they had all imagined. He wore a neat suit that Vance recognized as a Hugo Boss from last year's catalogue, accented with a slim fit Calvin Klein tie and shirt. His one concession to the prison environment was a pair of Combat boots, and even those looked like they might have been custom Danners. He was trim, with a small ponytail holding his slightly thinning, dark brown hair in place. Take away the fancy trappings and he could have been an aging Starbuck's barista working in a college town to pick up coeds. A degree in criminal justice from the University of Wisconsin hung on his wall. He addressed his guests in almost accent-less English.

"You're here on Vlad Berber I understand?"

It had been 40 minutes since Vance swallowed his pills and they were beginning to take effect, revving up his perception of the room. He looked over at Gould who launched into his act.

"Yes, we'd like to review his charges. I've got a note from the State Department indicating that I can question jail officials and review his files." Gould pulled a small flexible reader from his pocket to display the communiqué that he had arranged while in transit. He handed it to Carlos Regus.

"Very nice. But he has already been appointed a lawyer. You are free to review as much paperwork as you'd like. Stay awhile." Regus handed Gould a thick paper file held together with bailing wire. Gould carefully unwrapped the three inch thick package and was hit with page after page of Mexican court documents. He was looking for the most recent court order and within three minutes had found it. He handed it to Giletti, who read the file aloud.

"And Mr. Berber, having been found *not guilty* on the charges of manslaughter, is hereby remanded to the Reynosa, Mexico jail until such time as the charges for tax evasion are paid or two years' incarceration is served." The words ricocheted around Vance's hyper-sensitive skull like a gunshot in an elevator. This wasn't part of the profile he was looking for. He turned to Regus.

"He's not here on manslaughter? Who knows this?"

"We don't make a habit of broadcasting that kind of news like you do in the States, Mr. Vance. Berber was cleared of the manslaughter charge. He's here because he didn't pay his taxes on his winnings from cockfighting bets. It's that simple."

Vance felt the fire spilling out of his quest. His killer wasn't a killer. This kind of news was the last thing the campaign needed.

"How much does he owe?" Asked Gould.

"$25,000 U.S. Maybe $28,000 with interest."

Vance looked around the Commandant's office and spied a small plaque from a charitable organization, the Mount of Grapes. It bore an embossed image of a blind, limbless child being pulled in a donkey cart. The word "Gracias" next to the commandant's name told Vance, with his limited grasp of Spanish, that Regus had a soft place for crippled children, donkeys or the status of charitable donations. Although given their location it was more than likely just another money laundering scam for one of the drug lords.

"How would you like the fine paid with interest and a $20,000 donation made to the Mount of Grapes, in your name, in exchange for helping us tell our version of the story to the news about his release?"

Regus regarded the men in his presence. They had clean money and connections, not the dirty drug cash that he had been handed by the cartel for years. They could be useful allies, should he suddenly desire to change countries. He had something they needed, but he wasn't going to just hand the keys over. These men could come up with more than cash. Regus snapped his fingers and the two guards stationed in his office left the room. He walked around his desk and sat on its edge, looking directly at Vance.

"I like your way of thinking. Very direct. I must consider it. We have comfortable guest rooms here. You stay the night and we talk over breakfast. Then we go see Berber together. I feel this could be the beginning of a business relationship." He pressed a buzzer on his desk, summoning the two guards.

"Llevar a estos hombres a las celdas de lujo...vigilarlos. Son invitados."

Vance turned to Giletti with questions in his eyes. His chief of security reassured him.

"That's how they work down here. Don't worry, they didn't take our weapons and the cells will probably be OK. I'll tell the pilot to shut down the plane and sleep with one eye open."

"I just need ESPN," Gould commented as they turned to leave the commandant's office.

Reynosa, Mexico, Reynosa Jail: A windowless cell
Tuesday, December 19, 2017 12:12 AM
It was just after midnight when Regus announced his presence at the door of Vance's "room," a windowless solitary confinement cell with an upgraded bed, rug and an old flat screen wall mounted television set. Vance was reviewing the weekend *New York Times* on his rubbery Smart Phone.

"I trust you're comfortable Mr. Vance?"

"Like the view."

"I'm ready to release Mr. Berber to you. In the morning, of course."

"We'll pay the fine and donate to whatever charity you pick."

"There will be no fine. And there is only one charity: Me."

"How much and where?" Vance scrolled through the apps on his phone to a cash system login wall.

"You will send $100,000 to this address." He handed Vance a piece of paper.

"Little steep for a tax bill don't you think?"

"Then leave now, we'll release Berber to you and put a tax lien on the plane for his fine. You can get through the border on foot, the Mexican way."

"Let's not quibble over small change. $75,000. Half now. Balance when we are gone." Regus took a few paces around the room.

"Alright. And there is one more thing."

"How much for the overnight stay?"

"You're bringing in another passenger. Me."

"Hmm...might be a little hard for you to make it through U.S. customs with the immigration lockdown."

"We're not going through immigration. I'm not on the manifest. Your pilot will make an unscheduled stop at the abandoned airstrip written on that slip of paper. It's long enough to accommodate your plane and on your direct route to Chicago. No one will know except you and me and the pilot and your team. We will never see each other again."

"You cost me 100 grand anyway."

"Why, Mr. Vance?"

"Because the pilot's going to want 25 to keep his mouth shut and interfere with the plane's monitoring system. You can't just land anywhere anymore. The grid's everywhere."

"That's your problem, Mr. Vance." They shook and Regus left.

If Regus could deliver the kind of animal Vance was looking for the $100,000 he just spent was a bargain.

Jack Vance approached his father's bedside and looked up at the monitors that were a dynamic portal into what was left of his life. He hadn't seen the old man in years, only to receive a garbled call to come to a hospital because there wasn't much time left to talk. The chart outside the door read 'multiple gunshot and knife wounds.' What the hell was a 75 year old man doing with injuries like that... he should be in for a stroke or cancer or something most normal people lose their lives to. But not his father. No sir, *had to do everything the hard way.*

"How did..." But the old man cut him off, as usual.

"Follow this lead." Benjamin Vance pulled the sheet back from over his body, revealing a Cohiba cigar box. He handed it to Vance. It contained a Soviet OTs-33 Pernach automatic pistol emblazoned with the crest of the Cuban National Police.

"And find out."

"Find out what? Speak to me for once in your life. What do you want?"

"Find out...who killed me." A rap on the door pulled Vance out of his dream and back to consciousness and Mexico. It was 5:45 AM.

CHAPTER TEN
Carrie and the White Whale

Manhattan, New York
Tuesday, December 19, 2017 7:00 AM EST

Roger Drab had mid-1980's stamped all over him. He wore a blousy Brooks Brothers shirt, loose fitting, multi pleated Men's Warehouse suit, French Shriner loafers, a narrow (limited edition) Member's Only belt and wide Macy's house brand tie. He was quite content with a style that masked his girth, and modern trim fit tailoring only accentuated it. Drab wasn't a physically big man, but felt that his success in maintaining an agency of roughly 35 people for nearly 20 years was enough to pause conversations in any room he entered. Like a warder checking on inmates he did a personal head count every morning. Each busy employee was just another log that fueled his steam train of an ego.

Despite the embarrassing little monthly calls that he took with his trust-funded mother to secure the funds to make payroll, Drab felt that he had truly built a business and a reputation all by himself. He was so proud of his history that he made it into a public document through his LinkedIn profile. While his suburban neighbors were out gardening, Drab spent his Saturday morning's editing his online presence. He was immersed in the hyperbolists's black arts of polishing words and amplifying the insignificant. Drab felt that every single minute of his life was important and worthy of documentation, in the vein of William Manchester's multi-volume "*The Glory and the Dream*." Drab's profile collectively covered every aspect of his "working life," with long dissertations on his linear evolution into an advanced marketing professional, beginning at age six.

The first 10,000 words of the LinkedIn bio chronicled his early "professional career," starting with his childhood business of picking up dog feces from neighborhood breezeways. He added to his income in grammar school as a paid snitch for any numbers of teachers, working his way up the ladder. By Junior High School he was being compensated by his principal to report on teachers who didn't reprimand students who he had ratted out. Drab learned that the value of knowledge was only limited to the number of people who would pay for it.

In college he worked as the classified ad manager of the student newspaper, routinely up charging groups that he felt were not representative of his world view, like homosexuals, minorities and the disabled. His short history of working for other people after college, specifically the PR firm of Portrait Nobelly, received only 200 words, before segueing into the next 30,000 words documenting the founding of his own firm. His profile ended with a long list of the many bronze trade association awards he had won.

Drab was a member of the New Nixonians, a quasi political party that preached policy over transparency and advocated the return to a monarchy system in the U.S. He didn't broadcast this fact, but kept his rally garb of red ski mask and blue sheet in his office closet. Drab had maneuvered himself into the chairmanship of the Business Marketing Society (BMS), a position that allowed him to, among other things, select meeting speakers and appoint board members. He used these contacts and the organization's money to cherry pick potential clients, offering them board seats and access to "thought leaders" that he flew in to address monthly meetings.

He had found, however, that despite all the crafting and planning and skulking and back room deal making, that Drab and Associates always remained one step behind Jack Vance and Blowfish. Blowfish won the bigger accounts, took home the gold awards while leaving the Honorable Mentions for Drab. Vance's agency was known as the *"creative shop"* to Drab's *"I guess we'll use them"* shop. It was a shadow Drab never felt comfortable inhabiting and his revenge had been to steal Blowfish personnel whenever he had the opportunity. He once joked at an Ad Fed cocktail party that he had more Blowfish employees than Blowfish. And now he had an opportunity to add another charm to his bracelet, albeit a damaged one.

Drab would have been content to keep the battle on a strictly business level until the night that Vance crossed the line. The incident had been personal, visceral, and the act of a man that was truly driven by Satan. Drab truly felt that what Vance had done revealed that he bore the mark of the Beast and that it was his charge to rid the world of such scourge. Drab knew that at some point in time their orbits would cross and he would have the opportunity to plunge his dagger into Vance. Maybe this Christmas he would find gold in this lump of coal standing before him.

Roger Drab assessed Tom Agness, sitting across the desk from him. He had to give the little shit credit for getting this far. Stinking drunkard or not, the kid might have something that he could use to hurt Vance. If he had been good enough for Lee Burnout at one time, maybe he could be of some use to Drab and Associates. At least for a few weeks or until his information turned into something. Then he'd kick the little agency orphan back to the shit stream sewer where he belonged. The thought reminded Drab that he had promised to drop a case of Evian water at his church for the weekend's fundraiser.

"Alright Mr. Agness, what have you got?"

"I can give you a list of all the Blowfish clients and their contacts. I know who is spending what. I have direct access to the entire client side."

"An intern can find that out in an afternoon by going through press releases and MediaPost. Give me something of value or I'm afraid you've wasted your time."

Agness fidgeted in his seat. He didn't expect to blow through his small cards so quickly. He would have to play his whole hand now.

"Vance is doing a launch for MVN Online. He headed off somewhere to..."

Agness was interrupted as Drab's secretary stuck her head in the room.

"Sorry, Mr. Drab, but you wanted me to inform you if there was any news anywhere on Jack Vance or Blowfish? Take a look at your monitor." Drab's west wall, the one with the 12th story semi-skyline view of lower Manhattan, shimmered to life. It became a 6 'x 10' monitor, tuned to CNN. The words "breaking story" flashed across the screen. Brinke Badwin, director of International News, strutted across the screen.

"And on the celebrity front, we have just received an exclusive news feed that Vlad Berber, the man-slaughterer, is that correct? The contestant *accused of manslaughter* on the 2015 reality show 'Survivor Chernobyl,' is at this moment being released from a jail in Reynosa, Mexico, where another manslaughter charge has just been dropped. Let's see what happening." The words "*amateur video*" played across the screen as Commandant's Regus' face came into focus, clearly standing in front of a poorly lit Mexican jail cell.

Vlad Berber, dressed in the dirty remains of Propper tropical duty pants, Bates waterproof tactical boots and a greasy Hooter's tee shirt blinked up at the camera. Through the grime that covered his body you could see the brick of muscle that made Berber into such a popular character. His trademarked buzz cut blond hair had grown out into a long, stringy mass, just barely covering his eyes, red with anger. He glowered at the camera, saying nothing, unmoving.

Silence for more than a few seconds has a dreaded name in the news business: dead air. Badwin didn't like its scent one bit and was about to cut to a commercial when Berber, the celebrity "manslaughterer," stirred and looked straight into the camera. He spoke in a thick accent tailor made for an American viewing audience. Berber had practiced for months, mimicking Robin Williams' Russian accent in the movie "*Moscow on the Hudson*," before auditioning for "Survivor." It was a much better version of Russian than his own.

"Maybe I don think so. Maybe I don want to go." Without warning the transmission ended.

Brinke Badwin, who made a career out of on-camera professional bemusement, looked over her shoulder at the image that wasn't there, turned to the screen and said,

"Well, there you have it. Looks like Vald Berber, the 'manslaughterer' of 'Survivor Chernobyl' is out of a Mexican jail. If he wants to be." She made a shrug so practiced it could have been copyrighted.

"What a world, what a world."

Her producer cut to a commercial.

Roger Drab wondered if the first rivulet of sweat would appear on Agness' upper lip or over his eyebrows.

"Was Vance going to Mexico, by chance," Drab asked, trying not to let his vaginal crease of a mouth curl into a smirk.

Agness could save this. There was one little tiny bit of Drab that was intrigued. All he had to do was think like Vance, what would Jack do? Shit! *Had he really thought that?* What a jerkoff. He had bills to pay. It was time to make this work.

"That's what I came here to tell you. He is cooking up a massive high profile campaign that is tailor made to explode, if one were privy to all the details. If we work this right it will be his biggest failure, he'll be begging to sell you Blowfish." Agness played a hunch, calling up the slitter app on his phone and wagging it in front of Drab.

"Look at what's trending now: Berber/loser; Berber/drop/dead," the feed's played out in three word bursts from around the country.

"It's already becoming a joke. Give me time and resources and we'll tie Vance right into this brewing fiasco. It will be an *anti-campaign campaign*. You don't have the time to research Vance to get this right. I know his moves. I know what he's plotting. Why do you think I was right here with you when they made the announcement? I knew it was going to happen. But you don't get the rest of the story until I get a job." The chum was in the water now.

Drab looked at him. Maybe the microscopic turd shaking in front of him held the missing piece to end his ten year long quest. It wouldn't cost much to find out and he needed a new whipping boy to verbally abuse. He made a note to "call mom for money" on a pad on his desk.

Something Agness saw when he entered Drab's office suddenly clicked.

"*I am not a crook,*" he blurted out.

"What, Mr. Agness?"

Agness motioned at the small bust of Nixon that served as a bookend for Drab's collection of Reader's Digest magazines.

"New *Nixonian*? I am too! I worked for the party's founder Ron Gaul!"

Drab chewed over the revelation and the proposition. He prided himself on the efficacy of his gut reactions, and quick decision making.

"How long will it take you to put this anti- campaign campaign together, Mr. Agness?"

"45 days."

"I'll give you 30."

"And I have a job?"

"See Mrs. McGuire for a cube assignment Monday morning." Drab fished a small pink slip of paper out of his pocket and handed it to Agness.

"And pick up my shirts. They're at Del Floria's tailor shop around the corner."

As Agness left Drab's office he realized that there really was no place for honesty in the race up the corporate ladder. The old Blowfish tagline had nailed it, truth *was* overrated.

Chapter Eleven
VIP Personal Stash

Reynosa Prison, Reynosa, Mexico
Tuesday, December 19, 2017 6:30 AM CST

Vance needed an insanity break. He sat down on the dirty wooden bench next to Berber, pulled out his recently refilled flask and took a long draw. He didn't have a lot of time to talk the Russian back off the ledge after this bust of a press blast. He was back to stealth marketing.

"You can't stay here Berber, can he, Commandant?" Regus shook his head.

"I can have the guards dump him outside the door or in your trunk, whatever you want." Berber tightened. The old menace that made him famous flashed across his eyes and charged through his muscles. It was palpable; Vance could feel it. That's what he was looking for. Berber tucked his chin and rose into a natural fighting stance. At 6'5" the man was made for violent reality TV, and that was about it.

"First man who touch me, I tear off his arm. Second man, I feed him arm. Who hungry here?"

Giletti rose, his hand slipping to his side. Gould took the action as a cue to back out the door. Regus' two guards were already in the hallway. Nobody wanted to tangle with the Russian.

"Relax Vlad, you're a free man, you can't stay here. Come with us, we can talk it over."

Vlad looked up at Vance.

"It was men like you made me what I am: hated...a killer. I can't go anywhere, do anything. Everyone afraid of me...because of your fucking *TV*. I went along. I deserve this place. Is my world. " He sat and folded his arms.

Vance stood and walked over to Regus.

"He doesn't go, you don't go. Connect the dots. Let's talk."

They exited the cell.

"Have your guards bang him over the head and drag his ass to the airport for me, for us."

"That could take an hour, if I can find a guard to go in there. The regional commandant saw CNN and is on his way here. He'll want to be paid before he lets you leave the prison for the airport. If he gets here first our deal is off. *You* connect the dots."

"I don't give a shit who I pay. Let him come."

"You have 200 grand? Want to lose a man or two? He's cartel. They're all about sending messages. I can stand a couple more years here until the next marketing guy comes along. Your choice."

"How long?"

"Maybe thirty minutes."

Vance put his arm over Regus' shoulder and started walking him away from Giletti and Gould and the guards. He spoke quietly.

"Can you somehow heat that room up without Berber knowing it?" Regus considered the odd request.

"Mexican jails aren't heated Senor. But I may have something." He whistled for a guard and instructed him to place space heaters against the wall of the adjacent cell.

"Do you keep confiscated contraband here Commandant?" Vance asked.

"Evidence must be maintained until trials, of course."

"Could I see the room?"

"Why, Mr. Vance?"

"Motivation, Mr. Regus. I believe that your room may hold the motivation that Mr. Berber needs to leave your jail with me." Regus pulled Vance aside.

"I will give you anything you want for the next 15 minutes. After that it may be out of my hands and you will need a lot more than what you gave me to leave this place with that man."

"Where's the stuff?"

"Down the hall. Let's go." As they walked through the corridors Vance could hear the morning music of the incarcerated. Screaming, laughing, moaning, water running, animals braying, vehicles racing; he felt like he was outside a county fair in hell. They approached the evidence room and Regus ordered it unlocked.

"You have two minutes, find our solution."

Vance entered the locker and shut the door behind him. He was alone in a long, narrow, steel shelved ancient brick room that would be the ultimate "cover of the year" for *High Times Magazine*. Bales of confiscated marijuana piled floor to ceiling made a stoned castle for the mice and rats who had taken up a long and clearly comfortable residence. The castle's moat was composed of hundreds of clear bags filled with multi colored pills, bricks of cocaine and glassy shards of crystal meth. But that's not what Vance was looking for.

He approached an examining table filled with hundreds of small plastic boxes of chemical evidence of wrongdoing. As he rummaged through the packages, squinting carefully at the labeled contents, something caught his eye: a container of white powder with an old yellowing label that read *"Carlos Escobar, personal."* Vance stopped and looked at the Holy Grail he just unearthed. He carefully opened the lid on the drug lord's private stash, fished in a finger and helped himself to a good sized snort. Even though this supply might have been almost 30 years old, it had enough kick to buzz him to clarity. He had another, and another. Within seconds his mission was clear and an ounce bindle of the precious Escobar evidence was in his pocket.

Three minutes later Vance exited the room. Regus was nervously waiting outside the door, distinctly alone on the corridor.

"I'll need a couple of your men."

They returned to Berber's heated cell. Regus motioned for two guards to stand by while Vance entered alone. He loosened his tie and sat down next to Berber. The room was stifling.

"Hot shit in here man, you like this? Let's go. I've got a plane waiting."

"So leave, Mr. Executive."

"Call me Jack." Vance extended his hand; Berber reluctantly shook it. In the back of his reptilian brain Berber knew that everyone was potentially an asset.

Vance pulled his flask from his pocket; he motioned towards Berber.

"Dovgan?" The word caught Berber's ear and stuck.

"*Russian* Dovgan?" Berber hadn't so much as heard the name "Dovgan" uttered much less tasted the national spirit in years.

"Friend brings it back from St. Petersburg. Best thing for the heat, eh? Of course you don't have to have any. You can just sit here and sweat and feel sorry for yourself."

Berber accepted the flask, took a sip, verified the authenticity of the beverage, and proceeded to drain the flask. He wiped his mouth.

"You have good taste, Executive. Maybe you not so full of sheet." Vance hadn't counted on Berber downing the entire 12 oz. flask. He had mixed the vodka with some of the rare DMT that he found in the evidence room and added in a dose of vintage MAOI to allow for oral ingestion. The combination would yield an intense psycho-physical high that would render Berber open to suggestion. It also generated strong erotic reactions. Vance hoped that he could complete his mission and get Berber out of this cell before the Bear

started humping his leg. The drug ramped up quickly. Its full effects would be felt for hours and this dosage could keep Berber out for a day, if it didn't kill him.

Berber prided himself on his acute situational awareness. It was strange that he hadn't noticed the Executive glowing. The man in the tie had a warm, welcoming firefly light gently leeching out of his skin and shimmering on his suit. It made Berber feel good and he hadn't felt good in a long, long time. He handed the empty flask back to Vance. No need to keep something that belonged to this kind, glowing man.

"Can I open the door for you Vlad? Maybe it will cool things off." Vance rose and Berber watched him. He didn't want the Executive to leave. Vance returned to Berber's bench and sidled up to him.

"Let's talk about the future, Vlad. I want to put you back on TV. I want to help you help people. Is this something that we can talk about or should I just leave you alone in this cell?"

Vance feigned standing. Berber pulled him back down. He didn't really want the glowing man to leave him in this cell. He tried to talk but his tongue felt like a lizard tail being dragged through a muddy gutter of vomited fur balls.

"I... hate... this... cell. I hate... these people and everyone in this world... hates me."

"We can change all that, Vlad. Let me help you become...popular again."

Vlad liked what the glowing man was saying. He was sick of this cell and these small people and this damn heat. He missed being famous. And he really liked that vodka. Berber stood up, grabbing Vance by the waist and hoisted him over his shoulders. The Executive felt like a warm scarf. It was time to leave. Berber took a step forward and felt his legs stretch. He looked down. They had turned into slithering octopus arms with thick, wet suction cups that stuck to the hot stone floor. He gently lowered Vance down to the floor in front of him and pointed to his feet.

"We stuck, Executive."

Vance signaled for Regus and within 90 seconds the Big Russian was on a cart being wheeled towards Vance's waiting Escalade. As they cleared the last gate and reached the prison's main entrance Regus halted the procession. He instructed the two guards to turn the cart over to Gould and Giletti and walked with Vance to their vehicle. The driver activated the rear gate and all four men worked to move Berber into the back of the vehicle. Regus motioned at a dust cloud in the distance.

"Regional. We need to go." Gould entered the vehicle followed by Giletti. As Vance was about to enter the two guards approached the vehicle. Regus waved them away but they continued, signaling to wait, that a call had come for him. Vance hopped on board and pulled Regus in with him. He turned to the driver.

"Get us out of here. Now." Nothing happened. The guards got closer to the truck. The driver turned.

"You keep me waiting all night Senor and now you are in a rush? Maybe I forget the route."

The guards had arrived at the vehicle and started working the doors.

"Deal with this, Chuck!" Vance barked.

Regus was sweating, looking like he'd melted into his seat. Giletti shoved his way up to the front seat, drawing his Glock as he moved. He cracked it across the driver face, opened the driver's door, reached over, unlatched it and pushed him out. He slid in behind the wheel, threw the Escalade into gear and hit the gas. He punched up local attractions on the dash mounted GPS and within 60 seconds they had a route that would get them to the airport in under ten minutes. Regus was coming back to life.

"I would have your pilot get ready, they may phone ahead."

Vance moved into the passenger's seat, prepared to receive the stink eye from his professional security man.

"We're giving him a ride to the U.S."

"And he didn't tell anyone. And they wanted more money. I've been to this rodeo."

"And?"

"And they're so fucked up down here they wouldn't stop us at the airport without getting paid first. Of course if Mr. Whoever in the fancy car is Cartel, then they might listen.

"Bingo."

"That's great Jack. "

"So..."

"Tell everyone who has a gun to very carefully make sure it's loaded and the safety is off. Just in case we need to actually use them," Giletti ordered.

Vance looked back. Regus had his hand on his weapon and was looking down the road for the commandant's car. In the chaos of the escape Stu Gould had worked the Python loose and was nervously looking out the window, not sure what had just happened or what was going to happen next. Either way he would like the opportunity to shoot someone. It would be a hell of a lot more exciting than finishing the briefs on the desk in his office.

Within thirty five minutes Vance and his team were entering Texas airspace on their flight path North in the chartered jet. The "escape" had been a non-event. Apparently no one knew where Vance and his team were headed once they had lost their pursuers, leaving the airport personnel at zero alert.

Berber was strapped into a seat, long gone on the drug cocktail rapidly working its way through his system.

"He must be having a great time in there," Gould said to Giletti, nodding at Berber's obvious arousal.

"Thanks for reminding me, I'll take my gun back now counselor," Giletti responded, with an open hand. Gould sheepishly fished the Python from his waistband and handed it to the security agent. Vance stood up and spoke to the cabin.

"The departure didn't go as smoothly as we had planned and I want to apologize to everyone for the confusion. We'll be dropping Mr. Regus off on the way back to Chicago."

Vance moved forward in the cramped space, patting Regus on the shoulder as he walked past him. He'd have to cut a deal with the pilot now. Regus didn't appear on any manifest, so it was just a matter of money.

The deserted airfield in Kansas was just where Regus had indicated and an easy landing for the plane. It was a clear day and everyone took advantage of the short stop to stretch their legs. Vance spoke with Regus in the shade of the tail.

"I'll have the rest of the money sent to your account within the hour."

"Keep it. You are a man of your word Mr. Vance, in more ways than one. What you gave me was enough." He extended his hand.

"That money will be in your account anyway Commandant. Hang onto it... maybe I'll need it someday."

Vance fished his deck of burner phones from his pocket, fanned them out, selected one and handed one to Regus.

"In case I might want to make a withdrawal. Leave it in the sun and it'll always be charged." Regus slid the phone into his wallet.

"Let me know if you make it up north...for a Badger game or something."

"Badger? What are you talking about, Mr. Vance?"

"That degree on your wall...from Wisconsin."

"It came with the office. This is the first time I have been outside of Mexico."

"Pity you're not here legally, Mr. Regus."

"Why is that, Mr. Vance?"

"I've got an opening for an account executive and you're a natural bullshitter."

Twenty minutes later Vance and his crew were airborne and he was on the phone in the plane's small lavatory, sniffing more of the vintage Escobar private cocaine stash. He called Naomi Stiles. It was critical that the stage was properly set for the moment when Vlad Berber reentered the world.

"Dig up everything you can find about Berber from his season on *Survivor*. What he wore, where he lived, what he ate, what he drank. Get him a room at the Four Seasons and get that doctor that you use, the one with the psychoactive drugs. I don't even want to know his name. When Berber comes to he needs to feel like he just stepped out of the pool after a good night of drinking and fucking. We're going to make the whole Mexican jail adventure into a dream and the reality show into his new world view. Got it?"

"Yes, Mr. Vance, one night drinking and fornicating coming up."

"I said fucking. There's a difference."

"I'm trying to help you cut down on some of the abusive language, Mr. Vance. Drinking and fornicating."

"If he was trying to make babies he'd be fornicating, Ms. Stiles. But that's not what the host of *Some Will Die* does with his evenings. He fucks, Ms. Stiles. Frequently and with abandon. We're in the language business. Colorful or not we're paid to use the right words!"

"OK sir, one night of imaginary drinking and fucking coming up."

Vance rang off, considered his rare cocaine stash, and determined that properly rationed, it might see him through to the end of this campaign and into the first weeks of his retirement.

CHAPTER TWELVE
Chemical Dawn

Four Seasons Hotel suite, Chicago, IL
Friday, December 22, 2017 10:30 AM CST

Vlad Berber was sure his eyes were open now. He had been walking through the desert for days, but the sun hadn't made him squint like the light now streaming in from the window he was facing. He turned his head. The pillow under him was soft, firm and cool, like every ad in every magazine said a pillow should feel. He pushed himself up from his bed and looked around at the palatial room that lay before him. He knew this hotel. He had stayed here, in this very room years ago when he was THE celebrity from *Survivor Chernobyl*.

He felt as if a long dormant program was kicking in as he marched towards the bathroom and regarded his clean shaven face in the large mirror over the sink. He relieved a full bladder of avocado colored urine and walked back to the living area. A bottle of Kauffman vodka from Moscow sat in a vase, chilling on a tray. He poured himself a glass, sat down on the broad striped couch and picked yesterday's copy of the Komsomolskaya Pravda.

His standard outfit of Propper Tactical jungle pants, Bates combat boots and a Blackhawk Kev-lon shirt lay over the couch, where he had thrown them off before going to bed. He lifted the shirt and felt the heaviness he was looking for. Berber slid his hand into the custom made internal pocket and produced a modified .40 Walther PPS. So strange, his long dream about some hot prison in Mexico, then the desert and now, everything seemed so...right. The phone rang.

Berber didn't like heads-up glasses or connected contact lenses and never owned a smart anything. He was a "dumb phone" kind of guy. He, (at one time) was able to wrangle a lifetime contract for plain old voice-only service from AT&T in exchange for an advertising endorsement. His old Nokia rang merrily on the couch. Apparently, he hadn't misplaced it somewhere along the way, because there it was. He regarded it like a long lost pet come back to life, and touched its familiar keypad.

"Hello?"

"Vlad, it's Jack, how's the boy this morning? You presentable? I'm coming up."

"Jack..."

There was a rap on the door. Vlad opened it and regarded the overly cheery, highly styled man in the hallway. He knew him. Why?

Vance marched past Vlad. He had a short window to sell his illusion and counted on Berber's famously Luddite tendencies to leave what he was uncertain of unvetted. His first order of business was to start the alcohol flowing to lubricate the situation. They had kept Berber under for nearly three days while Stiles' crack psychopharmacologist had done a *Manchurian Candidate* on him. Vance scanned the room: the phone, the paper, the clothes, even the gun on the couch were all there. Stiles had done her job. He filled Berber's glass to the brim with the vodka, duplicated the order for himself and handed the confused giant his medicine.

"Pey Dadna! We earned this, eh!"

Vlad accepted the drink and followed Vance's suit, draining it. Vance steered Berber to the cocktail table and pulled out a small projector.

"Do you remember the program? What you're supposed to do this afternoon?"

"I...you mean *the show*? You're talking about *the show*?" Fragments were returning to Berber. He had been in some reality show in Mexico, but it was canceled when the sponsor pulled out. Now he was on another show. But this one was good. He would be helping people. And this man, he was the one who fixed everything. He created another show. He was a friend.

"That's right, Vlad, *the show*. Sit down. We're meeting with the clients in a little while. We need to sell *the show* to them. We need to sell you. Let's review the pitch."

Two hours later Vance and Berber were standing in front of Sidney Brill and company in the spiffy new MVN corporate offices. It was dog and pony time again. Brill eyed him, knowing the punch line with Vance was always preceded by a dollar sign.

"Gentleman, I'd like you to meet Vladimir Berber, the new face of *Some Will Die*. The cornerstone of our MVN launch campaign." Berber stood. He knew his place on this buffet table, having been run through it during all the *Survivor* beauty pageants.

"One of *many* shows we have planned," quipped Brill's programming exec, a heavyset pudge-ball who was all of 28 with a visible nervous twitch. Vance didn't respond. The little prick thought he could afford some cheek at Vance's expense because his boss was writing the checks. Vance thumbed the remote in his hand and the conference room screen filled with a stream of charts and spreadsheets. Brill recognized Berber, but like most people in the room couldn't put any association to a name that had been out of circulation for five years.

"Welcome to the team, Mr. Berber...your name is familiar, but..."

"Manslaughter in Chernobyl... and Mexico!" The pudge-ball sparked up again, clearly beside himself with his mastery of important cultural facts.

"Mr. Berber was shooting a reality show in Mexico. The press got very creative with their interpretation when the show's sponsor pulled out."

Vance needed to brush past the associations that didn't fit Berber's drug induced scenario as quickly as possible. The whole double man-slaughterer card wasn't going to work anyway. He refocused the conversation.

"We have gone through all the potential audience scenarios. You'll find copies of our data in your file folders on your server. Gentlemen, we feel that the best time to launch the premier episode of *Some Will Die* and the network is against the 2018 Super Bowl."

Brill stood up. Sure, Vance had put together an impressive program in an incredibly short period of time, but this was insane, whose money did the man think he was gambling?

"Not again Vance, *where's the real presentation!* Why not after the game, when three quarters of the potential audience isn't watching something else?"

"Because if we can pull it off, you will make history, I will make you rich and you will be guaranteed an audience for at least...a season. And that's pretty good these days." Vance sat while Berber remained standing. Brill shook his head.

"And just what makes you think that you can possibly deliver the kind of programming that will make this country tune out the Super Bowl?"

"Insurance, Sidney. The head injury settlements have reduced the Super Bowl to a flag football game. Our country is jonesing for something that organized sports can't deliver anymore: *violence.* I'll show you why we have gone out of our way to deliver Vlad to the table."

Vance nodded to Berber. The large Russian coolly picked up a conference room chair and threw it through one of the picture windows, shattering it. The bitter wind gusts from 50 stories in the air would have turned any paper in the office into a whirling vortex, if paper was still being used. While the room was still in shock Berber strode over to the fat little sniggering, twitching executive, picked him up, carried him to the open window and held him by one leg over the street.

"Give me ten crunches, Fatty. Now." The pudge-ball, shaking with too much fear to scream, flailed wildly, grabbing air. Berber gave his leg a squeeze.

"Relax! Give me a crunch!" Urine began running down the executive's inverted face. He looked at Berber through his tears and started crying for his mother.

"Vance!" Brill yelled. But Jack waved him back.

"Careful Sidney! He might drop him!" And the collective executive suite took a step back and watched as the surreal entertainment played out.

"I... I can't," the squirmy little fat man managed to squeak, his ruddy face filling with blood.

"You can!" Berber put his other arm on the man's other leg and steadied himself.

"We do it together." Slowly the man started to curl up.

"One!" Berber yelled. Pudgy curled again and again and again, feeling steadier and stronger with each motion. Berber counted faster.

"Five, six, seven, good!" Suddenly the fat little executive, whose twitchy snideness had formed the protective shield over his girth, stopped focusing on the fact that he was being dangled by his legs 600 feet in the air and began to want the 10. *He could do this.*

"8, 9...10!" Berber pulled the man back into the conference room and lowered him to the floor where he promptly collapsed. Berber pulled him up, then spit in his face and kissed him on the lips.

"Not many men do what you just did," Berber exclaimed, genuinely proud of his victim.

The executive held a urine and sweat soaked hand out to his tormenter.

"Thank you. I never...ever could have done that. Ever."

Vance looked at the room.

"Anyone feel like watching a football game now?" Vance asked.

The victim fainted. Within five minutes the assemblage had resumed their seats and the conference continued. Sidney Brill yelled over the howling wind from the broken window.

"Alright, Vance, let's say you can pull off something interesting and let's say we do agree to attempt to go against the Super Bowl. How does the launch figure in?"

"We launch simultaneously. We will host a massive launch party at a secret location, introduce all your shining new stars, and yourself. You'll be just like Disney and Hefner. We show the world your world, then segue into the official *Some Will Die* contestant introduction and weigh in."

"And where do these candidates come from?"

"Auditions, promoted hyper-locally, at some of the most obese cities in the country. We'll enter this whole thing on a massive wave of mystery and buzz, going town to town. We promote the amazing pay-off, The line is, *your fat is your ticket to nirvana*. Do you love it!"

"What about the ad campaign?"

"We get farther making people wonder. We don't release the name of the program until two weeks out and the invitations to the live weigh in are sent out 24 hours in advance. You want everyone to know about something? Tell someone it's a secret."

"What is this gambit going to cost us? The game's in a month, you telling me you can pull it all together that fast?

"Well, it won't be cheap."

"Is it a number that's going to make me unhappy?"

"Probably."

"Very unhappy?"

"Yes, but when the wound heals you won't have a scar."

"Just give it to me now, Vance."

Jack Vance pulled his thin black custom Dunhill wallet out of his pocket and extracted a folded, light green piece of paper. He unfolded it and held it out for the entire board to see.

"A blank check Vance? Jesus you have some balls."

"I can always have Berber do another demonstration."

CHAPTER THIRTEEN
Nefarious Arrangements

MVN Office, Chicago, IL
Friday, December 22, 2017 1:15 PM CST

Vance wished that there was something besides air between himself and Berber in the elevator. The man who had just thrown a chair through a 50 story office window and then dangled someone out of it was as calm as if he had spent the day smoking Mexicali Red. Berber was clearly the kind of psychopath who could roast puppies on a spit while buying cookies from a girl scout. It was just a matter of time before the Beast devoured Vance's leash and his arm along with it. Vance eyed the floor indicator, hoping that he wouldn't piss himself before hitting the street. Vlad was instructed to throw the chair at the window, not through the window, and have someone do crunches on the floor, not in the air.

"How you feeling, Vlad?"

Berber turned and put his hand on Vance's shoulder. The smaller man almost fainted.

"That what you wanted, Executive? Fear, compassion? Are you comfortable with the edge?"

Vance responded with one of his autopilot catchphrases, "You're a natural, Vlad. We're going places with this."

The elevator slid open and Vance felt the cool rush of lobby air pushing back the sweat gathering on his scalp. He was just glad the police weren't waiting for them.

"Let's get a drink at the Hard Rock, Vlad."

The pair walked east towards the Hard Rock Hotel. They arrived at the bar and found the same bartender Vance insulted just a week ago. Berber took a seat and smiled at the man. Vance slid a $100 bill across the bar to smooth any tension in advance.

"Triple Belvedere. Rocks. And whatever my friend wants."

"What I want is to celebrate, Executive! Our game is on! I will start with that bottle there!" Berber waved at a bottle of Stolichnaya on the wall.

Vance excused himself to the men's room and immediately pulled a burner phone out of his pocket. He dialed Naomi Stiles at the office.

"Berber almost turned a presentation into a murder scene. Get the Doc, we need some more programming."

"Berber needs to be *out* for that, Mr. Vance. Where are you?"

"Hard Rock."

"Get him back to the room."

"He wants to party."

"Get a room there."

"And..."

"Knock him out."

"I left my knockout drops at home today...*what was I thinking!*"

"I'm sending Jimmy over, then Doc. Just get him upstairs."

"Send a hooker. That'll get him upstairs. Use the Amex, we'll get points."

"OK boss, one Mickey-slipping hooker coming up. Anything else?"

"Yeah, you still have that Valium script, right? I need about 30 milligrams?"

"For Berber?"

"God no, for me."

CHAPTER FOURTEEN
Class Reunion

New York City: Drab and Associates Offices
Friday, December 22, 2017 6:45 PM EST

Agness was becoming accustomed to his cubicle, which was a bad thing. He had started to connect with other former Blowfishers on staff, even going out for beers after work one evening with a few of them to exchange Vance stories. Word was already on the street that he jumped to Drab. The story was "broken" by a local Chicago gossip blogger who ran *The April Report*. Agness actually leaked it himself, to increase his marketability. Internal scuttlebutt was that he was working on a special project for Drab, which excused him from any other client obligations. But that hadn't stopped Agness from poking his nose into a few meetings and throwing out some suggestions. It almost seemed like a real job, but it wasn't.

He had been 'hired' for one thing: develop a plan to destroy the Blowfish campaign and ultimately Vance. But that plan was nowhere. Drab wasn't known for his patience, he would expect status reports and intel updates. Agness had been rolling the clues of Vance's program around in his head, but they still added up to nothing. Vance had kicked him out of the conference room before he heard the whole pitch. Like a poor hangman player, he had three letters and a whole lot of blanks to fill.

Agness went over it again. Vlad Berber, a reality show about losing weight and the name *Some Will Die*. But what about the rest of
the MVN launch? He could win a battle against a show but lose the
war against the network. His desk phone rang and Drab's angry
face filled his mind. Was this it? He answered without looking at
the screen.

"Agness."

"Tom, it's Bill, Bill Neville."

Agness paused before responding. His stint at Blowfish seemed
like a dim high school memory at this point. Had it only been a
week?

"Bill? How the hell are you? You're gonna get your ass reamed if
Vance finds out you're calling me. You at the office?"

"No, I'm in New York. I quit Blowfish an hour after you were
fired. I'm radioactive in Chicago, no one will touch me. I need
something, Tom. Heard you were working for Drab. Maybe
there's..."

"You said an hour after? So you heard the *Some Will Die* program?"

"Yeah, made me ill. That's why I quit. Sickest thing I ever heard.
Vance is over the edge on this one and I think he put out the word
on me. So maybe there's something at Drab."

"Maybe."

Agness asked Neville to meet him at the Algonquin Hotel bar,
hung up the phone, pulled his one remaining credit card out of his
desk and headed for the elevator. He bounded to the Hotel, his ex-
uberance helping him defy the laws of gravity. This was it. With
Vance's complete launch plan he could develop a scheme. He *was* a
strategist after all.

Neville wasn't at the bar. Agness found him sunk deeply into
one of the overstuffed chairs in the lounge, his posture reflecting
his mindset. He clutched a stained paper Starbuck's cup like a child

clinging to a blanket scrap. Agness would have to change Neville's chemical makeup if he expected to get anywhere.

"You look great, Bill." Agness sat and signaled for a waitress. Neville was suddenly all elbows and knees on the edge of his seat.

"You think there's something at Drab, Tom? I'm not cut out for this whole unemployment/job search thing. You landed there right away, they must be hiring."

"Yeah, if they hired me they'd hire anybody, right? Sure, they're hiring."

"I didn't mean..."

"I know. You're excited and you're scared. *So was I.* But you have an inside edge now. You have me." The waitress appeared and Agness ordered two Belvedere martinis.

"So you could get me in there...maybe at the same level I was at? I don't think I could take a demotion, Tom, I really don't."

Agness let the moment breathe. He sat back in his seat.

"Pity you can't even smoke those e-cigs inside anymore, eh? I could really use a puff about now. How about you Bill?"

"They use the same titles over there? I mean I was the Group Supervisor, I guess that's like a Director level at Burnout. So what would they call me at Drab?"

Agness pulled his Smart Phone off his wrist and laid it out in front of Neville.

"You seen these Suzuki phones yet? Fucking amazing." Agness donned a pair of Serengetti HUD Smart Glasses and blinked his right eye. A photo of a very clenched up Neville appeared on the flexible phone. Neville's vanity briefly overrode his employment obsession.

"Not the most flattering, but the whole black and white thing is sort of cool. Now about..."

The drinks arrived and Agness picked his up, indicating that a toast was in order.

"To the new Drab and Associates Group Supervisor, Director of all things written for the press. Just meet me at the office in the morning and I'll get you all squared away."

Neville looked at him for a second, smiled, and picked up his glass. The tension flowed out of his body as he drained the entire four ounces of vodka. Agness took a sip and put his glass down.

"Now tell me about the whole program Bill. How does Berber fit into *Some Will Die?*"

"I'll tell you what I know Tom...and what I don't. What I know is that *Some Will Die* is one chunk of the launch, and that's going to happen in six weeks and Berber is the host. They start auditioning for contestants soon. Like next week. They launch the network and the show concurrently."

"Where, how?"

"I don't know, he said it was a surprise."

"Six weeks? Exactly six weeks or six weeks plus or minus? Is this a soft launch or a hard one? How can you launch a whole network in *six weeks!*"

"I don't know, seemed pretty hard to me."

"What else do you have Bill, seems kind of...*squishy.* You sure he didn't say six months?"

"No it was 40 something days. That I know."

"40 how many?"

"I dunno, what's six times seven, 42."

"There's a big difference between launching on day 42 or day 49, Bill. What the hell day was it?"

"I don't frigging know. I was too busy being revolted by the whole thing to memorize the exact date."

"42 then?"

"I think it was more. "

"44?"

"Jesus I don't remember Tom. More than 42 and less than 50. I know it started with a four."

"Ok. What else have you got?"

Three hours later Agness was hoofing it across Midtown towards Penn Station. It was 11:00 PM, too late to get a flight but just in time to catch a train. He had left a giddy Bill Neville at the Algonquin bar, with instructions for the waitress to keep feeding him drinks until a $200 advance tab ran out.

Agness' plan had started to develop as Neville unpacked Vance's program. He would have pointed out the fragility of the whole campaign at the launch meeting, if he hadn't been fired. Now he was going to be the hammer at the door of the glass castle. Jesus, hadn't anyone thought out the repercussions of a program based on hate and death? For all his glimmer and genius Vance was one shortsighted motherfucker.

There was something else in play here. Neville had provided more pieces to the puzzle, but left before securing the critical element: how was Vance planning on launching? He knew the man well enough. There would be a lot of sizzle followed by a surprise boom that would capture the media's attention. He still didn't know what that boom was or where it was going to happen, five and a half weeks from today. And it didn't matter at this moment. He knew enough to start taking the thing apart, to launch a creative counter strategy that would buy him the time he needed to fill in the blanks.

He entered Penn Station, made his way to the ticket counter and purchased a round trip for the midnight train to Washington DC. He had a little time to kill so he picked up what he'd need for the next day's work: a pre-gelled toothbrush, disposable razor, one shot of Kenneth Cole Vintage Black cologne, a pint of Absolute and a few breath mints. He grabbed up a copy of the *Washington Post* and found the cleanest bench he could on the freshest smelling car on the train. Agness settled in, unrolled his Smart

Phone and sent Neville's photo to the building security station in the lobby of Drab and Associates' building with the message:

"If this man approaches and asks for entrance to Drab and Associates, call the police. He has been harassing our offices and we fear that he may be dangerous. Please call me if he shows up so I'll know it's safe to go to work."

He sat back and sipped his vodka. It would be a long ride to his morning meeting in DC.

Chicago, IL: Hard Rock Hotel Suite
Saturday, December 23, 2017 3:00 AM CST

Dr. Earnest Trapp was an old friend of Naomi Stiles. She made his acquaintance when he was working for the CIA and she for Google. Drugs and programming were his specialty, and today Vlad Berber was putting all his talents to the test. Dr. Trapp wiped light latex liquid concealer over the slow dissolving psychoactive patch that he had affixed to the lower part of Berber's back. It would be almost impossible for Berber to see or find it. The patch itself contained a numbing agent and the concealer made it invisible. It was designed to make him susceptible to the storyline that they had worked on planting in his subconscious and to ever so slightly deaden his sociopathological impulses. They wanted a beast, just not a wild one.

Trapp started packing up while Vance, Stiles and Jimmy Welles stood around the bed. They had just collectively watched a three hour psycho-pharmacological-cosmetological intervention. Vance spoke first. After all, he was paying the tab.

"Well?"

"It either takes or he'll be in a trance for the next six weeks."

"And if it's a trance then what?"

"Then we sedate him, yank out the patch, give him 24 hours of enemas to flush his system and you've got your monster back."

"And what does he remember at that point?"

"Almost everything. Maybe he'll even want to go along for the ride, provided he doesn't mind being drugged, kidnapped, deceived and manipulated."

One of the burners in Vance's pants trembled. He pulled it out and looked at its screen.

"It's me."

The reality of "personal texts" was a million miles from where Vance was now standing. The little bit of him that wasn't focused on business and his current crisis took a jackhammer to his clinical core with the message: take a break. He moved from the bedroom to the bathroom and closed the door behind him, pressed the phone's speech-to-text button and whispered into its mike.

"Who?"

"DNADate. You: Mr. Business Acronym. Me: Not."

"Thought you were gone."

"Lke yer pix, if it's reel."

"So I get a 2nd chance."

"Until U pull sum biz babble on me again."

"K, how bout sum ROI for your work. Meet FTF and I buy you a drink."

"Too personal too fast."

"Your number then. Let's talk."

"Maybe later."

"Your name then."

"U first."

"Helluva666Guy."

"Not UR scrn name."

"Jack."

" ... "

"Chloe. What you do Jack666?"

"Think too much, drink too much."

"Send me a bdy prt."

Vance thought for a second, then slid his flask out from his jacket, sat down on the toilet seat and positioned it in front of his crotch. He snapped a photo and sent it in his response text. Within 15 seconds he received his response: Chloe sent a photo of her legs, skirt hiked up over tanned thighs, with a tumbler held between her knees. Her text read:

"We'll have lots to tk abot."

Vance ended the conversation. It was a nice diversion, but the real world had a noose around his neck and it was tightening.

PART TWO
JUST ADD WATER

CHAPTER FIFTEEN
HOP

Washington DC
Saturday, December 23, 2017 8:00 AM EST

Agness made his way to the grubby New Hampshire Avenue office of the Human Obesity Party (HOP). The group had been formed to demand more rights for obese people in an era of growing private and public restrictions. The Party's founder, former Georgia congressman Louis "Gekko" Potlatch, was known variously as Gek, Gekko, Pot or Potty, depending on the audience. Agness wasn't sure what the proper address would be at this stage in Potlatch's career and decided to keep his approach formal. HOP was the perfect tool for Agness' plan, providing he could convince their founder that he had their best interests in mind.

Agness found the office's hand lettered nameplate on the building's legend and pressed the buzzer. A bored female voice chirped through the ancient speaker.

"HOP Party."

"Tom Agness of Drab and Associates in New York to speak with Congressman Potlatch."

"New York? Third floor, second door on the right."

Agness climbed through the run down, mid-century un-modern, feline fecalized apartment/office building. He hadn't been in a rat trap like this since he stopped scoring synthetic mescaline for an old girlfriend when he was a student at the University of Illinois, Circle Campus. The HOP party's door was easy to find despite the lack of lights. It was the only one decorated with old signs, boxes of leaflets and empty pizza trays. He rapped on it, each knock pushing it open a little more. Either they didn't believe in locks, couldn't afford them or had nothing to hide or steal.

Agness entered the headquarters, a cluttered and filthy two room office that was probably a flop house bedroom at some time in its seedy past. A petite woman wearing a fly fishing hat and vest sat at a desk made of piled boxes. She was somewhere between 40 and 60. Agness couldn't tell if her grey hair was part of some quasi punk affect or an Act of God. She smiled, revealing several missing teeth, and then spit a plug of tobacco into a cup. He settled on Act of God just as she asked him his "biz-ness."

"Here to see Mr. Potlatch."

"From Neeeeew York huh? Well, Okay." She turned to bellow across the eight foot expanse of paper, plastic and God knew what else.

"Mr. Potlatch! Visitor from Neeeeew York!"

Primitive intercom system, but it worked. The office/closet door on the other end of the main room opened to reveal the moving cane tip that presumably was being held by former Congressman Gekko Potlatch. Agness approached and saw the arm attached to the cane attached to the body of the 500 plus pound man. He was curled like an old swollen sea sponge behind a desk crammed into the closet. Potlatch was awash in the same sea of clutter that had begun out in the hallway.

Agness wondered if Potlatch ever left this pit. He discreetly looked out of the corner of his eyes for Porta Poddy or a bucket with a hose. Agness worked his way through the narrow channel between six foot high piles of boxes to Potlatch's office and took a seat on a two by six that lay across a sideways filing cabinet on the floor. Time, gravity, diet and public opinion had reduced the former firebrand Speaker of the House into a wheelchair bound ember of his flamey old self.

Potlatch had started his career as a Georgia Democrat. He was thin and glib, with a Ph.D. in World History. His dissertation had been on the practical application of Nazi propaganda tactics in political campaigns. His colleagues joked that he was the next Goebbels of the Democratic Party, easily winning over four terms in the sixth Georgia congressional district. He was on his way. Potlatch took a page from the Clinton playbook and engaged in the nonstop campaign, which meant nonstop door to door, event to event and plate to plate glad handing. There was a cost.

By his second term he had doubled in size and by his third was discreetly slipping into big and tall stores. On the day he was appointed Speaker of House, the veiled cocktail chatter concerning his girth and career arc had turned into news. Potlatch was still haunted by the *Atlanta Constitution's* headline: *Party Passes the Plate on Potlatch Presidential Play*. The word was out. If he didn't curb his fork he'd never get the nod, no matter how smart or prophetic he appeared.

Potlatch waddled on stage during the 1992 Democratic National Convention and was greeted by several hecklers scattered throughout the audience with signs that read "A hundred chicken's in every POTlatch" and "Good to the last POTlatch." His temper got the better of him and he engaged in a verbal sparring match with the disruptors on national TV. He resigned the party later that day and joined the Republicans, never knowing that his own former party had paid the protestors to push him over the edge.

Potlatch found a home in the Republican Party until 2008, when his weight had ballooned to 450 pounds and he required a lift to make it onto the stage to deliver an address at their national convention. To his dismay he was confronted with the same heckling response, albeit with different signage. He resigned the party the next day to join the Tea Party. That lasted until he lost his seat in 2012 and was heckled out of a Tea Party trailer rally in Juno, lead by the former governor of Alaska and the former Congresswoman from Minnesota. They were affectionately known as the "*sycho sistas.*" He was denied membership when he applied to join the Libertarians.

Alienation was the catalyst for Potlatch's innovation when he formed the HOP in late 2012. HOP gave him not only new acclaim, but something that had been missing from his political experience: love. Looking down at the man, Agness could see that he was, if anything, a passionate proponent for his cause.

"Mr. New York! What can I do for you?"

Potlatch extended his cane across his desk, expecting Agness to shake it. He wore a concealing black cape and was surrounded by several laptops, ham radios and Morse code keysets. An old Smith and Wesson .44 magnum was draped over the back of his chair, a Remington 700 sniper rifle next to the window and the butt stock of a sawed off shotgun peeked out from under a pile of *Washington Times* newspapers in the corner of his desk.

"It's Mr. Agness, sir, and it's an honor to meet *my* American hero."

Agness "seated" himself on the plank in front of Potlatch's desk.

"It's this country that's the hero Mr. Agness, I'm just a servant for our liberties. What causes you to cross my door today, sir?"

Agness noticed that Potlatch had casually let the cane lie across his desk, its tip pointing squarely at his chest. He peeked down its glinty rifled cavity, .45 mm in diameter. *Great.*

Agness leaned across the desk to Potlatch, moved his body out of the line of fire and lowered his voice to add emphasis, playing on Potlatch's legendary paranoia.

"There's a brewing conspiracy sir, and I have some data that I'd like to share with you. It's a threat to your work. This conspiracy will push the abuse of obese people to a new level. Let me show you."

Agness unrolled a three dimensional viewer. It looked small and foreign in the tangle of greasy aging technology on the desk. He narrated through the presentation that he had put together on the train ride. The argument hit every piece of legislation HOP was working on defeating or having passed. Agness felt it was one of the best 15 minute pitches he had delivered in his career and one of the few he had constructed by himself. Potlatch's eyes grew bigger with each slide. When Agness finished he looked up at the angered, quivering fat man with the most helpless, 'please guide me Jesus' look that he could muster.

"So Congressman Potlatch, what do we do now?"

"Do they know that you know this boy? Do you have protection?"

"I don't think they know and I have no protection. *Should I?*"

This was going better than Agness could have wished for. He had positioned *Some Will Die* as a secret lobbying tool for FIT America. FIT was an organization that was aggressively pushing an agenda to place a fat sin tax on every aspect of U.S. life and commerce, from packaged consumer goods to public transit. Their motto, "Overeat: overpay," was easy to understand and already creating buzzy gatherings. Agness had invented the whole connection on the train ride to Washington. It was perfect, and made perfect sense.

"I never put anything past those skinny FIT bastards."

"The whole show will create so much ridicule in this country that obesity could become issue number one next election.

"And we'd have another skinny in the White House. Sickening."

"Next thing you know there's the incentive for being...not obese."

"Reduced air fare, insurance premium reductions..."

"A tax credit for health club memberships!"

"It's unholy. By God, man. What is this country coming to?"

"Nothing that can't be stopped, sir."

"Who knows that you know about this?"

"Just you and me, and my source. We can trust him. *They* don't know that I know. Yet. But I don't know what their next move is. Just where to look and who to ask."

"You need to find out more."

Potlatch opened a drawer in the side of his desk, extracted a serious looking cordura bag and slid it over to Agness.

"This is your bug out kit, in case they get on to you."

Agness opened it and found a small 9mm Glock, a HAM transceiver, approximately $1000 in traveler's checks and a military issue smoke grenade. He was in.

"So what's our plan, sir?"

Potlatch leaned across the desk.

"You keep your ears on," he motioned to the radio, "use that to communicate. We need to organize the troops. You tell me what their moves are. We will bring the heat, in public. They make a move, we make a move. It's up to you son. You found this. It's too dangerous for you to come here anymore, they might be watching. I'll come to you."

"So you want me to tell you what their next move will be, is that it, like spy on them and then let you know what they're planning and you'll do...what? We need to work on a planned response. You and me."

"This is political, boy. We organize and surprise. They hold a meeting, we hold a rally. They stage an event, we stage a riot. The press catches on quick when there's a protest. We get our word out. We respond quickly, we are flexible, like Gumby. Our tactics conform to their actions. We are being victimized and we're not keeping our mouths shut or putting our forks down over this."

Potlatch picked up the microphone on his desk and pointed to the dial.

"Frequency 30.004. We check in every night at 02300. I'm Foodie. You are Rook. When you call I'll meet you at noon in Columbus Circle the next day. I'll be the man in black, in a wheelchair. Go. It's too dangerous for you here, now. We don't want them to know we're working together."

"So I'm supposed to use a shortwave radio, no phone here?"

"We are living in a world that's always listening boy. It's against the law to turn off your cell phone, remember. My friends on the Hill tell me that these radios will be outlawed soon. Yes *we use blasted shortwaves here!*"

Agness was jumping up and down inside his head. The man was psychotic! Just the kind of scud missile he needed to torpedo Vance's program. Agness stood, grabbed his bag and turned to leave. Potlatch slammed his cane down.

"I need to know when they're going public. We work from there. I'll get the troops and the messaging. You find me a location and a date."

"I won't fail you, sir."

"And Mr. Agness, put on a few pounds."

CHAPTER SIXTEEN
First Call

Milwaukee, WI: Humboldt Park Band Shell
Thursday, December 28, 2017 8:00 AM CST

They began lining up around the Band Shell at 5:00 AM, standing as close as strangers allowed themselves to stand in the pre-dawn, guaranteed-to-be cold limbo week between Christmas and New Year's Eve. Blowfish put the word out using hyper-localized tactics. The attendees had read about it on paper tray liners at fast food diners, seen quick ads before illegally downloaded porno movies, saw notices printed on urinal cakes, circulars on car windows, been spammed through their phones with disappearing messages, received targeted social ads and read the details on sandwich boards being paraded in front of popular fatty watering holes and food stores. All the messages had been the same: *Your weight is your ticket to Nirvana: cash it in at the Band Shell on Thursday morning!*

By 8:00 in the morning nearly 3,000 people were tamping down the snow caked grass around the small, provincial looking A frame Band Shell, each hoping for the vague promise of the buzz. The signage on stage was equally mysterious. No actual programs or names were cited, just a reference to the "New star of the MVN lineup," whatever that meant. Large images of exotic destinations, fancy cars, and before/after photos of heavyset men and women allowed the viewer to fill in their own narration. It was one of the standard Blowfish techniques: provide just enough details for the customer to sell themselves.

The Band Shell audition was being streamed through a variety of online outlets, with bumpers indicating the next audition cities. Crawlers under the broadcast read: *The MVN network is coming to your Smart Device*, and *we're making history, be a part of it this February*. There was excitement in the air. Something new was happening, in Milwaukee of all places. Things like this hadn't occurred since the salad days of Laverne and Shirley, 40 years earlier.

Vance peeked out from around the curtain on the side of the band shell stage and surveyed the crowd, swaying like one large multi-colored blob of Jell-O on a frozen asphalt plate. He trained his field glasses on the audience, scanning the wearable tech, assuming that Milwaukee would be a couple of years behind the national curve of non-FDA approved illegally implanted and skin grafted devices. Everyone carried some kind of always-on recording device these days, powered by the notion that their daily lives were actually interesting enough to remain digitized in second-by-second moments for some later generation to review. It represented a large, brown thunder cloud full of shit as far as he was concerned. But he needed the eyes of the world on these events, and the collective lenses of this audience would provide that.

Naomi Stiles and her team ran through the data they were collecting from the attendees, looking for the day's five finalists. Everyone who entered the band shell had signed a waiver with retinal scan; they were then stamped with a thin RFID tag that would vibrate if they were selected. The retinal scan also provided access to their records through a backdoor that Stiles secured from a friend at the IRS, the warehouse for U.S. human intelligence.

Stiles contracted a former psychiatrist and profiler from Homeland Security to construct an algorithm that would select the candidates with the highest probability of self destruction, culled from IRS' weight and income data. It wasn't foolproof, but it shrank the pool enough to allow them to select, with at least an 85% probability, candidates who would more than likely risk/do anything for fame and fortune. And if they went on to win, they could also be counted on to succumb to temptations that would lead them to excess and death. Vance reserved the final candidate selection for himself, relying on gut instinct and photogenic appeal.

At that moment one of his burner phones vibrated, indicating that he was receiving a text. He pulled out his Oakley's and read the message.

"Ready to take it up a notch?

"Who..."

"Chloe. Last week's txt grl."

"Cd nev frgt U."

"Sk of txting. UR #?"

Vance pulled another burner out of his pocket and gave her a New York number. It rang immediately and he answered it.

"Chloe I assume? Got a taste for beer? We're in Milwaukee."

"You take a nosedive in the social register just flying over that place Mr. Jack. I'm in Buenos Aires, and damn proud of it."

Her voice had a smoky Suzanne Pleschette-ish inflection. To Vance it was a welcome respite from the upbeat "yes, anything you say sir," chirpiness that was affected by all the ass kissing, scared shitless marketing account managers in his life.

"How about Rockford on Tuesday?"

"Getting worse Jack, I'll be in Caracas."

"Topeka, Friday?"

"San Jose, Costa Rica, not California."

"Tampa, Florida?"

"Do you work for Wal-Mart Jack? "

"My interests at this moment are in alignment with some of theirs. How about you? You distributing Hawaiian Tropic or something?"

"I like to make people feel sunny Jack. Is that photo you posted honest?"

"About a year old."

"You're not a serial killer? Married?"

"Which is worse?"

"Unmarried serial killer."

"Then you get a shot."

"What does that mean? You give me your number?"

"No. It means if I stay interested and if we are in the same place at the same time and it's not as shitty as the kind of places that you seem to frequent then I will be at the same bar as you at some point. I will check you out from across the room and if you look like your photo I will let you buy me a drink. Or I might even buy you one myself."

"I lost track of where this was going after the fourth *same*."

"I got your number Jack, keep your phone on. It's a burner I bet."

"So what. I don't have your number and you have my burner."

"Pre-ban I imagine, right, Mr. Kong?"

"Looked it up already?"

"Your responses were a little slow, I needed something to do."

"Give me your number and I'll give you a real phone."

"I'm doing a little more research on you first Mr. Jack 666 Kong. *If that really is your name.* To be continued..." She rang off.

Vance didn't mind the distraction, frankly, he could use it. He hadn't been laid in a month or drunk in a week in preparation for this and the subsequent auditions. Milwaukee was the first, followed by Topeka the next day, then Tampa, Florida the following week. They planned on criss-crossing the country, stopping in cities and towns with a high percentage of obese people, announcing the program as they continued. They'd hit several cities through the middle of January, generating excitement and gathering momentum for the big launch on February 4th.

Blowfish would release the location to the televised weigh-in just 24 hours out. The lucky invitees would be sworn to keep it a secret and word would spread like the Black Death. The network launch would occur that same day, with the anticipated fever over *Some Will Die* providing the necessary eyeballs to power the network. He was playing it down to the wire, but with the deadline that he had in mind, there was no other move to make.

Vance felt his business Smart Phone vibrate. Stiles sent him the list of 30 potential finalists. It was time to select. As he went through the faces he walked up to Vlad Berber, busy combing over the crowd from the side of the stage. Vlad was wearing his "uniform," a pair of light combat pants, boots and a black tank top bearing the *Some Will Die* logo: a bloody fork with a pair of crossed barbells. The program they had scripted for today would become the template for the audition tour. Vance patted him on the back.

"Let's go over it again."

"We know the drill executive. Just like army."

Vance was insistent.

"Amuse me, what are we doing here today?"

"I announce we're looking for contestants who want to be rich, famous and thin. I call out the ten names that you give me. One by one. Each person I test onstage. We do some exercises, I toss out five and we come away with five. The we go to next shithole."

"Excellent." Vance turned to Stiles. "How many people do we think are watching us?"

Stiles stabbed at the flexible screen draped over her tanned knee.

"Maybe 20,000. Mainly here."

"We need to grow this thing." He turned to Berber, "Make it happen, Vlad."

Blowfish had hired a popular local morning DJ from Milwaukee's top ranked WCOW to keep the crowd entertained while the area filled. He was in his mid-70's, wearing a Member's Only jacket, and bobbed energetically around the stage. His large head of upswept white-dyed-blond hair could be seen from the air. Most of the jokes he told had been lifted from the Borscht Belt playbook and de-Judified for the local Milwaukee audience. *Also Sprach Zarathustra* began playing over his monologue and he shifted into his ringside voice. The show was beginning.

"Hello dere MilVaukee! Who wants to be a TV star!" The response was tepid.

"I didn't hear anything! Let's try this again" He looked down at note card in his hand.

"Who wants to lose all their extra weight and feel like a million bucks?!" A bottle hit the announcer in the leg, followed by a series of catcalls. He threw down the card and practically stuffed the microphone into his mouth.

"Who wants to be rich and famous and sleep with a different movie star every night?" The crowd barked and hollered their approval of the suggestion.

"Here's the man that's going to help you do it! Give it up for the star of Survivor Chernobyl...the baddest Russian since Stalin...Vlad Berber!"

Berber walked up behind the announcer, took the microphone from him and let the applause knock him back. God, it felt good. His assistants rolled out several pieces of exercise equipment, ranging from barbells to kettle balls. He would use these to test each contestant's abilities and give those watching a flavor of the show. Vlad was a no-nonsense performer, preferring to let his body and his actions make the point. He pulled a transparent reader from his pocket and called out the first name.

"Homer Gillespie!"

A bald, middle aged man wearing sweat pants and an untucked golf shirt made his way from the second row to the side of the stage, where he was helped up a short flight of stairs by two guards. He was 5'4", carried all of his weight in his belly and had already sweated through his outfit. Berber regarded Homer's thick, drippy extended hand and snapped on a blue latex glove before shaking it. The audience applauded.

"You want to *die*, Mr. Gillespie?"

Vance, standing in the wings on stage right, felt his legs suddenly grow weak. Vlad was instructed to keep the show's name in stealth mode. He instinctively felt through his suit for his flask, then remembered that he had left it in the hotel. *Jesus, what was he thinking?* He looked over at Stiles and out at the several paramedics next to the stage.

"No sir, Mr. Berber. I want to lose 150 pounds and live on an island with a movie star!" Berber slapped his back.

"That's it! Let's see what you do." He regarded his play set for a moment then picked up a 15 lb. kettle ball.

"We try some simple swings, yes?" Berber demonstrated a perfect swing. It was graceful, elegant and powerful, as if he was directing a video for Men's Health. He called out the muscle groups involved, the proper number for a set, and enumerated the benefits of a rigorous workout with this simple weight. Then he handed it to Homer. The fat man immediately dropped into a crouch, pulled down by the weight. He recovered and began swinging. Berber moved behind him and watched his form, ready to kick his ass for motivation.

"Fast...higher...let ball do work."

Gillespie was beginning to catch on. An approving murmur, like a collective burp, rippled through the crowd. The fat man smiled, feeling in control of something besides a fork for the first time in his life. The *'Laverne and Shirley'* theme issued from the loudspeakers and Gillespie began churning, developing a rhythmic flow to his exercise. Berber, motivated by his initial success, pulled out the Russian drill sergeant and started shouting for more, kicking Gillespie's behind to help him swing higher.

"Work it Homer! Feel it!!"

Sweat flew off Gillespie's body as he crouched down then exploded back up to the crescendo of the song's chorus "Always...always," losing his slippery grip on the weight's coated metal handle. The kettle ball arched over the barricade and plowed, like a wayward red shell, into the audience. Gillespie flew backwards into Berber.

The tightly packed group in the front row could barely breathe much less make way for the inert flying bomb. It careened directly into the stomach of one Eva Brownowsky of Mequon, Wisconsin, who promptly vomited up the two pound bag of Cheetos and the Double Super Gulp 7/11 Jolt cola she had consumed on the drive down to the show. The police and paramedics shoved the audience aside as they pushed through the sea of fat to the prone woman. Vance looked down at Stiles.

"Are we protected on this?"

"Everyone here signed a waiver when they scanned in. We're bulletproof, to a point. That accident just started a trend. We're up to 85,000 uniques."

"Tell Vlad to do some more damage."

The paramedics placed Ms. Brownowsky's vomit splattered frame on a reinforced cot. She gave a weak 'thumbs up' as they wheeled her away. Berber regained his composure onstage and helped Homer to his feet. The fat man stammered.

"Oh God...I'm sorry." Berber's natural abilities as a showman drew him up. He seemed to grow in stature, commanding the audience's attention away from the momentary tragedy.

"She alright! Ms..." he paused, waiting for the woman's name to be whispered into his ear through his headset.

"Eva Brownowsky of Mequon!" He paused again, "Ms. Brownowsky is second contestant!"

The crowd roared with applause. From their station at the side of the stage Vance smiled. He looked over at Stiles.

"We just went over 100,000 viewers in the past thirty seconds, just on our feed. The crowd is streaming this everywhere."

"With people like this we don't even need the media. Screw em for not showing up."

"The accident is everywhere."

Vance looked down at Stiles and smiled. "*Fat* is the new *fuck*, baby."

CHAPTER SEVENTEEN
Liar's Poker

New York City: Drab and Associates Offices
Thursday, December 28, 2017 9:45 AM EST

Tom Agness crouched in the stall farthest from the door of the Drab and Associates men's room. He whispered into the short-wave transceiver that Potlatch had given him.

"Foodie this is Rook. Foodie, this is Rook. Do you read me Foodie?"

A "dial-up" slow 30 seconds passed before he received a response.

"Rook, you're off schedule."

"Emergency, Foodie. I am sending you some files. We must meet. We need to mobilize and act."

"Clarify Rook, what is happening?"

"Look at the *files*. One is a video of the Some Will Die event. The other is your HOP Manifesto. You need to watch the video and post the Manifesto. It's the first stage in our response! We need to meet tomorrow."

"*You* wrote *our* Manifesto Rook?"

"Edit it, change it, whatever, just get it posted! We need to get out stakes in the ground now! You need to call out that event for what it is!"

Agness pulled a pre-ban burner phone from his pocket; it was another trick he had learned from Vance: always have a pocketful of untraceable devices. He sent a file of the Milwaukee show audition to Potlatch.

"Read your email Foodie and call me back on the number I am sending you! We need to meet!"

"I don't like phones, Foodie."

"Reception bad here, Rook. Just call the number it's pre-ban."

Vance had not been idle in the past week. Agness knew the playbook. Blowfish would tease the market with several auditions, let the buzz and the speculation build, then announce some type of news when a critical mass of potential viewers was reached. They'd repeat the formula for the actual launch. He'd need the location of the next audition cities to appease Drab and feed Potlatch's army. The game was on. He just had to move as quickly as the Blowfish team. The information had to be out there. He left the men's room and was intercepted by Patty Labrea, the head of HR.

"Mr. Drab would like to see you." She had a paper file tucked under her arm. Patty wasn't an Agness supporter and a sudden meeting request with his new boss was never a good sign.

They entered Drab's office together and she shut the door, remaining standing while Agness took a seat in front of Drab's desk. This felt un-good.

Drab enjoyed making people wait. He wrapped up typing on his vintage KayPro computer, priding himself on his ability to communicate in DOS, and regarded Agness. The window monitor filled with video of the morning's Milwaukee audition.

"My data expert tells me that more than 100,000 people were watching this *unknown program*, featuring *Vlad Berber*, the man we were talking about just a week ago. Why am I discovering this on my own? I need you to explain to me what you are bringing to this party Mr. Agness? *Where is your anti-campaign campaign?* It's been a week!"

Agness felt the room start to swirl. He didn't know if he was having a panic attack or a stroke. He tried to steady his vision by fixating on a tiny shiny spot on Drab's bald, Elmer Fuddish forehead. Patty Labrea handed Drab the folder she had been carrying. He removed a single sheet and laid it on his desk.

"This is a bill, Mr. Agness, for one week's worth of office space, advance money and a portion of the office utilities. You will owe me this money upon termination of your employment at Drab and Associates. You have exactly ten seconds to talk me out of changing you from an employee to a receivable account. Go."

Tom Agness was too young to have a heart attack. At 35? No way. But the sudden ringing in his ears was so loud he couldn't hear himself think, let alone formulate a response that would save his "job." It was over. He began to rise from his chair when the burner phone in his pocket vibrated. *Hail Mary*, this was it. He took it out and slapped it on the desk, hitting the speakerphone. Only one person in the world had the number.

"Agness here."

"Rook! Use your code name."

"You received my file *Congressman Potlatch*? Are we ready to discuss an organized protest against the *Some Will Die* program now?"

"It's Foodie, Rook! Stick with the code! We can't have this conversation on a party line! Meet me at the designated location at 01200 tomorrow. And be careful Rook, they're listening."

That was it. The room had stopped spinning and he refocused from the spot on Drab's forehead down to the man's eyes. He was searching for any signs of softness.

"Would you like to come along to the meeting tomorrow... Mr. Drab?"

Drab unfolded his arms. Maybe the little shit was actually doing something.

"Congressman Potlatch, of HOP?"

"That's correct."

"And you have been in communication with him..."

"And his network of 100,000 motivated obese people across the country."

"To organize a protest against Vance's program?"

"Yes. We're working out the details. Blowfish is operating in stealth mode. They won't release the agenda until they're closer to launch. We're going to push that window and make this into an embarrassing national debate. The last thing Vance wants is the spotlight. He works much better in the shadows."

Drab let the moment play out. He could see little beads of sweat gathering just under Agness' tight hairline. Another reason to hate the little prick: he *had* a hairline. Drab turned away from Agness and hit the intercom button on his vintage desk phone.

"Cancel my lunch with the Deacon tomorrow, Ms. Barnes, I'm taking the afternoon with Mr. Agness. We won't need any reservations." He looked up at Agness.

"Lunch is on you, Mr."

Agness left the room silently, hoping it wouldn't prove to be the last time he ordered out in New York.

CHAPTER EIGHTEEN
The Sure Thing

Topeka, Kansas: Denny's Restaurant
Thursday, December 28, 2017 11:00 AM CST

Jimmy Welles knew that if he completed this assignment successfully he would be cemented as the 'go to guy' in Vance's world. He had taken charge of the whole mission, from finding the suitable candidate and initiating the preliminary discussions to flying in ahead of the as yet publically unnamed *Some Will Die* audition tour to close the deal. He was a man of resources who would take the place of that self aggrandizing scumbag Tom Agness.

Word on the street was that Agness had joined up with Drab, but no one was going to tell that to Vance. It was the last thing he needed to hear in the midst of this campaign. Drab and Agness deserved each other: a liar to fuel the interests of an obsessed paranoiac. Why Welles had been passed over in favor of Agness at Blowfish still bugged him. Welles had street sense, could hustle, wasn't a drunk, kept the companies' interests in mind. And he was a BlAsian; the fucking John Shaft, Nick Fury, Bruce Lee ass kicker that Blowfish needed in its C-Suite. It was all going to change with this campaign. He would prove his value and find the word "Senior" in front of his title before the Groundhog saw his shadow.

Welles was sitting at a side table in a greasy Denny's by himself, stirring his translucent coffee and watching the grounds swirl around the bottom of the mug. His identity was obscured by his Blackhawk Alias glasses. They projected another face over his, forming an electronic mask. He had selected the Prince-face program for this meet, figuring that everyone liked Prince, even Hillbilly types. In the right light the system was almost foolproof. His victim's would have no clue to his identity.

A smoky old police van, its door badge crudely covered by camo spray paint, pulled into the parking lot outside the Denny's. A heavyset 60-ish woman in a ratty *Sportsman's Guide* down hunting parka eased out from behind the wheel and walked around the vehicle to assist her passenger. She opened the side door, blocking Welles' view. A pair of legs touched the ground and the van rose a few inches, almost breathing in relief as its load was discharged. The man connected to the legs emerged. He resembled a 600 pound stack of tires sandwiched into a track suit. The man stood six feet three tall and wore a pair of faded green overalls, muck boots and a thin windbreaker.

The pair lumbered towards the diner, entered, squinted, and spied Jimmy Welles, whose $300 handmade Italian tie immediately branded him as 'not of this place.' As they approached Welles could see she was wearing a beat pair of CmyWorld Personal Transmission glasses. Those had to go. Welles stood.

"Mrs. Bigelow? Could you please remove those glasses?" She looked him up and down then pulled them off her face. The last thing Welles needed was any record of this meeting.

"Ah need em for reading Mr..."

"Keep them off or the meet's over. There's nothing to read today."

Welles smelled opportunist. He held out his hand.

"John Smith. Call me Mr. Smith. And you must Mrs. Bigelow's son, Ben."

Mrs. Bigelow demurred Welles' hand. He looked down to see her skin, scaly with eczema, and silently thanked her. He placed his hand into Ben's fleshy baseball mitt and shook. The large "boy" attempted to speak, then immediately began coughing.

"We better get Ben into a chair," the woman urged.

Welles had three chairs ready. They helped Ben ease into his seats, and then assumed theirs. Welles wanted to make sure that their data validated their claims. He looked over at Mrs. Bigelow.

"Did you bring the medical records?"

She slid a chip across the table to Welles. He pulled a flexible screen out of his pocket and laid it on the table. Within seconds the screen filled with charts. Welles scrolled through them, pausing at some, flipping past others. A full minute elapsed before he looked up.

"No hope for a cure?"

Mrs. Bigelow's face crunched into an 'about to cry' grimace.

"There's none, Mister, I've got less than six months to live any way you slice it," Ben said, quietly placing his large hand on his mother's shoulder.

"Let's review our proposition, Mrs. Bigelow."

"Benny will enter the competition in Topeka tomorrow. He'll be selected to become a show finalist." She began to choke up.

"And what Mrs. Bigelow?"

"He will compete in the big launch program."

"Where Mrs. Bigelow?"

"On national TV, in February." Welles gave the pair a moment to compose themselves, regarding the medical records again for a moment.

"And then what Mrs. Bigelow?"

"He will...he will join God during that show."

"When during that show Mrs. Bigelow?"

"When they have him do exercises."

"Not before, not after, during that exercise, and all by himself. No drugs, nothing else."

"Right. And you give us $100,000 in cash. I mean me. Because Ben won't....he'll be at peace...with the Lord Jesus Christ." She started sobbing. Welles placed his hand over Mrs. Bigelow's, remembered the eczema, then quickly pulled it away.

"This must be so hard for you. We'll need to have our doctor review this and give your son an exam."

Ben leaned forward.

"I can assure you Mr. Smith, if I do so much as a sit up, this old ticker's gonna quit out on me. I've got an enlarged heart, diabetes, enlarged spleen, cirrhosis of the liver and I'm going blind to boot. If one don't get me something else will. Mom needs the money. I won't let her down."

Mrs. Bigelow pulled herself together.

"And the down payment of $25,000 comes today, comes now, for going along with the idea."

"Subject to doctor's exam, Mrs. Bigelow."

Her face morphed slightly from teary mother to negotiating businesswoman. It was almost as if a little bit of Meg Whitman was lurking beneath her surface, just waiting for an opportunity to scratch up to the daylight.

"We don't think you're going to find anyone else Mr. Smith. Who you workin' for anyway?"

"It's called HOP, Mrs. Bigelow, the Human Obesity Party. Did you read the manifesto our party published last night? We're condemning this show and all it stands for and want to send a message that will protect everyone like Ben. His death will have meaning, it will send that message."

"*Manifesto?*"

"It's like a statement. A long statement. And ours said that this show was evil and should not be taken lightly."

"*HOP*, huh? Hmmm..."

HOP was the perfect foil for the plan. It was amazing how they had fallen into his lap at just the right moment, almost as if it was planned by some invisible helping hand. He owed somebody a big thank you. Their Manifesto roundly condemned the entire program and they were just crazy enough to believably make a move like this.

Welles looked across at their faces and saw a strange mix of sincerity, desperation and greed. If he had handed over the cash without the doc's sign off it would come out of his paycheck. He was being shaken down by a pair of trailer-billies. Sure, the fat guy looked sick, but a big infusion of money has a unique way of healing just about anything.

"This going to happen like we think?" asked Welles.

"Mister, I feel like I'm havin' a grabber every time I squeeze a loaf. We need the money. You wan' me dead, I'm dead."

Welles pulled an envelope out of his pocket and handed it to Mrs. Bigelow.

"There's a new CVS about a mile down from the Amphitheatre. Meet the Doc in the ambulance in the rear of the parking lot at 7:00 AM. And don't spend all that just yet."

"We knows it. Okay..You be there?"

"Yeah, and I'll make sure you get into the competition line for the show."

Ben smiled and rose to stand.

"Thank you Mist...." He grabbed at his chest and fell back into his chairs, his eyes rolling back in his head while his mouth went slack. Welles bolted up.

"Not yet...Jesus...Ben!"

Mrs. Bigelow blocked Jimmy from approaching Ben while the fat man in the chair started to shake and quiver. She stuffed the envelope of cash into her purse.

"It's Mother Nature's call, a deal's a deal!"

Then Ben opened his eyes and started laughing.

"Relax boy, we was just funning you."

Welles felt the warm trickle of urine run down his leg. *Fuck*, he didn't need to christen a new Armani suit this way. Good thing it was dark enough to shield the stain.

He watched the pair trundle off back to their vehicle and wondered if their van's oily blue smoke trail on the road was the last he'd see of them. Twenty five grand could buy a lot of propane for their trailer.

CHAPTER NINETEEN
Plan A

New York City: Columbus Circle
Friday, December 29, 2017 9:55 AM EST

Drab walked briskly for a man of 60 who seemed to spend all his time crouched over an old computer. He remained several steps in front of Agness as they maneuvered through the busy Manhattan morning. It was one of Drab's power plays, staying a few feet ahead of the competition. During his stint as a balding 22 year old intern at Portrait Nobelly he was hell bent on getting to the head of the line before the next guy, even if it was a toilet staff. Agness leaned back a little and regarded the man pushing through the crowds ahead of him. God, *Drab must have been abused relentlessly in the schoolyard.* They arrived at Columbus Circle and Agness caught up to him.

"I don't see anyone." Drab was impatient, searching the moment for failure.

Agness pointed to a black figure in the distance.

"Look lower, he rides a wheelchair." To the North of their entry point sat Potlatch, looking like a crumpled Orson Welles in a large cape and fedora that protected him from the icy spray of the surrounding fountains. Drab and Agness approached him like two retarded foxes stalking a crippled rabbit. Agness extended his hand.

"Congressman Potlatch. Glad you could make it, sir."

Potlatch looked up, his hands didn't move.

"I'm sorry I've forgotten your name, Rook. Was it New York?"

"Unimportant, sir."

Potlatch gave Drab an up and down review while Drab returned the silent appraisal with a down and up, their heads were tracking in opposing unison. Potlatch looked back over at Drab.

"Your assistant?"

"Associate. Congressman, we'd like to talk about plans for the demonstrations."

Potlatch signaled and three men wearing dark Blackhawk tactical pants and sports coats emerged as if they had been newly spawned from the surrounding bushes. One of the three took steerage of Potlatch's chair while the other two assumed flanking positions on Drab and Agness. Potlatch motioned them forward.

"Let's walk gentlemen. This city is full of drones and cameras. The concrete has eyes and ears." They pushed forward around the Circle. Potlatch reveled in these moments. These men had given him a new mission, a target, a raison d'être. It was exactly what he needed to revitalize his all too-quiet-lately organization. They had the sensitive intelligence that he needed to regain the national limelight. Rook was an honest soldier. Potlatch had a sense for things like that. He would deliver. The "associate" could be a wild card. Older, suspicious, with an air of sneakiness about him. Potlatch had met many like him during his travels and knew how to handle him. This was his moment, he would call the action.

"We have been busy, Rook, in our own way. HOP does not squander media coverage on camp fires. We want bonfires, events that will light the imaginations of the next generation of believers. The video you sent me was vulgar and discriminatory and inflamed us as much as it hurt us. Many members found it and are tracking it. The HOP manifesto we published last night makes our case. But unless we provide direction, our members may act on their own. I trust that's why we're meeting today."

The group stopped and Potlatch and his three handlers all looked at Agness. Drab responded to the question.

"Roger Drab, of Drab and Associates, Congressman, and a pleasure to meet you."

Potlatch regarded Drab, he still didn't like him and wasn't about to move to shake his extended hand. Drab slowly lowered it and continued.

"Our interests are the same, Congressman, and I'm willing to put my agency's resources behind this effort."

"So what's the plan, Mr. Drab?"

"Let's take a page from the Viet Cong. We start by annoying them, making our presence known during their city by city audition process, building empathy in the press."

"We do bonfires, Mr. Drab, not little sorties."

"Tet offensive."

"Excuse me?"

"We build to that bonfire, our Tet offensive. On the day the group that produced the audition you saw launches their new network we conduct a massive protest that disrupts their launch party and their show."

"*New network*? There's more than just what I saw?"

"Lord yes! They're putting a whole series of programs out and they're going to launch it sometime soon. We find where, grab the press that they've scheduled and drive our message home. We accuse them of framing a whole network around messages of exclusion and hate. Nothing alienates potential sponsors faster than the wrong kind of controversy. This is definitely the wrong kind."

"OK, say we go with this plan. What's the schedule?"

"We start hitting the auditions next week. They've got one in Tampa. We'll send some protest messaging over to your offices. Just get your people assembled, we'll stir up the press."

"And we do this for how long?"

"Until the launch. Then we take them down."

"And that is?"

Drab looked over at Agness.

"Mr. Agness?"

"Sometime in February. First or second week. We're nailing down the hard date."

Potlatch had spent enough time in Congress to know a bluff when he saw it.

"When exactly and where exactly?"

Drab interceded, sensing a way to turn this missing data point into a bargaining chip.

"Just get your people together for phase one Congressman, when we get closer to the launch date we'll review the second part of the plan."

Potlatch looked up at the pair. He'd give them a couple of weeks to prove themselves before taking control of the entire operation himself.

"Okay, we meet again in middle January. Send your documents over Mr. Drab, I'll deliver the HOP to Florida. How many people do you need?

"About 20 tons should do it."

"I don't find that funny, Mr. Drab, it's the kind of thing one of those cretins from FIT might say."

"FIT?"

"We won't let you down, sir. Those FIT bastards won't know what hit them." Agness interceded by ending the conversation. He hooked Drab's arm and pulled his boss out of the Circle. Drab disentangled himself before they had taken ten steps.

"What the hell does FIT have to do with this, Agness?"

"It was a tool to get him on board."

"Switch up the truth on everyone else but me, Agness. You just gave away your castle, *Rook*, better hang onto your queen."

Chapter Twenty
One More Rung

Topeka, Kansas
Saturday, December 30, 2017 5:45 AM EST

Welles hadn't slept all night. He had drunk coffee, worked out in his room, penned a chapter of the marketing book he was writing, sent out texts and emails, posted status updates, monitored the morning newscasts, and it still wasn't 6:00 AM. He left the Motel Six that Missy Slats had so graciously booked him into and headed over to the Gage Park Amphitheatre. It had cost Blowfish $300 to book the facility, as non-residents. They reserved it from 8AM-11AM and weren't anticipating the huge crowd they had in Milwaukee. There had been virtually no press for this event and the Amphitheatre only held 200. This event literally had one purpose: to secure their shill without drawing too much local fanfare. Then his phone rang.

"Jimmy, it's Missy. The Town of Topeka's been calling about the event. Seems a few more people showed up than we anticipated. You want the number?"

"Already on my way. Deal with it there. Have Gould look over our event insurance and make sure that we're covered on this."

Welles received his first dose of reality about a half mile from the location when he was stopped by the Topeka Police on SW 6. The reason was clear: traffic was blocked all the way to the Amphitheatre. He pulled his rental Chevy over to a side street and left it. The only way he'd get to the Bigelow meet up on time was on foot. He made the CVS by 7:10 AM and activated his Blackhawk Alias mask as he walked around to the rear of the store's parking lot.

The ambulance was there. He opened the rear door and saw Bigelow lying prone on a gurney, a doctor bent over him, shaking his head. *Shit, had he died already?* He walked over to the local physician who had been hired along with the rest of the crew. Besides Berber, Welles was the only other representative of Blowfish in Kansas. Vance wanted their exposure kept to a minimum for good reason. Mrs. Bigelow stood outside the ambulance, looking at him strangely as he approached. Welles nodded hello to her and jumped into the back of the ambulance.

"How is our candidate, doctor?"

"A medical miracle."

"Why?"

"Because he should be dead."

"So he's not, right?"

"No, at this point his heart can't pump enough blood to keep him awake for more than 15 minutes at a time. He's asleep."

"So what do you think in terms of the future?"

"If he doesn't move from this cot, maybe a month." Welles stepped out to Mrs. Bigelow.

"Looks like we've got a deal."

"A deal? Who are you, mister?"

"Smith. From yesterday. Remember, that's why you're here today."

"Man from yesterday looked like Prince. You look like dat black president we had. You sound like Smith but you don't look like him." Welles looked down at his Smart Phone. In his haste he had selected the wrong fucking mask.

"We work together. And we're both named Smith. Mr. Smith told me to make sure you got to the Amphitheatre on time and make it through the line to get Ben checked in."

"Huh."

"So...let's go."

"Funny thing, mister."

"What?"

"That so many skinny black guys named *Smith* is workin' for an organization bout fat people. You sure you ain't with the show, Mister? I imagine a guy dyin' on the first show would help with them ratin's, you know."

"HOP is an equal opportunity organization, Mrs. Bigelow. We don't discriminate against skinny people."

Kansas International Airport, Platte County, Missouri Saturday, December 30, 2017 8:00 PM CST

Jimmy Welles would never set foot in Kansas again. He had 40 minutes to kill before his flight back to Chicago, enough time for a cocktail and a quick scan of the news. He entered the bar, not expecting to find his boss waiting for him. Vance had ordered two drinks and handed one to Welles.

"Congratulations, kid. You should have seen the numbers; we're blowing the doors off this thing. Video everywhere, people were snapping and sending from the God damned line on the highway! Thought this was a low profile thing but what the hell."

"Nice to see a friendly face. Why did Berber get the limo and the chartered flight and I'm riding coach?"

"They give you a hard time out there?"

"Goes with the job, right."

"You ready for Tampa now?"

"Tell me I've got some backup this time."

"Sure kid. Now that the sticky stuff is done. It is done, isn't it?"

"Oh it's done, Jack. You've got your launch ratings boost in the bag. Mrs. Bigelow was a little snoopy, not the roll over hick we maybe thought."

"She gets her money she won't care. Berber, he doesn't know, right?"

"Clueless in so many ways. I did my thing, he did his."

"That's a professional talking. I'll join you in First Class back to the city."

"Upgraded?"

"Comes with the title, *Senior Account Group Supervisor.*"

Vance picked up his glass and clinked it against the one waiting for Welles. He had just secured the younger man's absolute loyalty, and they both knew it.

CHAPTER TWENTY ONE
First Salvo

Chicago, IL: Blowfish War Room
Thursday, January 4, 2018 8:00 AM CST

The hospital room was clammy and oppressive. Vance couldn't breathe. He woke in a sweat in the chair next to his father's bed. The Cohiba box with the Soviet pistol was still on his lap. He was sick of the old man's cryptic clues. If this was his last night on earth he'd answer a few fucking questions before he checked out. Vance stood over the bed, reading the weak vital signs. Fuck it. He tapped Ben Vance on the chest. Nothing. He slapped him lightly on the right cheek. Eyes flickered. Life.

"Jack. Jack what the shit are you doing?"

"Wake up. Stay with me. I want some answers."

"You interrogating me? YOU?" Ben Vance started laughing as well as he could with one lung. He was awake now.

"Who were you spying for, Dad?"

"Spying? I troubleshoot. I put out fires. Spies wear suits and go to cocktail parties and pretend to be diplomats. I got my hands dirty for the right reasons, boy. Remember that. For things that mattered."

"For who?"

"Not for the government. Pay sucks. I worked for people who needed help."

"So you're a mercenary?"

"Mercenaries hurt for a living. I make things right. Put together the clues, you're a reporter, right?"

"Why did you give me the gun?"

"Because I want you to find the bastard it belongs to and pay him back."

"For what?"

"For killing your father, idiot!"

Vance awoke, again. He was at his table in the War Room. He looked up at the cloud and into the live feed from morning's audition in Tampa. The over head view from the top of the stage revealed a healthy stream of rotund Floridians. From a distance it looked like the start of another successful day. He called down to Welles.

"How we doing, Jimmy?"

"This place can handle 20, 25,000. Should be okay. No weirdness yet.

"So I can get back to some other company business today?"

"Yeah, I got this."

Vance ended the call and laid out a couple of lines of his precious Escobar cocaine stash and snorted them. Better than coffee in the morning, he said to himself, then called Naomi Stiles into his office. She was joining him on a new business call with Waist Watchers. They were pitching the CEO on a fat awareness program based on the obesity awareness created by *Some Will Die.* Vance's creative department had outdone themselves with a deck on why fat was about to become the hottest new trend of the year and what they could do to capitalize on it.

Drab and Associates Offices: New York
Thursday, January 4, 2018 9:00 AM EST

Roger Drab and Tom Agness knew their messaging was bullet-proof, designed to draw just the right kind of negative media attention to the Tampa protest. It had to work. They were both strategic geniuses after all. If the tactics failed it could only be for one reason: because Potlatch's group screwed it up. They watched one of the audition feeds on Drab's office monitor, waiting for the moment when the scheduled unrest began. If the plan was followed the way they scripted it the protests would start after the second contestant was announced, then the organized mob would storm the stage.

The plan called for the protesters to work their way towards the front then unfurl their signs and banners in a manner that would create an edge to edge wall of messaging. It would capture the top 40% of screen real estate on any device. Their research showed that interest in the programming picked up after the first 20 minutes of the show. No one was supposed to move before then.

They watched with the volume on low as a local radio personality warmed up the audience. Drab impatiently shook his foot. He knew what was going to happen if everyone followed orders. True to script, Also Sprach Zarathustra blasted through the loudspeaker at ten minutes into the programming. Vlad Berber appeared on stage, made his comments and called up the first contestant. Drab checked his watch. Thirteen minutes in. His foot twitched faster, a fact that was not lost on Tom Agness, who was just as anxious as Drab, but for different reasons. One thing his tenure at Blowfish taught him was that the only aspects of a campaign you could count on were those that you directly controlled. The list didn't include Potlatch.

At the fifteen minute mark Drab watched a wave of signs start popping up roughly around the front half of the audience. He bolted up out of his chair, kicking the nearest litter basket across the room.

"Sit the fuck down!!" He screamed at the monitor. "God fuck it what are those idiots doing! It's not time."

The signs remained static, almost as if those holding them didn't know what to do next. A few moved back while others disappeared entirely. Berber didn't notice and if he did, didn't indicate it on camera.

"What the hell are they doing?" Drab screamed at the screen.

"I think they're protesting."

"Not the way I want. Get Potlatch on the phone."

"What's he going to do? It's happening now."

Drab threw his shoe at the screen.

"Do something you fat, fucking idiots!! Protest!"

Tampa, FL: Florida State Fairgrounds
Thursday, January 4, 2018 9:20 AM EST

Welles surveyed the protestors through his binoculars, trying to put the messages together. The Florida State Fairground band shell stands were swollen well past their capacity. The police reported that 35,000 were packing into the area, with more on the roads. He had watched the signs pop up around the crowd and waited. Five minutes passed and nothing was happening, the signage remained unmoving, the action on stage was uninterrupted. He called Vance.

"You got a second?"

"We're closing the Waist Watchers account, you'll be on it when this program wraps. What's up?"

"Little bit of a wildcard, some protestors."

"Good! We're expecting some response. Make sure the media knows."

"You're the PR guy."

"Oh yeah. What do the signs say?"

Welles read the signs through his field glasses.

"*First FAT, then everything else! It starts with Fat and ends with Race!* And here's an interesting one, *FIT hates FAT.* You know FIT?"

"That health organization. What the hell do they have to do with this?"

"There's more FIT stuff, and now they're moving towards the stage."

"Everyone?"

"Just the FIT signs. Hold on, a few are hitting the stage area. Okay, what's our response here?"

"Let them come up. I'll get CNN."

Welles called up Vlad through his earpiece.

"Vance says carry on. We're going to let them on stage. Put on your charm, invite them to join us."

Vlad Berber saw the blobby bodies working their way, fat leg after fat leg, up the stairs on either side of the stage. They came one by one, the stage hands holding their signs for them as they ascended. He gave them time and within ten minutes roughly fifty protesters were assembled on stage. Vlad addressed the crowd through the PA system.

"Anyone else? Thanks for coming! Who wants to lose weight and be superstar?"

He walked from person to person offering the microphone to anyone, stopping at a short, twentyish man in a Kevin Smith style belly-covering shirt that ended halfway down his thighs. He was a lightweight at no more than 315 pounds.

"You, can I help meet your goals?"

The man blinked several times before answering.

"Help yourself hater! *You shill for FIT!* Put someone else in a concentration camp! Fuck FIT! He yelled through the microphone, waiting to be joined in a chant with no takers. Berber cast his eye up and down the twitching man and idled up to him, smiling. He placed his hand over the mic and whispered into his face.

"I bet women be all over you."

"What?"

"Bone structure. How you keep them away now?"

"Really?"

"I not shitting. Drop sign, you in."

The man slowly lowered his sign, looking around at his peers. In their collective state of confusion they may have felt that this was part of the protest. Berber put his mic to his mouth.

"I help everyone here who want to do the work! Fuck fat! Next three peoples drop signs I make into sexy symbols. You want it? Prove it!"

A murmur went through the fifty protestors onstage. In less than three seconds the signs began to drop. The man in front of Berber kicked at his sign and spat.

"Fuck fat!"

The rest of the signs dropped and the crowd flooded Berber. At that moment several news drones appeared on the horizon and flew in low over the Amphitheatre, focusing on stage crowd. Each wore a different network badge. The news had been sent automatically by a program that scrubbed the Internet and Mobile universe for hot spots based on public feeds. Each outlet had its own algorithm; the first two *Some Will Die* events had generated enough material to place the auditions on top of the watch list. The social activity surrounding this event just tipped the scales for Fox, CNN, NBC, ABC, Cock Brothers Network and BluffPo. The auditions were now indexed as the tier one news.

Welles' Smart Phone chirped. It had to be Vance.

"Do we have a star or do we have a fucking star!"

"He was on autopilot, Jack. I never saw anything like it. The man has a steel spine."

"We just broke a million views a minute. Nice work, boy."

"Who put this protest thing together?"

"I dunno, but if I find out I'm gonna kiss em! I think we can put FIT on our short list, this plays out the way I think it will they're gonna need some crisis management!"

CHAPTER TWENTY TWO
Plan A Revisited

Washington DC: HOP Offices
Thursday, January 4, 2018 5:30 PM EST

Roger Drab could cite a dozen reasons why he was furious. He was forced to take the red, red eye from New York to DC. It was fucking cold. He was carrying his own bag and he was entering some run down shit hole of an office to have a face to face with a wildcard who was unfortunately the critical linchpin in the plan to destroy Vance. He didn't know who deserved his first salvo of anger: Potlatch or himself for buying into this cockamamie scheme. Drab found the office, opened the door and followed the stench past Potlatch's "secretary" and into his broom closet office. The former Congressman looked up.

"You're early, Mr. Drab. I like that."

"What happened with the messaging, Congressman?"

"Your messaging didn't address the enemy, Mr. Drab."

"And just WHO is the enemy, Congressman?"

"FIT. Those skinny creeps have been nibbling at our lunch for years."

Drab sat down on the board across from Potlatch. He allowed himself the luxury of a good five second foot twitch before responding. Potlatch may have been able to sway the country and various parties at one time in his career, but it was men like Drab who put the words in his mouth. One on one Drab knew he had the edge.

"You're wrong, Congressman. The enemy is bigger than one little lobbying group. The enemy is a new idea on the marketplace that has reduced your people to a tool for ratings. You're cannon fodder for a campaign of discrimination, and you're allowing the opportunity to deal with it slip between your fingers."

Potlatch let the man's words settle in. He had studied the broadcast and watched his true believers falter in their approach to the stage then collapse into the enemies' hands. Drab continued.

"You expect different behavior in other markets? *Get real Congressman*, these are your people and this is how they will act. They aren't ready for what we need to do. We pull them back for now."

"What about the next audition?"

"Forget it. Our campaign is Tet. Like I said the first time we met."

"Tet?"

"A statement was made, small and confusing, but the nationals were there. News likes a reason. People are wondering what it is all about. We need to put a meaning to it. You are going to add some meaning to the mess. You are about to go on the campaign trail, stir the pot, cause questions about the program."

"Press conferences?"

"Just like the old days."

"Then what?"

"We curl up and wait until we find out where their program is launching, where they're making their big splash in February and then *Tet it*. They think maybe we've gone away, we're defeated, that we're just waging a word war now. They won't expect a massive sneak salvo on their day of glory."

"What's different? You just told me my people can't do the job."

"We will train a crack group of 500 true believers and deliver them to the site of the broadcast. These HOP members will know how to protest. It will be a surprise attack. Tet."

"So we're leaving nothing to chance, Mr. Drab?"

"Nothing."

"I soften up the field with talk and you bring in the trained troops, that right?"

"Let's fry these pricks and I'll put you back in office. How's that for a deal?" Drab knew the only thing that could transform Potlatch from an unpredictable thorn to a controlled mallet was the possibility of making his yesterday into tomorrow.

"Whatever you want, Mr. Drab, just say when and where."

Drab stood and looked down at his new servile partner.

"Call me Roger, and call me a cab."

CHAPTER TWENTY THREE
Eventus Un-interrputus

The Art Bonito Amphitheatre, Jefferson Township, NJ
Wednesday, January 10 2018 9:55 AM EST

There was no room for surprises during the New Jersey audition stop. Word had spread like honey on a hotplate. Still unnamed, the media dubbed the auditions as the *"Vlad Berber Fitness Show,"* giving it an identity to rally around. Vance, Welles and Stiles watched the gathered crowd through several monitors located in the Amphitheatre's Green Room. Vance had invested in extra security and bumped up his event insurance coverage to 30 million. He expected and was looking forward to more fireworks.

"So the HOP party engineered that Florida protest? Where the hell did they come from? Thought Potlatch was history?" He asked the room.

"Funny, they didn't issue a statement or anything. Not like the Potlatch I remember. Tampa Police couldn't get anything out of the whole three interviews they conducted," Welles responded.

"Let's see what they have in store for us today. We should send the Congressman a basket of chicken for making our ratings. Looks like about 10,000ish. Nai?"

"Don't call me Nai. Try Naomi, or Ms. Stiles. We registered fifteen thousand twenty minutes ago," Stiles responded.

"Have a drink and settle down."

"Go ahead Mr. Vance, I have work to do."

The groundswell in numbers had relaxed Vance to the point where he felt it was safe to resume a little morning drinking. His flask contained a light blend of Belvedere, ginseng and peppermint oil with a little of the magic Escobar powder mixed in for good measure. He was trying to wean himself off coffee for health reasons, and found the cocaine was just as effective as a morning stimulant. Stiles finished assembling her contestant list and transmitted it to Vance, who began picking through it before sending his final selections to Berber.

Vlad Berber felt the flexible Smart Phone wrapped over his right arm vibrate and looked at the screen. A clock counted down and he heard his theme music rise through the speakers. The names of the selected appeared on his wrist and he strode on stage. A buzzing wave of small drone cameras rose up out of the crowd. There were hundreds of them, each one sending out a live stream of the event, accompanied by the narration of the self-appointed embedded reporter broadcasting to any one of the fifty popular social network platforms de jour. Word was out all right.

Berber began his standard monologue, ignoring the drones that slowly buzzed closer and closer, until three of them, almost simultaneously, crashed into his face. He batted away at the annoying cameras and more joined in, capturing the moment. Within 30 seconds he was enveloped in a swarm of cameras.

"Get off me," he yelled batting at them. Berber fumbled in his pants and pulled out his Walther.

Vance was in crisis mode.

"Jesus fuck, he shoots at this crowd and we're screwed! EMP this now!" He yelled.

Jimmy Welles was already racing to the stage with two security guards when the controlled pulse hit, sending out an electromagnetic signal that shut down every device in the area. The drones flew off aimlessly, their ground and broadcasting capabilities suddenly cut off. *There would be no broadcasts of gunplay.* Stiles leaned back in her chair, covered with sweat; she had thrown up a "technical difficulties" screen to their official transmission just before triggering the pulse. With any luck all the outside world saw was a true fuzzy moment.

"I think I got it in time."

"Hell of a morning to start drinking again," Vance mumbled under his vodka breath.

Welles managed to make eye contact with Berber before he was able to pull his weapon into view.

"Put it down Vlad, everything's okay." Welles motioned to the crowd, hoping the Russian understood the bad press that guns reliably generated. Berber slowly slid it back into his waist. He was surrounded by at least 40 inert drones. He picked up his microphone and looked over the audience.

"I appreciate...but too much of anything not good for me. Even... attention."

The crowd burst into applause. Vance watched from the corner of the stage because the Green Room electronics had been knocked out by the pulse. Pity no one outside the arena could watch this. Berber saw him and strutted over.

"What you do, executive?"

Vance handed him a piece of paper with several names written on it.

"The show goes on Vlad. Pick ten this time." Stiles joined him to watch.

"What did the numbers look like before we went off the air?"

"Couldn't even count."

"So we're dark. Adds to the allure of the show."

"Okay. I didn't see that in the plan."

"Keep the signal jammers going. No more chances. Let them talk about what they saw later. No HOPers yet, huh? How about his reaction?" Vance spoke nervously.

"I think a little of the old peeked through and a little of the new took over." Stiles responded, crossing her legs.

"So we *think* the patch is holding the beast in check too, right?"

"I hope so...we don't have manslaughter insurance."

Francus Tavern, New York City
Wednesday, January 10 2018 8:00 PM EST

It felt good to be back in the city, back in a place that Vance knew and loved, surrounded by accents from a happier past. His little group of Berber, Welles and Stiles had taken over a corner table in the Francus Tavern, one of New York's oldest restaurants. It was also the site of some of Vance's fondest pre-blackout moments. They were on their fourth order of mussels and second bottle of Oban when Jimmy Welles tapped Vance's arm.

"You better look at this." He placed his Smart Watch projector on the table and held up the back of a menu for the screen. The words *"CNN exclusive...HOP press conference"* flashed across the menu's shiny, wiggly surface. Former Congressman Gekko Potlatch, apparently broadcasting from a Washington DC studio, sat in front of a microphone, holding what appeared to be a black and white 11 X 14 photo. Vance hushed his table and directed everyone to watch; they all listened through their Sawtooth headsets.

"I address the nation this evening with a grave warning. There is poison brewing that represents the beginning of a new era of hate and violence. We, as Americans, are helping popularize it!" Potlatch held up a murky photo of Berber pulling his gun out of a back carry holster.

"This was taken just this morning's at Vlad Berber New Jersey show." Potlatch continued. "This photo was shot on film during the audition call for a new reality show that is based on ridiculing and castigating an entire segment of our population...overweight Americans! It is a photo of international man-slaughterer Vlad Berber, pulling a gun to celebrate the cult of hate and violence that he is helping propagate, city by city. The producers of the program shut down all transmissions to keep these images from appearing. But they couldn't muzzle the truth, and this image proves it."

Vance put down his drink. All eyes were on the broadcast now. Suddenly he didn't feel so buzzed.

"This program is called *Some Will Die*, and it will appear on a new network about to launch. It is being engineered by a media Svengali named Jack Vance, who runs a company called Blowfish Communications in Chicago. Vance is using the despicable tools of hate and violence for one sole purpose: to build up an audience for a new network to pump this bile to every mobile device in the country. They're calling it MVN and I'm calling for a public protest! Do not let Vance and his cronies use hate to sell soap! Call your cellular provider and tell them that you want MVN blocked from your phone! First obese people, then thin people! Then you, whatever you weigh, look like, eat, drink, think. Once hate starts, it doesn't stop..."

Vance slammed down Welles' projector, shutting off the broadcast. HOP wasn't missing from today's party, they were laying in wait. One of his burner phones rang. It was Sidney Brill.

"What the fuck, Vance! Was this part of your plan?"

"Meet me at my office at 5:00 AM. We have this."

"You have what? I'm getting calls from Verizon and AT&T. If we lose the carriers over this we're fucked. Get it! Without them there is no MVN."

"I said we got this. Don't talk to anyone. Especially the press. And get your friendliest suit out of the closet." Vance rung off, he turned to Naomi Stiles.

"Get us on a flight out of here tonight. Call a midnight meeting. Tell Mayhew I want everything he's got on Potlatch and HOP. And get us, I mean me and Brill, on all the morning shows. *Talk shows.* We're going at this now."

"You have a plan, Jack?"

"Ask me at 4:50 AM." He looked over at Berber.

"Give me that fucking gun, Vlad." Berber stood up. Vance stood up.

"Give me that gun or so help me God I'll make sure you never set foot in this country again if it costs me every last cent." Berber glared at Vance, pulled out his weapon and handed it to him. Vance passed it over to Welles.

"Get rid of this now, the water's a couple of blocks away."

Vance's burner phones started ringing. He looked down to see calls coming in from CNN, Fox, NBC and ABC. They all had his number. It wouldn't be long before every network and news outlet wanted a response.

"Let's go. No one's sleeping tonight."

CHAPTER TWENTY FOUR
Medium Sized Brains

Blowfish War Room, Chicago, IL
Wednesday, January 10 2018 11:45 PM CST

Jason Mayhew had done his homework. By the time Vance, Welles and Stiles returned to the Blowfish office, he and Stanley Best were prepared. Chuck Giletti was stationed by the front door, waiting for any trouble. Vance entered the room, took his seat and glared at the cloud.

"I don't want a show, Jason, I want some recommendations."

"Jason and I have a whole pile of research we want to go through with you, Jack..."

"Good. So what's the plan? This is no time for a slide show. I'm going to be on the morning news with Brill in six hours. Give me some words now."

"You're the plan man, remember Jack? I'm the research man. You put our ass into this fire. You want this or not?"

"Take your 15 minutes, give me the show. Maybe juices will flow. Somewhere."

Mayhew let out a long breath and stood up to begin his narration. Within fifteen minutes everyone in the room was a shallow expert in the long career of Gekko Potlatch and the spiraling descent that lead to the founding of HOP. He concluded and sat back in his chair, waiting for a response from the room.

"So what do we all think we're going to do now?" Vance asked no one in particular.

"We go head to head. Potlatch is crazy, call him out. You can goad him into going over the edge on national television and it's done," Best offered.

"Unless he gets the sympathy vote. He's in a fucking wheelchair, Stanley. He practically called me Hitler! He's got victims, we've got...ratings and ad sales and a guy with a gun wearing combat boots! On screen we're the bad guys. As a matter of fact *we are* the bad guys!"

The table turned red, the response algorithm reflecting Vance's displeasure with the idea.

"Ignore it. Go forward. Let everyone else make the call. We have no comment. He's nuts, it's clear," it was Stiles turn to enter the area. The table swirled, changing from grey to orange.

"We let everyone else tell our story and roll with the punches? How does that help with ad sales or the launch of the program? The carriers are already losing subscribers. Don't you people fucking get it? Potlatch is winning this game!" Vance was getting frustrated. That's what you got in Chicago, medium sized brains.

"We're above it. We're launching something big, something special. He's one lunatic," offered Mayhew.

"In a country full of the same lunatics that we're banking on! Only he's got 100,000 card carrying followers and a picture of Vlad holding a gun. *Our star and a gun.* We might want to ignore it but the media won't. They love this shit. If I had that photo it would already be a screensaver in every newsroom in the country. He's got his boot up our ass and you guys want to hand him a jug of Vaseline," Vance said wondering whether to have a drink or not.

"It's a three day media cycle story, Jack," offered Jimmy Welles.

"And if we had six months or a year we could let this die. But we got three weeks, and then we're back in the news again. You want to add a gunshot on top of this knife wound? This has to go away.

You all need to tell me...what do people like more than hate?" Vance collapsed into his seat, feeling like he had just delivered a William Shatner act three Star Trek soliloquy.

The table was turning red again.

"Then postpone the whole damn thing," Naomi Stiles threw up her hands.

"Jimmy, what have you got?" Vance asked.

Welles wasn't keen on entering the hot box. He knew that Vance would come up with the solution, he always did. The room was just a way to distract him while his reptilian sense figured it out, deep down in the bowels of his brain.

"What you said."

"I didn't say anything."

"But you will. You always do. You're just jerking yourself off for a little while before it comes to you. And when you do I'm right there, Boss."

One of Vance's burner's rang. He walked to his bathroom, touched its surface and routed the call to his bathroom's speaker.

"Vance."

He laid out a long line of his Escobar white gold and bent down to snort it.

"It's Chloe. I'm between planes at O'Hare."

Vance inhaled his line quietly.

"How long?"

"Couple of hours. Saw the news, didn't know you were so famous...Jack Vance."

"So I'm out of the potential married serial killer category and you'll graciously meet me in my hour of need, eh."

"Yeah. I thought you might like to talk."

"What I need are new ideas."

"I solve problems Jack. I think I know an answer to yours."

Vance peeked around the corner into his War Room. An argument broke out and the idea cloud exploded with a graphic stream of conflicting images. He looked at his watch. This was getting nowhere. Welles was right, it would come to him but it wouldn't come here. He shouted into the speaker.

"I'll meet you in the O'Hare Hilton Bar, 40 minutes."

O'Hare Airport Valet, Chicago, IL
Thursday, January 11 2018 2:00 AM CST

Vance didn't like leaving his beloved 2017 Bentley Continental GT Speed Convertible with valets, or anyone for that matter. When he parked the car in public lots he took the time to find the remotest space, and then set up a sensitive short range electronic jammer. If anything touched or nudged the sheet metal on his vehicle the jammer triggered a signal that scrambled all the electronics in the area, which included the operating systems of neighboring vehicles. The "perp" would be stuck until Vance returned. He had yet to see the technology in action, but with the way things were going, maybe tonight would be the night.

Chloe had sent her coordinates to Vance's Smart Phone. She was now a little dot on the screen wrapped around his wrist. He walked into the lower floor of the airport and crossed the baggage area to the underground walkway that would take him to the Hilton. He could smell its booze soaked carpet before he saw the signs; some scents just couldn't be steam cleaned away.

The facility showed its age and was surprisingly lively for the hour. He moved through the dim lights past little clusters of name tagged drunks from some convention somewhere. Vance followed his signal. The advanced GPS technology could bring him to within a millimeter of anything, outside. Here, buried under thousands of tons of steel and concrete and wire, with every cubic inch of space saturated by particles and waves, his device told him that he was standing on top of her. At least she was in the right place.

He worked his way through the floor towards a well dressed woman with medium length sandy blond hair seated at the bar. She had two martinis, one in her hand and a fresh one waiting to be enjoyed. Vance came up to her side and picked up the drink, slightly startling her.

"To new friends."

She looked at him for a moment then leaned her glass in to his and clinked.

"You're better than your picture, Jack. Frazzled, but better," the woman spoke in a husky voice that Vance now decided was 2/3 Suzanne Pleschette and 1/3 Lee Remick.

Vance took the chair next to her. Chloe was every second of a well preserved early forty-something, wearing a neat navy business suit that showed off her tanned, personally trained legs. Her overall look was tight. She was more interesting than beautiful, with a slightly exotic appearance and coloring. She wasn't the girl down the street, unless you lived in Belize. She appealed to Vance, not in a bend-over-the nearest chair way, but in a challenge, conquer and keep for a few months way. A vintage Cartier Tank Francaise watch, black pearl necklace with matching earrings, Vertu gold lame Smart Phone and Hermes handbag defined this woman as a certain class of business professional: expense accounted.

"Thank you...I think. How long do you have?"

"I can always change my flight, darling. You, on the other hand, probably have some appearances scheduled for the morning news."

"Did your homework already?"

"The BluffPo had a fascinating piece on you tonight. Read it while I was waiting. I feel like I know you."

"Was the word Scumbag in the title?"

"No."

"Give them a few more hours, they'll change it."

"Talk to me, Jack. Anything you want. You're the man of the minute. "

"I thought our first meeting might be a little less rushed."

"And involve a bed at the end of the first bottle?"

"Second bottle."

Vance was too tired to keep up the repartee. Any other night but this one. He had left the office to clear his head, distract himself from the problem while his subconscious worked on solving it. His system always worked, provided he could wait long enough for the solution to pop to the top like the answer cube in a fortune telling plastic eight ball. Chloe was the distraction that might make it happen. He looked at his watch. 2:15 AM. He would give this temporary muse another 20 minutes to stroke his cerebrum into coughing up the goods. Vance took a long draw on his slowly warming martini and stared hard into the distance.

"You're not really here, are you?"

"I'm working on something."

"What can I do?"

"What do you do?"

"I fix problems, Jack...political issues."

"Are you an attorney?"

"No, more like a concierge. I get things done."

"I'm looking for some answers. Do I need to fill you in? *Do you smoke?* I need a smoke tonight."

"I smoke. Let's go."

Unfiltered Galois were beyond an acquired taste, you either grew up with them or you didn't. Try finding one in a U.S. schoolyard. Vance accepted the cigarette from Chloe while they exited the hotel's front entrance into the cold January morning. It was going to be a quick smoke. She handed Jack her lighter, a vintage Zippo with an enameled crest on its side. He lit her butt, than his own, absently sliding the lighter into his pocket.

"God I miss this," Vance inhaled deeply. It had been five years since he had a cigarette. Chloe took a small draw off hers and huddled into Vance, she wasn't dressed for this weather.

"I'm cold."

Vance put his arm around her. "What would you do if you were me right now in my situation?"

"What's your deadline?"

"I'll be in the Green Room for the Today Show in two hours with my client."

She took another puff off her cigarette.

"Put your other arm around me."

Vance hugged her into him, warming her. He could feel her shivering slightly. It felt good to hold someone, to be protective. She looked up at him.

"People like free things, Jack. It makes them forget everything else."

Vance thought about her statement. He looked down at her. She had just given his cerebrum a hand job. He dropped his Galois and stubbed it out, turning her towards the hotel entrance and walking them back inside.

"Let's get you warm."

"Keep the lighter, Jack."

"What?" As they crossed into the hotel entrance he remembered putting her lighter into his pocket and reached for it. They stood in the vestibule.

"Go to work, Jack. Give it back to me when you see me again."

Then she kissed him and Vance kissed her back. But he had already left the room, his mind white boarding a plan. "Go. Leave. I'll see you again."

Vance felt the tug of responsibility. He was back on the horse. He looked down at Chloe.

"Thank you, Miss..."

"Battista." She slipped the pack of cigarettes into his pocket.

"To keep the lighter company. Do your job. We'll pick this up."

"Promise?"

"Unless you become a serial killer."

Vance started laughing.

"What's so funny, Mr. Vance?"

"I already am...*Some Will Die*, remember!"

"Lifted from Ligner's *Marketing Ethics*. An oxymoronic title if ever there was one. Standard reading where I went to school."

"And where was that, Chloe?"

"Universidad de La Habana."

By the time Vance retrieved his car it was 3:15 in the morning and he knew exactly what he was going to do. He called Stiles and put her in charge of delivering Sidney Brill to the NBC Studios at 5:15 AM. He made sure that they were booked for a complete round of morning exposures, CBS, ABC, CNN, Fox and the Cock Brothers Network, formally WGN. He told her to bring Welles. He'd be chauffeuring them from studio to studio in Vance's Bentley.

Vance pulled the car into the cell phone lot, retracted the front seat, closed the privacy glass and set the alarm for 4:15 AM, allowing himself a quick nap. He had a fresh shirt and tie in the trunk. By 10:00 CST the situation would either be resolved or he'd be on his way to a new career, as a greeter at Wal-Mart.

Chapter Twenty Five
BOGO

NBC Studios, Chicago, IL
Thursday, January 11 2018 5:15 AM CST

"What's the plan, Vance? Why are we talking about you and your fucking controversy with fat people and not about our God damned network launch in three weeks?" Demanded Sidney Brill. Brill had cut himself shaving this morning. He dabbed at a small wound next to his mouth. It opened whenever he spoke and now it was threatening to leak all the way down to his collar. Brill and Vance were in the NBC Green Room, waiting to be interviewed by the new network hot shot hosts in NY while the Chicago locals twiddled their thumbs and waited to deliver the traffic and weather reports.

"Remember when we first started talking Sidney and you were so proud of your comedies and your dramas and your news?"

"The things you convinced me wouldn't sell?"

"Yeah. Today you're selling them. That's all you're selling. Here and at our next stop and our next. I'll manage the crisis."

"What do you mean and the next?"

"We're doing everyone this morning, Sidney. NBC, ABC, CBS, Fox, the Cock's and then CNN."

"Why CNN last?"

"Because they're going to try and blow this up, but we're not going to let them. We'll play our hand with these softball interviews... by the time we get there this will be in the bag."

"You're managing a crisis today, Vance, where it goes from here is up in the air."

"Remember your media training, Sidney...*great question*, three messages?"

"Shut up, Vance. If I didn't need you now I'd fire you."

Brill and Vance were seated in front of a nice image of the Chicago skyline, looking at the large, projected, short white haired face of Chesterton Rogers, the natty new host of the Today Show. Chesteron was conducting his interview from the New York office and wanted to prove himself to the Today show audience as someone who could ask "likably tough" questions. He wasn't supposed to be too challenging, that wasn't the Today Show thing.

"Thanks for coming in, Mr. Brill and congratulations on the pending network launch. Just when is that?"

"Great question, Chesterton! We'll be releasing the exact date shortly. And let me tell you about our lineup! We've got some of America's favorite stars in the *kind of roles you've always wanted to see them in*. For example..."

"Speaking of shows, let's talk about *Some Will Die*. Mr. Vance, you were cited as the mastermind behind this new show, what can you tell us about it?" asked Rogers.

"I can tell you the rest of the title...*And Some Will Live*. Our show is about hope, Chesterton, and the general public has responded. Our auditions were so successful that we actually have a surplus of candidates and are cutting the tour short. We're done! The next time you see them will be on the show's official network launch in a few weeks."

"Did I hear you right, Mr. Vance? No more audition stops?"

"That's your exclusive, Chesterton. The *Some Will Die* and *Some Will Live* road show is officially over. And as a little treat we're going to introduce you to a few of the wonderful people who you'll meet on our launch. Have your tech pull these images off your server."

Vance produced his Smart Phone, tapped it a few times and waited a second. Two images filled the screen: the before/after of a woman who had clearly lost a tremendous amount of weight.

"Meet Betty Dratch of Milwaukee, Wisconsin. She joined up on our first audition and was so motivated that she asked Vlad Berber for some additional training and coaching. Under his guidance she has already lost 30 pounds."

Jimmy Welles had been instructed to keep the Bentley outside the studio door no matter what happened. Vance and Brill were on a tight schedule. The car chimed 6:00 AM as the pair emerged from the NBC studios and the two men hustled to the back seat.

"ABC, Jimmy," Vance barked, shoving Brill into the rear seat and slamming the door.

"Well?" Vance asked Brill.

"You bought yourself another show, Vance. When does the shoe drop?"

"The rest of the networks will be watching. They'll want to step up the game. *Good Morning America* has moved towards rougher stuff since they added John Gregerious."

"What's rougher supposed to mean?"

"Just stick to your TV Guide speech. I'll handle the nasty questions."

ABC Studios, Chicago, IL
Thursday, January 11 2018 6:10 AM CST

Vance hadn't expected his network to fly morning show host John Gregerious in from New York for the interview, but there he was, waiting to meet them as they were dusted and seated in their chairs at ABC's Chicago studios. The smallish anchor and former

White House Svengali reached across and shook Vance's hand while they waited for the commercials to run.

"New York hasn't been the same without you livening things up, Jack."

"What have you got, John? We already gave our exclusive to NBC."

"Yeah. I saw that. Nothing personal Jack, but I think I'm going to ask the questions on this show."

"Okay, John, you do that."

It started before Sidney Brill knew what hit him. One minute Vance was chit chatting with the morning host and the next minute the green light was flashing and all cameras were pointing at him. Gregerious fired the first question at Brill.

"Were you aware that Mr.Vance had an armed man hosting your show, Mr. Brill?"

Brill wasn't ready for this question. It fell outside of the scope of his training.

"Great question, John, and the answer is no."

"No that you didn't know or no as in no he didn't."

"No to both and no I didn't see anything anywhere about this."

Gregerious directed Brill to the monitor over his shoulder. It filled with the live image of an elderly man holding a camera and an 11 X 14 photo.

"This is Mr. Billy Bradenton who was in the second row of the *Some Will Die* audition in New Jersey yesterday and he has a photo he'd like to share with us. Mr. Bradenton, could you please hold up the photo that you took?"

Brandenton held up a black and white still with his shaky 70 year old hands. The camera attempted to focus on it, then stabilized and froze on the image. With a little imagination the frustrated form of Vlad Berber could be seen reaching for his weapon while fending off a swarm of amateur camera drones. It was grainy and printed slightly off center on photographic paper. The camera cut back to Bradenton. Gregerious continued his interview.

"Tell us what you saw yesterday, Mr. Bradenton."

"Well, I was there because I collect celebrity photos...and there ain't many celebrities big as Vlad Berber in my book. I staked out my spot way early. Well, so, he gets on with his show and all these other people with their gadgets and what not started getting, you know, in his face. Think it spooked him so he went for his gun. I always knew he carried it, just never seen a photo before. 'Til now, that is."

Gregerious directed his attention back to the cameras.

"Mr. Brill, did you know that your host was violating New Jersey's firearms law? He's here on a green card! He can't carry any weapon, much less a concealed one. and much less in the state of New Jersey in a public facility. If this becomes a police matter will you be replacing him as your host?"

Vance was done with this sneak attack. He spoke up without asking permission, but didn't direct his question at Gregerious or Brill. He looked up at the screen behind Gregerious.

"Is that the camera you used to take your photo, Mr. Bradenton?" Vance squinted at the large black camera dangling from Bradenton's neck.

"Why yes, sir, it is. This camera's shot everyone from Pete Townsend to The Rock."

Bradenton looked down lovingly at the worn black bodied camera.

"That a Nikon F?"

"Sure is, sir, you know your cameras."

"Plain prism?"

"Plain prism."

"No light meter, shoots film, how'd you gauge exposure, Mr. Bradenton?"

"Instinct."

"No date stamp on your photo, must have processed it yourself?"

"That I did. In my own darkroom. Hard to find anyone to do film anymore."

"Would you like a new camera, Mr. Bradenton, a digital camera?
"

"Matter of fact I'm getting one. No more manual focusing."

"Did this show pay you for that photo?"

"That's where I'm getting the money. Yes, sir."

"Then you'd have to say that ABC has a financial stake in that photo you're holding, right?"

"Them and Mr. Potlatch. They both paid me."

Vance turned his attention to Gregerious.

"Kind of hard to see anything in that blurry, undated photo you bought John, or was it manufactured? You can do a lot in the darkroom. It's the original Photoshop, remember? Got any more shots? *Any more witnesses to your accusations?* With all those cameras in the air you've got to have seen something."

Vance pulled a burner phone out of his pocket and laid it on the table in front of him.

"312-989-8818. That's the number of this phone. Mr. Brill and I are prepared to offer $10,000 in bitcoins right now to the first person who sends in a legitimate digital, date time and stamped photo of Vlad Berber holding a gun at yesterday's audition. Ten grand. Right now." Vance looked into the camera, then over at Gregerious. The morning host cleared his throat. This wasn't part of his program. Three seconds ticked by before he pressed a small button under his desk and the dead air cut to a commercial break. Vance saw the red light come on and stood up, grabbing Brill by the arm. He looked down at Gregerious.

"You can tell your viewers that we had more important people to talk with, John. See you back in New York. Keep the phone, maybe it'll ring if you stare at it long enough."

They exited the studio and found the Bentley waiting for them by the front door. Vance opened the door and let Brill get in, then took the front passenger seat next to Jimmy.

"Go to CNN."

Jimmy Welles put the car into gear. Brill, still in semi shock from the experience, spoke up.

"I thought we were going to CBS, then Fox. Save the roughest for last."

"Not anymore. We're bringing the fight to them. They're not expecting us for an hour. They want an interview. It's going to be on our terms. I've had it with the sneaky media bullshit. We're telling this story today, our way, right now. This is over."

CNN Studios, Chicago, IL
Thursday, January 11 2018 6:00 AM CST

Vance and Brill parked behind celebrity expat UK newsman Percy Trojan's limo and surreptitiously followed him into the CNN studios. They crept up behind him while he announced, in his polished British accent, that he had arrived to conduct the morning's big interview.

"And we're ready to do it now," Vance said, startling Percy. The former wiretapping London newspaper editor had been recently rehired by CNN. Hearing Vance's voice he suddenly became all flushed and ruddy.

"Jack Vance! We're not going on for two hours. Have a seat and I'll get to you when we're ready."

"We can go on now or we can go on never," Vance responded, shoving past the host and into the studios.

Drab and Associates Offices, New York City
Thursday, January 11 2018 7:15 AM EST

Agness and Drab had been watching the morning news programs, playing a game of invisible chess with Vance and Brill. They were keeping their best move for last: the scheduled surprise studio appearance of Gekko Potlatch on CNN. They had arranged for Potlatch to appear in an exclusive face to face to be moderated by their ace in the hole, the "British Bulldog," Percy Trojan. They counted on Potlatch to reinforce the messaging that would set the stage for their planned professional protest at the network launch, provided Tom Agness ever discovered its location.

If Potlatch kept on message they could pull this off. In his wheelchair, in person, with the conviction of a man wronged, the Congressman could be very persuasive. They were surprised when their monitoring service suddenly shifted to CNN. They were supposed to be watching the show on CBS. It was two hours too soon.

Percy Trojan had practiced all sorts of faces for the camera: outrage, bemusement and today's special, angered disappointment. Working with guidance from Roger Drab, he was planning on luring Vance and Brill into a conversation on the social and cultural impact of their show then springing Potlatch on them. He had rehearsed the scene in his mind: it would generate instant viral media and he, Percy Trojan, would be credited with putting it together. Drab's facilitation and assistance would remain a secret. It was going to be perfect, a real network coup.

But all of a sudden there was Vance, sitting across the table from him, two hours early. He tried calling Potlatch but had been unable to raise him. His ace was missing. Without the sucker punch this was just going to be another 40,000 foot interview that followed on to the other network "exclusives." Nothing viral, nothing memorable, a squandered opportunity at greatness. Trojan directed his first question to Sidney Brill, hoping to goad him into saying something incriminating, inflammatory or offensive. At this point he wasn't picky.

"Thank you, Mr. Brill and Mr. Vance for coming down this morning to discuss your new network and specifically your controversial show, *Some Will Die*. Can we take the nature of the show, which I and many others would call discriminatory and demeaning towards obese people, as an indication of your overall approach to programming, and an indictment of a society that would find such hateful content...amusing?"

"Great question, Percy and I'm glad you asked. As a matter of fact the response to *Some Will Die* has been so positive that we've already found all our contestants, ahead of schedule."

"I saw that this morning."

"And we're bringing a whole lineup of terrific programming to your devices in just a few weeks. You'll find all your favorite stars *in the roles that you've always wanted to see them in.* There's something for everyone Percy, even you if you get tired of this network."

"Do you have any reaction to the very public gauntlet that former congressman Potlatch threw down last night in response to the New Jersey audition?"

"No. He has his opinion, that's what makes the show so amazing. It brings out something in everyone. We welcome all points of view."

"I am sure that if Mr. Potlatch were here he would point out that the only party extracting value from *Some Will Die* seems to be the carriers. If I understand this right your contestants will have just six weeks to lose half their body weight?"

"To win, yes. And not everyone will win. But everyone will lose something along the way, a lot more than they would lose without our show."

"Like their lives?"

"That's a matter of personal choice and Mother Nature. We're just providing a vehicle for the most amazing programming that this country has ever seen, all delivered right to your device."

"Why don't we try and get Congressman Potlatch on the phone and see what he really thinks about this."

Vance leaned in to the conversation.

"We'd like to give your audience an exclusive, Percy. The first 500 people who call this studio will receive a free subscription to MVN for life. And starting tomorrow, the first million people who call their carriers and sign up for a one year subscription will get six months absolutely free. Now what were you saying about calling someone?" The studio phones immediately began ringing and a very frustrated Percy Trojan slapped his hand on the commercial break button located on his chair.

Drab looked over at Agness.

"This is fucked. We're taking command of this operation now. YOU have one week to find the location of that event or so help me God, Agness I will deliver your head in a box to Vance myself. And find that fucker Potlatch."

Three minutes later the programming resumed. Vance and Brill were smiling. Percy Trojan did his best to corral the stampeding horses.

"It seems that the *Some Will Die* message of hate and violence has catalyzed a certain faction of society. Our phones haven't stopped ringing. What does that say about the American culture, Mr. Vance? Do you feel any responsibility for participating in fueling a culture of discrimination?" asked Trojan, trying to minimize his 'grasping for straws' vocal inflection.

Vance leaned in to the camera and looked directly at Percy, licking his chops like a cat about to swallow a bleeding, one legged field mouse.

"I have just one response, Percy: *have you ever been properly in love?*"

CHAPTER TWENTY SIX
You Call This Marketing?

MVN Offices, Chicago, IL
Thursday, January 11 2018 11:30 AM CST

Sidney Brill and Jack Vance were sitting in the MVN conference room, waiting for Vance's team and the MVN team to arrive. Vance's stream of morning surprises had bothered him to the point of nausea and he wasn't about to pay for cleaning his own puke off the floor without getting some answers in return.

"Where the fuck did that offer come from, Vance? You end-running us with the carriers?" Brill didn't know whether to kiss Vance or kill him after he sprung his "offer" live on international TV without consulting him. The two men shared an unquiet moment.

"Let's see what the carriers say Sidney, they've been giving away phones and minutes for decades, what's a little content."

"These things have to be negotiated, codes entered, you just can't throw offers out there."

"If it's money they'll figure it out fast. Don't worry about carriers collecting."

"And what about us? You're giving away our profits!"

"What profits? You haven't got a product, haven't turned the lights on, and haven't put anything out. You exist in people's minds, on Vlad's name, in the news, on the fucking bar napkin where the idea came from. Profits! You're a venture funded creation until we make you into something. The only one who's profited here is you, Sidney! You got someone else's money, my ideas and everyone else's talent. And a new Maserati to boot, so I'm told."

At that moment Jimmy Welles, Naomi Stiles and five nameless but trendy looking suits from MVN arrived at the conference room and took positions around the table. The smoke was still coming out of Vance's ears when Brill started talking to "his" group.

"Any word from the carriers?"

One of the nameless, a young woman wearing a dark business suit and glasses, touched the Smart Phone wrapped around her wrist and the conference table screen filled with a sales chart. The numbers shouted millions. She was clearly the one managing subscribers for the company.

"Verizon just sent over a case of Dom, AT&T wants to take you and your family to the Four Seasons on Lanai for the weekend and Orange wants to know what the international deal is. They can't take orders fast enough but just wish you had informed them in advance so they could have scheduled more operators. And we're making money. Nice work, boss."

Brill relaxed in his chair, letting the good news wash over him like a piss shower from Aphrodite.

"Okay. So what's next? What about our crisis? The gun? The protesting fat people?"

"We're fine, Sidney. It's already yesterday's news. Once we pump out the data on our successful numbers we'll create even more interest. Announce that you're extending the deal and sales will go through the roof."

"Along with your *blank check* bills, right?"

Vance took a moment before answering.

"No. Actually I've got a proposition for you. How does "no more bills" sound?"

"Sounds like T-Mobile. Are they in this too?" Brill asked.

"No. I mean no more bills for real, Not carrier chatter."

Brill and his entire staff focused on Vance. The Blowfish campaign burn rate had been climbing to nearly $100,000 a week. MVN's numbers wrangler replaced the carrier order screen with the Blowfish expense requisition spreadsheet. The columns steadily rose in size with each passing day. By launch date Blowfish was projected to have spent nearly ten million dollars on promotions, and that didn't include any advertising. Vance smiled at his staff and the MVN brain trust. Stiles quivered, she knew that he was about to throw another grandiose gamble into the mix. The man would never be satisfied with good old success.

"I'll guarantee you the biggest launch in history, Sidney and it won't cost you, I mean your investors, a penny. Blowfish will cover all the expenses, short of advertising. That means our time, the talent fees, whatever venues we rent, you name it, all the way through the launch. I want half of the paid advertising revenue from launch day. One day. 24 hours of ad revenue. That's it. And no more bills from this moment forward."

Brill looked down at the screen and let the proposition steep in his head for about two seconds.

"That includes the cab fare over here today right, Vance?" The room remained silent.

"And the lunch from Emeril's we just ordered in. Yes."

"Well then God damnit you got yourself a deal, boy!"

"Let's celebrate." Vance tapped his Smart Phone and ordered a case of champagne to the conference room. He knew his audience and looked over at Brill.

"Don't worry, on me. And yeah, it's the same stuff I drink," he said.

Blowfish Offices, Chicago, IL
Thursday, January 11 2018 2:30 AM CST

Naomi Stiles was the only one in the MVN conference room who hadn't helped drink the case of Dom while celebrating their new revenue partnership. She knew the numbers and realized that Vance was gambling the entire firm on the success of the launch. The Blowfish group had stopped at Binny's on the way back to their offices to pick up a second case, which they were popping and splashing all over the lobby. She pried Jack Vance away from Jimmy Welles and steered him in towards the War Room. Stiles couldn't remember the last time that she had seen him this drunk as she fended off his pawing hands and shoved him into his chair. Peggy Bump sat down next to him.

"Let's focus, Jack. Peggy wants to go over some numbers with us."

"Focus? Both of you? This is great, close the door!" Vance wasn't in a mood for business. He was exhausted from 48 hours of scheming and traveling and presenting and selling. Unless Naomi and Peggy had called him into the War Room for a long awaited ménage he really wasn't interested in hearing anyone talk about marketing, media or business.

"You've put us in a real vulnerable position, Mr. Vance," Peggy Bump spoke, filling the War Room cloud with a three dimensional spreadsheet that only an accountant could love.

"This is our current and projected burn rate. We can float the company on receivables and our line of credit, but unless you can deliver revenue by the first week in February, we're out of business. More than out of business, we're in debt to the tune of about $200,000. That doesn't include a dime for whatever you have in mind for the launch. *What do you have in mind for the launch?*"

"Don't worry."

"That's it? Don't worry?"

"Don't worry and hire some sales people. Make sure they're good on the phone. We'll need them on launch day."

"So that's it? What about the money for the launch?" Vance put his head down on the table and closed his eyes.

"We borrow it, against launch revenue," he mumbled, passing out in his chair.

Peggy Bump shook her head at Naomi Stiles,

"Who the hell is going to loan against a bet like that?"

"Knowing Jack? *Good fellas.*"

Jack Vance's Condo, Chicago, IL
Thursday, January 11 2018 5:30 AM CST

Vance looked up at the ceiling in his bedroom, amazed that plain white paint could spin. As it slowed down he felt he actually might be able to stand without falling over. He remembered meeting with Naomi and Peggy, then waking up in his bed. His money was on Welles driving him home and his doorman depositing him his bed.

He had been gone for days and hadn't received a single message on his home line. He activated his viewing wall and tried to resume watching Lee Marvin wade through bodies in the movie *Prime Cut.* Within three minutes he put the film back in the library, unable to remember what happened in the first third of and unwilling to commit the time to re-watching it. He thumbed through his collection of inspirational films by Heston, Marvin, Eastwood, Coburn and Bronson. There was nothing produced after 1979 that interested him and nothing was working today. He reached over, felt for a burner phone on the bed stand next to where he lay and punched out a text to Chloe.

"You near my town?"

After two minutes of waiting for a response he placed the phone down and got out of bed, staggered across his stark room and sorted through the contents of his suit on the floor. He found

Chloe's lighter and studied it in the light from his adjacent living room. It bore a familiar symbol. He walked over to his closet, opened the door, and placed his face near his recessed safe's retinal scanner. The small wall safe door opened and he pulled out the gun his father had given him. Both objects bore the same marks: a serpent encircling an island. Vance placed the lighter into the safe along with the weapon and crossed the room to his vanity. He should be celebrating, not attempting to fall asleep. With any luck he'd be a millionaire in a matter of weeks.

The FDA advises discarding old and unused drugs as they expire, but pharmaceutical connoisseurs like Jack Vance stockpiled them for future recreational purposes. Expiration dates were for the ill. He rummaged through his vanity and found a prescription bottle with a 1984 date. It contained something that he had been saving for a special occasion. Whether it retained any of its original potency was immaterial to him. Just the act of consuming it would bring back the kind of body high that had made Methaqualone one of the most legendary drugs in history.

He pushed down on the child proof cap, opened the bottle and dumped the single pill down his throat, flushing it into his system with some water from the faucet. This was possibly the last bona fide Quaalude in the world, and a fitting nightcap to the most tumultuous and potentially fortuitous week of his life. He walked back to his bed and took a long pull from the bottle of scotch that was always an arm's reach away, wherever he was in his condo. He read the ancient "do not consume with alcohol" warning that promised a better high if ignored, then tossed the old container into the trash.

Vance wasn't a collector, he didn't hold onto things for "sentimental reasons." He wasn't going to die with a desk and wall full of mementos, like so many of his peers who were content to revel in what they had done in their pasts. His action represented his world view: what happened yesterday is only important to those who can't make new tomorrows. Vance closed his eyes and felt the familiar drug's tingle starting in his fingers. Maybe it would slow down the spinning, or at least reverse its direction.

Chapter Twenty Seven
Training Daze

A Private Ranch: Myakka City, Florida
Sunday, January 21 2018 11:30 AM EST

It's not easy to gather, train and house 500 people who share the common appearance of unbridled obesity. Together Drab, Agness and Potlatch had discreetly rented a medium sized private ranch near Sarasota, Florida then recruited and transported 500 hard core HOP true believers. Their army of impassioned and inflamed members was about to become a highly trained protest mob with the sole mission of disrupting the *Some Will Die* premier and, with any luck, the whole MVN launch. Provided they could find out where it was all going to happen.

Agness was in the ranch's main house, discussing launch day tactics with Peter Krink, a seasoned political organizer from Berkeley who had been hired to put together their strategy. Krink brought in his own crew who were already making their misgivings about the "army" well known, after just 24 hours of training. Few, particularly those being trained, felt that they would be ready for an organized mass run on anything but a buffet in two years, much less two weeks.

Drab entered the room without knocking, taking both men by surprise. He wasn't supposed to have appeared on site for at least another three days. Agness excused himself from the meeting and directed Drab to a private office off the dining room where the planning session was being held. The two men didn't shake hands or even make eye contact, they had long since dispensed with any formality or pretence of camaraderie. They were each driven by the mission, and that was it.

"Early I see," Agness commented, closing the door behind Drab.

"Did he see me, do they know us?"

"No. Don't worry about it. As long as they're paid they don't ask too many questions."

"One question is too many."

Agness walked to a window and looked out over the ranch's back acreage. Clusters of roughly protestors ran through drills of crowd penetration, unfurling banners and tearing down a mock stage.

"When will you learn to trust me...Roger?"

Drab wrinkled his face at Agness' impunity. The man not only addressed him by his first name, he did so with his back to him.

"Watch your place, Agness. You're on..." Agness turned to face his boss.

"Thin ice, I know. You'll have my head. I know the threats. Fuck you, Roger."

Drab was furious. If he had been a fighting man he would have punched Agness in the head. Drab's preferred weapons of choice included the verbal stiletto, the back stab and the whisper campaign.

"You're done, Agness."

"Okay, Roger, I'll take the location and date of Vance's launch party with me. Have a nice day." As Agness moved towards the door, Drab stepped in his way.

"The date? You have it?"

"And the location. And the time. And fuck you."

"Let's talk, Tom."

Agness put his face into Drab's. This felt good.

"It's Tom now? I haven't gotten an hour of sleep a night since I walked into your office. I have been terrorized and stressed by your threats and I have delivered... over-delivered on my promises to you. More than anyone else on your God damned staff, and I should fucking know... you stole most of them from Blowfish! *You want to call me Tom?* You can lead this bunch of fatties to the Promised Land, *Roger*. I'm done." Agness pushed past him, walking deliberately towards the door. He was counting down from five when Drab called out to him.

"You can have Blowfish." Agness stopped and turned.

"I want it in writing. I've got a document ready for your retinal signature."

"Of course you do."

"And I'm being fair. I don't take possession until you do. If you don't you just owe me my new salary."

"And how much is that?"

"$150,000, starting now."

Drab gave the contract a quick review on Agness' flexible Smart Phone then scan signed it.

"Alright. Where the is the launch and how did you find it?"

Agness unwrapped the Smart Phone from his wrist and laid it on the table. He touched the face of the device and a small image of a calendar blew up on the office wall. The date of February 4th was highlighted with the words Super Bowl: Atlanta, Georgia. Drab looked at it hard.

"You've got to be kidding."

"Where else will all the press in the country be in two weeks? It makes sense. It's bold. He'll sit on the date and collect his audience that morning from the local population."

"Prove it."

"Every bus, every charter, every limo in the city is booked that day."

"What else?"

"The Encore Park Amphitheatre in Alpharetta has been booked. No musical acts scheduled, no Super Bowl events. And when I called posing as a city inspector I was given a copy of their event insurance document. Wanna read it or you trust me that it was issued to Blowfish Communications Group of Chicago. Illinois."

"We got him."

"We got the *Some Will Die* premier. I don't know about the launch."

"*Some Will Die* is all we need. Fuck the launch, we'll fill his pot with so much shit that he'll be drowning in the mess for the rest of his career." Then Drab did something that he had never done with an employee before, he extended his hand.

"Nice work. Everything locked down here?"

"For now."

"Good, because we have another meeting. Grab your coat, let's go."

Sarasota/Bradenton International Airport: Rental Car Pen Sunday, January 21 2018 1:15 PM EST

Drab's scheduling for his gambit was tight. He had calculated every detail to the second, down to the positioning of the vehicles and the timing of all parties involved. He knew when planes were to land and people were to show up. This was his campaign from start to finish. He crept his rented Chrysler slowly along the Hertz parking corridor outside the airport, looking for a specific car. He pulled up halfway in front of a late model Mercedes and turned off the vehicle. He had explained the program to Agness on the drive over and received complete and immediate buy in from his accomplice.

"This is where your natural talent comes into play, Mr. Agness."

"That's all I got? Looking like Vance?"

"For this meeting, yes. And your fast tongue. Sell it. Put on this hat and jacket and stay out of the camera over there." He slid a card over to Agness.

"There's $20,000 in bitcoins on this. You promised them $35,000. They get the rest when the job is done."

"Got it."

"And you know the..."

"Yes. I know what we want."

A black Hummer pulled in front of them and parked hood to hood, completely blocking the Mercedes. Agness exited the car as a man in a tiger striped jumpsuit, black combat boots, boonie hat and aviator sunglasses jumped out of the Hummer. Per Drab's instructions their positioning forced the man to walk around the front of his car to meet Agness on the far side of the two vehicles, out of site of the lot's security camera.

"You the guy wants security?"

Agness let the man see just enough of his face to recognize him later.

"Yeah. Jack Vance. You Chris Zales?"

"Yeah, BlackNight Security."

"You know the deal, right?"

"We don't take no shit from no fatties. If there's a protest we put it down."

"Zero tolerance. Teach them a lesson."

"And you pay us thirty five grand now."

Agness handed him a card.

"There's 20. You get the balance when I see the results."

"We said all now."

"Then make it nothing. I can find someone else."

"What kind of zero tolerance you looking for?"

"Hospital, blood, morgue. "

"You wants guys dead, Mr. Vance?"

"I didn't use that word exactly."

"Beatin' heads is one thing. We ain't hit men."

"Zero tolerance."

"Roger that Mr. Vance, but no killin...'"

"We'll see. And you never heard of me and you never saw me."

"I know the drill."

"Call you after the show and you can collect the balance."

"No. Meet you after the show and we can collect the money."

Agness saw the figure that he was looking for over the man's shoulder. He knew timing was critical. He gripped the security man's hand and shook it slowly, stalling the process until the man was literally ten feet from where they were. He looked up at the man and smiled, giving him a good view of his face. The he walked straight to his car and slid into the driver's seat, put the car into gear and backed out. He flipped the car into an open space and exited the area. Zales walked back to the front of his car, into the field of the camera and ran face to face with a man looking for a rental Mercedes.

Jack Vance really didn't have time for a new business call at this stage of the game. But when the CMO of the Publix grocery chain sends you a first class ticket for a meeting, you jump. Even if the meeting came out of the blue and was in Sarasota, Florida. They had sweetened the pot with a rental Mercedes and promised him that he'd be home before midnight, so he made the time. And now some asshole Hummer was parked in front of his rental car.

Vance approached the tall tactical Cracker standing in front of the ugly old SUV.

"Scuze me, that's my rental."

Chris Zales did a double squint at Vance as he opened the door to his car.

"Sorry. You just take off, Mister?"

"What're you talking about? We never met before."

"Oh yeah. I remember. We never met. Right."

Three hours later Vance was back in the airport, returning the car. This wasn't the first time that he had been stood up for a new business meeting, but it was the first time that he had been flown somewhere for the experience. He had taken advantage of the warm Florida sun to get a little color after he realized that his potential client was a no show. Returning with a tan wasn't his idea of success. Maybe he needed a little break from the ramp up. In a matter of weeks he'd be a millionaire running the hottest agency in the country. Nothing could stop him now.

PART THREE
CHESS ON A CHECKERBOARD

CHAPTER TWENTY EIGHT
Beginning of the End Game

Blowfish War Room: Chicago, IL
Saturday, February 3, 2018 6:00 PM CST

Naomi Stiles hated it when Vance knew she knew he was right. But he had nailed it, and beyond his reckless behavior, disruptively sexist attitudes and chaotic agency management, the guy had a gut for the ever swirling global media miasma. Just two weeks ago the entire team had been huddled around this War Room table, gnashing teeth and grinding fingernails into palms wondering if the Vlad Berber/Gekko Potlatch crisis would be the torpedo that finally put them under. But it hadn't. Vance pulled charmed snakes out of his ass and manipulated the crisis from a headline to an afterthought in less than a morning. It was effective, masterful and put them back on the game. *God, how she loathed him.*

Stiles stood, it was the only way she could get anyone's attention above the roar of activity in the packed War Room. The standard complement of personnel was swollen by a squad of advertising salespeople hired specifically to sell space around tomorrow's Super Bowl and the MVN launch. She raised her new Baume and Mercier Smart Watch to her mouth and spoke into it, projecting her voice over the room's speaker system.

"Attention, please. Let's quiet down and review our activities for tomorrow's game. Turn off all recording devices, glasses, helmets, phones, personal drones, skin grafts. What's said here stays here!"

Vance and his inner circle stopped chatting and looked up at Stiles. The additional 60 or so Blowfish and temp workers standing around the room hushed themselves and pulled out everything from small tablets to pads of paper.

"Alright, everybody has their lists. The game starts at 17:30 EST and our launch will begin concurrently. Everyone here has a number, a cube assignment and a list. We'll take in bound calls on a rotating basis. The goals will be posted on your cubicle screens every fifteen minutes. Beat them and you'll receive an automatic spiff, deposited into your account. We start calling the New York media firms tomorrow morning at 0500 EST. Peggy Bump will be overseeing the internal operation. Go home and get some sleep. Remember you have all signed NDA's on this entire program."

Within three minutes the room was cleared and Vance was back in charge.

"Everyone knows their thing for tomorrow or do we have to go through it again?" He gave the room a scan.

"Mayhew and Peggy will be running the home office and Naomi, Welles, Best, Giletti and me will be down in Atlanta holding Brill's hand and managing the launch. We've got an outside team running the *Some Will Die* contestant introduction and an inside team running sales. We can thank Naomi for putting all the resources together to make this happen."

The one thing Stiles hated more than Vance trying to grope her were his attempts at obsequiousness. She smiled curtly and returned to review the files on the desk in front of her.

"When are we releasing the location of the audition?" Mayhew asked. Vance had kept the final launch plans close to his chest during the past two weeks. Everyone knew he wasn't about to risk Potlatch and his crew pissing all over the party. The clock had run

out. They needed a crowd and couldn't remain in stealth mode for-
ever.

"We need a couple of thousand on the ground. Our audience is
the world now. Naomi and Welles have identified 2000 locals.
They'll receive invites at noon tomorrow. No one will be able to
assemble a protest in five hours. By the time our friends hear about
it the whole thing will be just about over," Vance paused. "Questions? Okay. Let's put this sucker to bed. If we hit our numbers everyone in this room is going to have the biggest post-holiday
bonus in the city. Get outta' here."

Ten minutes later the War Room lights automatically dimmed,
picking up the heartbeats of only three people: Jack Vance, Naomi
Stiles and Peggy Bump.

"You know we've technically been selling against our client,
Jack," Bump said, spreadsheets at the ready to prove her point.

"We haven't sold anything except commitments. We're *technically* closing all the deals tomorrow. Bitch slap me when I hand
you a personal check for $10,000." Vance responded.

"Better post date it, we don't have that in the bank now. That 12
million dollar line of credit you acquired is on fumes."

"You're on top of sales, Ms. Stiles, what are we looking at?"
Vance steered the conversation away from Bump. She was starting
to bother him, again.

"Right now, commitments of maybe nine million," Stiles offered,
not looking up.

"Which nets us 4.5 per your agreement, Mr. Vance. After taxes,
salaries and overhead we're down another million. If those commitments don't turn into sales, and those sales don't turn into
deals, we're out of business." Bump insisted, wanting her messages
to get through Vance's self delusional fiction of nothing ever going
wrong. In this case just about everything could go wrong and she
wasn't interested in losing twenty pounds to find a new job by
next March.

Vance pulled a cashier's check out of his pocket and slid it across to Peggy. She picked it up. It was for three million dollars.

"What did you use as collateral for this?"

"The agency, the receivables. The usual."

"Everything you used for the first loan?"

"Pretty much."

"Jesus, Jack. Now we're down 15 million! You need to clear 30 to break even."

"When is this due?"

"Monday, same as the other note. Not until midnight. Plenty of time. We'll have the money in hand Monday morning."

"Let's hope. Your agreement is a bit loose. We collect when they collect."

"And the transfers from the Bowl sales are instantaneous."

"To MVN. We sell and they collect, like a clearing house."

"And we get our cut Monday morning."

"Provided nothing happens."

"Like what?"

"Like who originated the contract. MVN's got their own sales team. Maybe an advertiser wants a whole season. Suddenly the lines get blurry."

"Sidney Brill's a man of his word. As long as he's running MVN we'll get paid. End of story. We'll cover this and the juice."

"Juice?"

"Interest. 25%."

"That what they call it? Who did you get this money from, Jack?"

"*Not* a bank."

"Really."

"Not a traditional bank anyway. More like a private bank."

"What's this lender called, I'll look them up."

"They don't advertise. You either know them or you don't."

"So lucky us, I guess. Without them we'd be doing this the normal way, billing the client for time and expenses. That would be terrible, right?"

Naomi Stiles had heard far more than she wanted to and was busy packing up her materials when Vance called her name.

"What do you think, Naomi? Are we gunslingers or shopkeepers?"

She turned on her way out of the room, wanting her presence on this conversation minimized if and when the federal agents or the mafia or whoever would be likely to rain hell down on this operation decided to review the room's data banks.

"I don't know Mr. Vance. We have some decent commitments, that's about it." *Fuck*, now he was walking her way, putting his hand on her arm and whispering in her ear.

"I promise you that as soon as we hit the forty million mark tomorrow you can take your bonus and your attitude and march your ass out of here." Before she could react he slid his hands down the back of her skirt, *inside her underwear*, and tapped her right ass cheek. She turned and slapped him across the face as he pulled his hand out.

He yelled before she could.

"*You see that, Peggy!* Blatant sexual harassment in the Blowfish offices! *What a place.* That Jack Vance, what a fucking asshole!" He looked over at her again. "Do a good job and you can collect a bigger sexual harassment settlement for a severance package."

Naomi left the room shaking and stopped to breathe before entering the dark foyer of the reception area. Her heart slowed down and she thought about Vance's hand on her behind. He hadn't actually squeezed her or tried to auger her lower depths. In a twisted kind of way it was a show grope, just enough to give her an excuse to sue him. Was he opening an exit door or throwing down a gauntlet? If the program went up in flames there'd be nothing to sue. He was right. She was motivated. Her breathing resumed at a normal rate.

She continued through the lobby and towards the front door, stopped and looked around, wondering for the first time if she would miss the place, and Jack Vance. She pulled a resignation letter out of her purse and placed it on top of the stack of mail on Missy Slats' desk. Given Slats' efficiency she was assured that Vance would receive it by next Thursday or Friday. She put her hand on the door and stopped, turned and snatched the letter back off the pile, then left. She had about two hours to get to the airport and on a flight down to Atlanta where there was work to be done.

CHAPTER TWENTY NINE
Players Assembled

Motel Six: Atlanta, GA
Sunday, February 4, 2018 8:00 AM EST

Potlatch always felt more comfortable in low key motels. He wanted to minimize being seen by anyone who might recognize him, like people who paid attention to the news. He was excited about his pending re-entry into the national stage. The men from New York had given his Party a new purpose. If the battle plans were carried out accordingly he might even consider another run at the presidency. He sat with a large paper map laid out on the hotel table before him, watching his "battle associates" pace. The next few hours would tell if they could keep it together in the heat of conflict. From where he sat, he wouldn't bet his next meal on it.

Drab and Agness paced around the small two bedroom hotel suite, following in each other's footsteps like figurines in a creaky old German Cockoo clock. The data they had failed to collect dragged on both of them like wet rope. They knew the location of the *Some Will Die* live weigh in but virtually nothing about the network launch. To make matters more interesting the challenge of keeping Potlatch's army hidden in Atlanta all week had been about as easy as stuffing a 12 foot boa constrictor into a Japanese condom.

With a little less than nine hours on the clock, chance and the missing data were the only factors Potlatch and Drab hadn't locked into a spreadsheet and timetabled with complete anal attention. Agness had put aside drink and sleep for the duration of the campaign, realizing that he would be overseeing final details in lock step with his two masters. Despite the glaring omission it all seemed to be somehow moving forward. With a little luck he'd be behind Vance's desk and wheel of his former boss's Bentley before the first cherry blossoms bloomed on the trees outside of Potlatch's Washington, DC office.

"How many HOP members are in town, Congressman?" Drab asked. He needed to make sure the man in the wheelchair understood who was really in command of this operation.

"I capped it at 1500, Mr. Drab. We have an exposure issue. If we show too much backside our enemies will be able to prepare. We need to retain the element of surprise."

"And we're communicating with these people..."

"Via shortwave, per our spreadsheet. *I suggest you consult the tab seven, on campaign logistics.* We've set up an encoded numbers station at this base. We send the signal and they go to work. They're in friendly camps surrounding the city."

"Camps?"

"Tab five Mr. Drab, *remember*? Trailer courts. Our constituency needs familiar surroundings. The liberal press is interested in the glitz and gloss of watering holes like the Four Seasons, not the Four Winds Trailer Court."

"What about the Amphitheatre, Agness?" Drab asked.

"Still setting up. All quiet," Agness responded, waiting for an inevitable series of questions that would lead to the bald man's next explosion.

"What do you mean all quiet? We've got 500 protesters waiting in cars. They need to get in there and mingle. Didn't you review *tab three* before this meeting?"

"The area is empty. There is NO ONE to mingle with," Agness

snapped.

"Are you telling me Blowfish rented an Amphitheatre for the event they've been building for a month and no one's showing up? Make sure *your man out there* is in the right location!"

"He's *our* man and he does not have the wrong location, sir, *sirs*. Maybe, just maybe no one has been invited to their event, yet."

"Highly unusual. Not how we would do it." Potlatch added, to amplify Drab's displeasure.

"Is this part of Vance's playbook," Drab asked, not willing to let the field mouse run away with a mere flesh wound.

"It could be. He'll want to outmaneuver any protest this time around. He doesn't need it. He needs respect and people watching the network launch. The local audience is just window dressing at this point."

Drab thought about this new data point then played out the assessment to his audience. "So he waits until the last second and sends out the invites. The numbers don't matter to him. 500 or 50,000, as long as there are enough people to cheer on the contestants. He's waiting because he doesn't want controversy. If he puts the word out a few hours before the event he'll almost guarantee that the HOP or any other group..."

"Won't be able to do anything in time to create a scene! *By God we've got him boys!*" Potlatch roared, slapping his cane on the thin, Formica table.

Several seconds of silence followed while the three men collectively pondered the implications of the Drab's revelation. Despite their hatred for their enemy, they had all secretly admitted to themselves that he was the better player. Until now. Now it seemed like they were actually creeping up behind him, sharpened blade in hand, and with Ninja like. His fall meant success to all three of them and they could taste the holy water of career salvation they had been seeking. It felt good. It felt warm. Potlatch looked down at his map and whispered, "Thank you, Mr. Vance."

CHAPTER THIRTY
Mindshare Warfare

Georgia Dome: Atlanta, GA
Sunday, February 4, 2018 4:45 PM EST

George Grecos worked his small, aging body through a gauntlet of sweaty butt cheeks and jock straps that filled the locker room occupied by the Denver Broncos, in the bowels of the Georgia Dome. Grecos had been generally unloved by the players and the press after a series of controversial on-air gaffes and outright insults that began in 2015. Was it early Alzheimer's mixed with a dollop of Tourette's Syndrome? No one knew. Maybe he just didn't give a shit anymore and decided to reveal his true self: a diminutive man who actually loathed the bulky giants he had covered his entire professional sports casting career.

Having run the gauntlet of beer, nacho farts and snot spitballs, Grecos found the one man who would speak with him: Jim Flux, head coach of the Broncos. With his cameraman/bodyguard in tow Grecos shoved his wet microphone into the coach's face.

"I won't waste time asking you whether you're going to win or how you prepared for this day...we've all heard your answers before. What can you tell us about the mystery man who rented out the two massive Club Lounges above, in this stadium?"

Coach Flux felt like shoving Grecos' microphone down his throat and drop kicking him into the middle of the pack of players.

But they had all been paid to restrain themselves from doing the sports announcer bodily harm. It was also in his contract to answer Grecos' questions, no matter how absurd they might be. His team, along with broadcast rights for this particular Super Bowl, were owned by NBC. Grecos, with all his pestilent intellectual boils and warts, had been their lead sports anchor since the 1980's. In short, it was hand's off.

"I dunno, George. How bout we talk about the game?"

"The game! Anyone can talk about the game. I've been talking about the game for 30 years. Let's talk about Madama! See her being wheeled up to that Lounge by Roger Cloosey? I'm not sure who *looked* older, whaddya think?"

Jack Vance and Sidney Brill relaxed in the Green Room of the South Club Room 200 feet above the site of the interview. They shared an unlaughed laugh as they watched Grecos relentlessly squander network air time wondering what *they* were doing *up there*. But Grecos wasn't alone. Every news channel had been covering the parade of limos that were disgorging A, B and C list celebrities at the Stadium that afternoon. The guests were shunted by an army of tuxedoed escorts to the heavily secured Club Lounges. In the past these celebrities would be found dotting the stands, today they were disappearing into shielded rooms and it was driving the media nuts.

Vance and Brill had been observing the celebrities flood into the Club Lounge's warm, wood paneled comforts for the past hour. The pair were hidden behind a large two way plasma screen off the cavernous main room. Between implanted chips, skin phones and traditional Smart Phones, it was impossible to confiscate all the communications gear that their guests carried or wore. The signs sternly forbidding any pre-game outside communications were roundly ignored by a crowd that didn't feel that rules ever applied to them.

To maintain the Iron Curtain of mystery, the Blowfish communications team had multiple signal jammers saturating every cubic inch of the both North and South Lounges. They had cleared it with the NSA and FCC beforehand and made a list of the people who would be officially Off The Grid during their event. The media manipulation was already working. The mystery lounges were slowly becoming the top trending news story on the planet, threatening to eclipse a game that hadn't even started yet.

Vance blinked twice and his Oakley Smart Glasses broadcast a feed to the small table projector indicating the magnitude of the global conversation.

"I'd say 'how could you ever doubt me, Sidney,' if I said things like that."

Brill took a sip of his second Boodles gin and tonic.

"You hunt, Vance?"

"Animals?"

"What else?"

"Fuck no. Never."

"*Hummph.* You own guns, right?"

"That makes me a hunter?"

"Usually, or a guy worried about the size of his sword."

"Where we going here, Sidney?"

"We got a saying in the world where people who own guns actually use them. *If you haven't missed you haven't been hunting long enough.* We'll see how this plays out when the day's over."

"You probably think I'm a Republican too, right?"

"Because you own a gun?"

"No, because I'm an asshole."

Vance had long ago figured out the solution for gun control: restrict them from anyone with an IQ under 130. That thinking wouldn't find him friends in any political party in this country.

Brill turned from Vance to survey the roomful of celebrities mingling with the cast members and directors and producers and advertising executives from MVN. The long suite was covered with monitors displaying a season full of new shows and promos, with two large projected images in the front carrying live feeds of the *Some Will Die* stage. Soon one would broadcast Sidney Brill's official launch speech. Brill looked over at Vance.

"Should we mingle?"

"Absolutely, Sidney...I want you to get my money's worth. Have another drink on Blowfish."

Vance stood up, it was his time to work the room and check in with his production team. If his plan unfolded the way it had on paper he will have masterminded the most successful network launch in history and made himself a millionaire for his trouble.

"Go ahead, Sidney, we're not joined at the hip."

Vance exited to the private bath located off the observation room leaving Brill to straighten the two gin and tonics out of his tie. He locked himself in the bathroom. The remainder of his Escobar stash was immediately in hand. He opted to gather it onto one foot long line instead of parsing it into little nibbles. It took him a full 45 seconds to consume it; the impact of the drug knocking his head back. His eyes bulged and the room went white for a second. He steadied himself, stopped shaking and felt 150% of his living capacity surge through his body. *Shit*, if only he could walk through every second like this, he'd be the fucking president already.

He pushed out of the room, glancing down at his Blancpain. In 24 hours the only thing that would remain of Sidney Brill and MVN in his life would be their money.

Vance let his newly found third eye guide him through the swirl of celebrities, knowing that Chuck Giletti, parked somewhere in the room, was keeping a constant watch over him. He stopped to point out the "cellular silence" sign to an annoyed Brad Slit, who had been attempting to make a call on his ancient early century anti-techo Motorola Razr phone. A phone like that was more of a statement than a tool these days, but that was Slit's brand.

He had never been enamored of stars and starlets. At the end of the day they all served one purpose: to sell advertising. He served the same God, but for a different piece of the equation. Every glittery sculpted smile and carefully tanned pair of high cheekbones was putting money in his pocket. Kickoff was less than 45 minutes away and the unwitting participants in this room were about to become part of the brightest day in broadcast and blackest day in NFL history. This was truly insurgent marketing at its diabolical best.

CHAPTER THIRTY ONE
Tilling the Soil

Motel Six: Alpharetta, GA
Sunday, February 4, 2018 5:00 PM EST

Potlatch and Drab were having little success working with one of HOP's wheelchair bound techs on finding a live overhead video feed of the *Some Will Die* audition. Maddeningly it was being conducted a short three miles away from their location. The word was finally out and people had shown up, by the thousands. They were relying on sketchy radio reports from Tom Agness who was now in the field. His job was not only to coordinate the "security team" as a Jack Vance impersonator, but also to work with the small army of organized protestors who had been trained for the event. The long nights of plotting were not playing out as planned on the large plasma area map, stretched out on the small hotel room table.

The HOP "troops" all carried powerful GPS transmitters in their shoes, allowing the two generals to watch their positional progress on the dynamic map. Potlatch insisted that all his field lieutenants use shortwave radios and communicate on several discreet channels that had been programmed into Agness' transceiver, instead of cellular devices. He made it clear to Drab that their activities were not the NSA's business. The reality of shortwave, however, was proving challenging in practice.

"Rook! Groups two and four are not close enough to the stage, squawk their squad leaders and get them into position." Potlatch barked into the handheld mike connected to his powerful RCI Ranger shortwave base station transceiver.

"What frequencies, Foodie?"

"They're programmed into your unit, Rook, access memory banks two and four," Potlatch looked disapprovingly up at Drab. In these circumstances it was "his man" pouring tar into the neatly firing cylinders.

"Thousands of people here... It's pretty chaotic, Foodie. I don't know if I can find or reach anyone. Nobody's picking up." Agness responded.

Drab was done with Potlatch's attempt at direction and the aimless progress on the map. He grabbed the microphone from Potlatch.

"Breaker...uh...Rook, this is PR Guy. Did you connect with security?"

"Who?"

"RD Rook. PR...RD."

"*Roger?*"

"*PR GUY*, ROOK!"

"Roger that, Roger." Drab slammed down the microphone. The last thing he needed was to be outed at this stage of the game. He walked across the room and turned on the old Samsung 2000 X 2000 flat screen monitor with his Smart Watch. He couldn't find any video feed of the *Some Will Die* audition. It seemed that the number one story of the minute was not the Super Bowl itself, but a party being held in the stadium's two club lounges. He motioned to Potlatch.

"They're not covering the game. They're covering some idiotic celebrity party at a box in the stadium." Potlatch left his intelligence table and wheeled over to take a closer look.

"Probably an old dotcom millionaire celebrating his last hurrah."

"Like McAffee?"

"Showy freak. Maybe Gates."

"Not his style. Branson. Way more Branson than Gates. But McAffee maybe if he has any money left."

"Doesn't matter. We have bigger fish to fry." Drab thumbed off the set and resumed his vigil with Potlatch over the moving map, watching their troops mingle into position. He made a loud, dramatic sigh. Somehow the fools he'd cast his lot with were sort of pulling it together. If the ship held together within 45 minutes they'd be delivering a death blow to their chosen enemy and using the ashes of his program to resurrect Potlatch's political career. Drab always wanted a congressman in his pocket. He indicated the map with his hand.

"Disruptive marketing at its finest."

CHAPTER THIRTY TWO
Press Watch

**Main Stage of the Encore Park Amphitheatre: Alpharetta, GA
Sunday, February 4, 2018 5:15 PM EST**

Vlad Berber had done something atypical specifically for the *Some Will Die* network premier/live weigh in: he purchased a new pair of combat boots. He wasn't superstitious, but the luck was all used up in the old pair that was issued to him while a member of the Russian Special Forces. After ten years it was time for an upgrade. Fifteen minutes on eBay convinced him that his new Danner USMC RAT military boots would bring him another decade of good fortune, or at least a little less bad luck. They were tight, but with enough ass kicking they'd loosen up.

He didn't believe in opening acts or Green Rooms, and sat in the middle of the stage with his 35 contestants standing in a neat row behind him. He had trained them well and was proud of what he had achieved. Tonight was not only the first weigh in, it was the official re-launch of his own career.

The Encore Park Amphitheatre grounds held 12,000 spectators and from his perch Vlad could see that the facility's 45 acres were packed. The 2,000 invitations sent out to randomly selected local households just five hours earlier had multiplied exponentially. He assumed that anyone who couldn't wrangle a ticket to the Super Bowl had decided to invite themselves to his premier. But it wasn't the tens of thousands of local spectators that he wanted. Berber was looking past all the floating amateur cameras and counting the large news drones that were hovering around the area, providing a feed that just needed a little fuel to catch the world's attention. Vance, in his madness, had pitted him against the Super Bowl, but Berber's guts told him he would win the moment. He had one mission with this soon-to-be memorable show: the return of the Big Russian.

Jimmy Welles paced back stage with one eye on Berber and the other on the crowd. In just a few minutes his secure satellite phone would chirp and he'd receive the official word from Vance, at mission control, that they were live. Over on the stage, in the line of obese contestants, Ben Bigelow, the man who was scheduled to die tonight, was sweating heavily under the color balanced Mobile Vision lights. Welles noticed a gathering yellow pool beneath his feet. *Shit*, was he flaking out? He scanned the front row and found Bigelow's mother, sobbing to herself. Whose fucking genius idea had it been to put her in the line of sight with her son! He looked back and forth between them. They were clearly making contact. Bigelow was mouthing "goodbye" and his mother was yelling "I love you, Benny!" God, *what if the network drones pick this up!*

Welles scurried over to the edge of the stage and found a tight knot of private security guards. Some wore dark blue tactical jackets and some wore black. Peggy Bump probably hired more than one firm for extra protection. He motioned to the nearest pair and they approached him.

"See that woman over there?" He pointed out Mrs. Bigelow.

"Flank her. She starts anything I want her out, discreetly."

"We take orders from one guy only and you're not him." Said the larger of the two, a razor shaven monster with a close cropped graying goatee, mirrored Ray Bans and gun bulge printing at his hip. His smaller associate kept a vigil on the crowd.

"Really? Who is that?"

"I can't say, mister."

"Let's try this. I work for Jack Vance. Jack Vance put me in charge of this whole show, where you are standing. So you work for me."

"You say Vance? You shoulda said so."

"Yeah? You know him?"

"Know him? No. We don't know him. Never heard'a him." The big guy leaned over to Welles and spoke in a hushed voice.

"I get it. No problem." He winked.

"Well. Okay then. Just keep it quiet."

"Roger that."

The pair slowly dissolved into the crowd. They had a good 200 feet and a thousand bodies between their location and their objective. Welles retreated to the security of the side of the stage. *That was weird.* Since when did Vance personally hire security?

CHAPTER THIRTY THREE
Go, Dog, Go!

Georgia Dome North Club Lounge: Atlanta, GA
Sunday, February 4, 2018 5:30 PM EST

The plan was to launch the network at the moment the game began. With the aid of a few pedestrian Tito's vodka and sodas, Vance had descended from his other-worldly cocaine perspective to a gentle 10,000 foot glide over increasingly familiar territory. He was seated next to a neatly dressed, rouged and powdered Sidney Brill. In the right light Brill actually looked a few days younger. Vance stood off to the side of his client, positioned to direct his cameraman, his producer and his favorite employee, Naomi Stiles. He gripped his GlobalStar satellite phone and kept one eye on a monitor of the NBC Super Bowl broadcast.

The football players were squaring off on the field below as the launch moment approached. Vance raised his hand to the cameraman and winked at Sidney, who was going to introduce the network in Walt Disney style. They watched the coin toss on the monitors. Denver won the toss and both teams retreated to their places on the field. As the ball was snapped back to the quarterback, Vance dropped his arm and yelled the start code into his satellite phone: *"Go, dog! Go!"*

Three things happened at once: the blacked out screens shielding both lounges cleared, the blinking red light on the camera trained on Brill went solid red and no less than three planes appeared dragging banners over the stadium. They read:

MVN.TV is live
Some Will Die today!
Punt the Game: watch MVN!

One thing didn't happen: Sidney Brill sat staring into the camera for a full five seconds before Vance ran his finger across his neck and pointed at the celebrity filled lounge. Bright lights filled the party room and the Producer activated the feed from the mobile camera trained on former bodybuilder and politician Gunther Schmuckafinger and his wife, professional trainer Gillian Michelle. They were positioned in front of the window overlooking the game. Gunther had been the backup plan, he would provide a nice accented segue for Vlad. The well aged geriatric bodybuilder practically swallowed the cameras trained on him.

"I vood like to velcome you to the vaunch of the greatest new netvork of the century: MVN online. Join me as ve tune in for the first live premier of da show de whole country has been buzzing about: *Some Vill Die*! Kick asssss, Vlad!" He raised his large arm, knocking a drink out of a Disney child star turned porn actress who had made the unfortunate decision of standing to his more animated right side. The network feed cut to an MVN show promo.

Naomi Stiles, ensconced in the back of the North Lounge Green Room, was following the network traffic for MVN. The live celebrity party was drawing in viewers, but it was the NBC advertisers that Vance wanted. His sales team was in direct contact with every significant media buyer around the country. Given the right audience share, he could count on pulling ad dollars directly from the game itself. He was guaranteeing an additional :07 second bonus for every :60 ad that pulled out of the game. If he could deliver the numbers he would gut the game of all ads and advertising revenue, literally leaving *nothing but the game* itself for viewers to watch. Vance planned on giving NBC their first-ever Super Bowl with no commercial interruptions. In an alternate universe he'd win an Emmy for it.

Pre-game commitments were still hovering around the ten million mark, but Stiles knew all too well that Vance wasn't doing this to break even. There was over $600 million on the table and he wanted all of it. As Peggy Bump had so cheerfully reminded everyone, failure meant losing Blowfish. Vance's "creditors" might have other things in mind for him, like hot instruments and testacies. As much as Stiles would like to see him take a fall, she'd rather see him succeed. It meant more money for her sexual harassment suit exit strategy. Blowfish didn't have a pension plan, so she had to make her own.

"We're not moving the needle yet," she said.

Vance decided it was time to open the floodgates.

"Down Dog!" He spoke into his satellite phone.

George Grecos was watching the game on his monitor from the press booth when he received a tap on the shoulder from someone who directed his attention to the bright lights pouring out of the North Lounge. He felt his Smart Phone vibrate and looked down at the text message on his wrist.

You're personally invited up to the North Club Lounge for the official MVN celebrity launch party and Some Will Die premier. Free top shelf booze! Free lobster tails! Celebrities by the truckload!

This made Grecos madder than hell: a launch party in HIS playground and he was being invited after the fact with the rest of the press riff raff! He wasn't going to take the bait. He thumbed his phone to the MVN channel and tuned in the *Some Will Die* launch. It hadn't started yet. There were no networks covering it and that meant an opportunity. Something bizarre had happened at every one of the auditions, why should the launch be any different? Let the lemmings follow each other for table scraps and celebrities, he was headed to where the action was, and his gut said it wasn't on the playing field. He signaled his director to cut from first down play coverage to his camera. His light went red and Grecos began talking.

"This Super Bowl has just borne witness to one of the strangest scenes in the annals of latter day sporting events. Right up there, in a loud, brightly lit stadium sky box, an upstart mobile network was just launched. *You heard this reporter right.* A network launch staged at the beginning of the Super Bowl! Virtually every reporter on the field was just invited up to sip champagne and slurp shrimp cocktails with stars and starlets. While the other press outlets race to cover this tawdry party, your intrepid eyewitness to history, George Grecos, will be heading to where the action really is…and it's not on this football stadium. No sir, ladies and gentlemen, we will be the first network to cover the *Some Will Die* premier. I will bring you that story. Live! Let's go!" Grecos signaled for his mobile cameraman to accompany him on his mission. Let the fools go to the party or cover yet another football game. He was after a real story.

Five minutes had passed since Sidney Brill was supposed to launch the network. He was still sitting in his studio chair, allowing the nice tingle of his fourth gin and tonic to bring him back to a comfortable reality. His vintage BlackBerry phone lay on his lap, its signature red message indicator lit. He knew who had called but wasn't ready to respond, yet. He felt Vance jab him in the side and looked up.

"We just landed Cadillac."

Naomi Stiles came up from behind Vance and Brill and tapped her wrist, commandeering the signal fed to the two way monitor in front of them. The screen filled with multiple images from news outlets across the globe: stories of the planes, the celebrity party and the launch had already eclipsed the Super Bowl. The most common headline read: *Audacious launch of new network disrupts Super Bowl.* She pointed at a feed of the players down below, looking up at the sky box, with the crowd following suit.

Brill blinked back to life.

"What about sales?" he asked.

Stiles tapped her wrist and the MVN bug appeared on the bottom of a Nike commercial.

"That's us. Right now."

Vance's ear cochlear device chirped. It was Stanley Best.

"Peggy says you're in the clear. We just took in 30 million in orders with promissory on another 60 if we continue to deliver."

Vance grabbed Stiles and kissed her until she was able to wriggle free.

"That'll cost you, Vance," she hissed, spitting his saliva out of her mouth.

"I can afford it." He looked at Sidney who had moved his stare from the screen to the phone in his hand, a strange smile on his face.

"We're on the road to 90 million! That the big six point buck you're looking for Sidney?" Vance didn't wait for an answer. He felt untouchable. Fuck everyone, it was his show and he had won. He pulled his satellite phone out of his pocket and called Jimmy Welles.

"Go live with *Some Will Die* in sixty seconds."

CHAPTER THIRTY FOUR
Friendly Fire

Encore Park Amphitheatre: Alpharetta, GA
Sunday, February 4, 2018 5:45 PM EST

Something told Tom Agness that he would be able to operate more effectively outside of the swirling thousands of spectators packed into the Amphitheatre grounds. He moved to a line of trees to the right of the stage on the upper elevations surrounding the area. He found the most climbable one. He managed to work his way to a seemingly sturdy branch twenty feet above ground. He could see what was happening on stage and positioned his devices on a thick array of vines, creating a little control center in the woods. His shortwave transceiver lay on the right, a flexible Smart Phone carrying the MVN feed was positioned in front of him and one of his burner phones lay to the left.

He studied the stage through a pair of light gathering binoculars. There was Jimmy Welles, directing things on stage right. The little cunt probably had his old title and his lips firmly fixed to Vance's ass. He looked forward to personally firing the bitch when he took over Blowfish. Agness slowly zoomed his glasses out at the exact moment when large flash pots were ignited onstage. The amplified light overwhelmed his lenses, immediately blinding him. He shrieked with surprise and dropped the binoculars. Even at his distance he felt the wave of heat from the incendiaries.

His tree shook as the Also Sprach Zarathustra theme song boomed through the area. Agness knew that the show had started. His shortwave squawked and he felt for it, this was the moment to issue the order to the ground troops! He fumbled blindly for the radio and felt it just before knocking it off the tree to the ground. *Fuck, what a fucking idiot!* He cursed himself, almost losing his balance and jostling the rest of his devices from their little perch.

He was blind and clinging to his branch. Vertigo set in. He hugged tighter, hearing an occasional chirp from the ground below. The stage noise was deafening and continued to shake the tree. He knew that Drab and Potlatch were calling him, expecting him to get ready to take command of the situation. He felt his foot slip and held tighter. Destroying the program was about the last thing on his mind. He just wanted to get out of the *god damn piss fuck* tree alive.

CHAPTER THIRTY FIVE
Generals at the Front

Motel Six: Alpharetta, GA
Sunday, February 4, 2018 5:50 PM EST

Drab hated cheap. He was frustrated, stuck in a low rent, stuffy room with a bunch of morons who couldn't even operate their own equipment. He felt sweat roll down his face and checked his pulse. 120. Fucking assholes were going to kill him on top of it. He paced the small, crappy cage looking for things to kick, hit or tear up. The toilet paper and towels had fallen in the first salvo of his rage, now he was eyeing the phone, TV and bed sheets.

"The show is starting! We need to activate your fat fucking army!" Drab screamed at Potlatch like a psychopathic little child who had run out of butterflies to de-wing. Potlatch was also sweating, knuckles turning white from gripping the send button on his shortwave microphone. He was flicking and clicking the controls on the faceplate of his radio.

"*Rook*, this is *Foodie*, acknowledge! Rook! Activate groups A through F! *Rook*! Respond!"

"Activate them yourself, Potlatch! Why are we waiting for Agness!" Drab hissed, lowering himself to Potlatch's level. Potlatch put the microphone down and looked up at Drab with a look of sheer incredulity.

"Because he has all the group frequencies programmed into his transceiver."

"*So what?* Call them yourself."

"They're encoded to his transceiver. *His* transceiver. We don't have the frequencies here. You understand what that means, *correct*?"

"Yeah, it means you're either kidding me or you're an absolute idiot."

"I'm protecting us."

"From what?!"

"*Are you mad?* The NSA! You want these communications traced back to us someday?"

"So you're telling me that the only way to initiate our plan is with Tom *fucking* Agness who might be out taking a shit in the woods!"

"You would know, Mr. Drab...*he's your man*."

"Screw him. We just need his radio."

"That's about the extent of it, Mr. Drab. The HOP won't move without their go signal. They're too well trained."

Drab started snickering, then broke down into an all out belly laugh that made him collapse on the bed. He indulged himself in a rush of endorphins before pulling himself up.

"That's the funniest thing I've heard all day."

He looked over at the large monitor. MVN was running a Fiat commercial. There was time to pull this out of the fire. Potlatch played with his laptop for a few seconds then looked up at Drab.

"I sent his coordinates to your phone. You should be able to find him."

"Me?"

"You expect me to wheel out there with you?"

"Who else have we got?"

"*Who else have you got?* I've supplied 2000 people and you came up with the key man who is now missing. You have *you*, Mr. Drab. *Go get a little dirty.*"

Drab pulled his Smart Phone from his pocket and thumbed up the personnel tracker app. There was a distinct yellow blob located just a few miles from where he was standing. He grabbed his coat and started for the door. Potlatch called out after him. Drab stopped and Potlatch tossed a small shortwave transceiver to him.

"We'll need to talk!" Drab let it sail past him to crash into the wall.

"Just watch the monitor. You'll know when I've found him."

CHAPTER THIRTY SIX
Opening Act

Main Stage of the Encore Park Amphitheatre: Alpharetta, GA
Sunday, February 4, 2018 5:52 PM EST

Gina Loretta, a curvy five foot five, 115 pound, apple scented object of nightly male lust had no objections to donning a translucent thong bikini on national *whatever it was.* She wore a lot less when she was working at the Cheetah Club. Besides, with her Brazilian there wasn't anything to see anyway. She didn't like having to pull her gum out of her mouth, but she conveniently parked it on the right handlebar of the wheelchair she was rolling out onto the *Some Will Die* main stage. The Old Geezer she was wheeling about must have been real important for someone to give her $200 for twenty minutes of her time, *whoever he was. Bald head's a bald head* as far as she was concerned.

The main lights faded and spotlights came up as wheezy comedian Bobby Sapphire was rolled out onto the stage. Gina Loretta dropped her grip on his chair, did a small curtsy and flit back into the wings. There was no change in the volume of murmur from the crowd. Sapphire attempted to lift himself out of his wheelchair. A large projector above the stage beamed a message onto a synthetic, controlled smoke screen: *Applause for Bobby Sapphire (When Larry Met Harry),* then filled with a 30 year old photo of the comedian. The crowd slowly began to clap as the identity of the man in the chair in the middle of the stage started to sink in. Sapphire breathed into his microphone...

"You look mahvelousss." The crowd started clapping and whooping as a message appeared in the smoke: *"$1000 to the loudest clapper!"* The clapping increased. A stadium cam picked through the faces in the crowd and projected them on the smoke screen. Sapphire attempted to rise again and screamed,

"Mein fuehrer, *I can walk!*" No one got the joke, but they continued to clap anyway.

Sapphire continued, "Welcome to the *Some Will Die* weigh-in... where everyone will look mahvelous, eventually." He began to cough, almost falling out of his chair. Welles knew the comedian was calling it a night and instructed Gina Loretta to fetch him from the embarrassing glare of the spotlights and cameras. She sashayed back onto the stage, allowed the cameras to get a nice angle of her ample backside and wheeled Sapphire off the stage.

Vlad Berber took his cue and entered from behind stage center in a cone of high intensity light, smoke and military drums. He spoke into a microphone suspended above the stage.

"From the bowels of hell called Chernobyl, I am back...back to help poor victims of a culture that celebrates obesity! I will return their bodies to natural state and give them pride, health and maybe..the fortunes of Nirvana!!" His arms swept expansively and the stage brightened. The show had begun.

Vlad was about to speak again but found his microphone had gone dead. He looked at the monitors embedded in the floor and read: FIVE MINUTE COMMERCIAL BREAK. His row of contestants stood at their erect best as the stage lights dimmed. While they disappeared into the darkness he marched off the stage to Welles.

"I do my show now."

"You are doing your show, Vlad. And the advertisers appreciate it."

Vlad didn't like the interruptions. It upset his rhythm, he wasn't a turn it on and off kind of guy. He also didn't like dealing with middle men.

"You tell Executive I don't stop now. My show is for the people. Your network can go to hell. Turn on my mike." He walked back to the stage, shot a look at Welles and started to speak.

"We begin program now!!!"

The crowd screamed in approval and the cloud above the stage filled with the typical Jumbotron bios everyone in the free world had come to know. The face of a middle aged woman made up as well as rolls of cheek and neck fat could be made up, filled the space. Her bio read:

Rose Hulbert: Plano, Wisconsin: disabled over-the- road trucker: Opening weight: 375 pounds.

A geyser of smoke and flames erupted around Vlad and an animal scale appeared from the floor on a platform behind him. At the same time a livestock cage slowly descended from above the stage and settled next to him. A short woman wearing a black spandex Neiman Marcus track suit with red velour stripes running down its side shoved her walker against the pen door and wheeled herself over to Berber.

"Ready to succeed, Rose? Show us what you do!" Vlad noted that he was still off the air. No matter, his crowd was here. He kicked her walker out from under her. She staggered as he stepped away then caught herself and steadied her position to a ripple of applause. Slowly, resolutely, she lurched, like a wounded manatee, up the steps of the platform. Every painful breath was lovingly mixed and amplified for maximum effect by the same sound editor who had worked on the *Saw* movies. She reached the top of the platform and slid one foot, then another onto the metal scale. The digital numbers above her spun like a slot-machine readout, stopping first at three, then six, then two. She looked up, stunned at the results. The spotlight focused on Vlad again:

"I give you Rose Hulbert!!" Vlad saw his show return to the monitor. He was on the air again, just in time for a wave of applause to be transmitted to his adoring fans.

"She joined us thirteen pounds ago! Only 162 pounds and four weeks left. If she makes it she will be millionairess! Rose!" The woman managed a weak smile and began to stagger before two burly stage hands rapidly sprinted up the platform and helped her down.

Chapter Thirty Seven
Treed

Tree Line of Encore Park Amphitheatre: Alpharetta, GA
Sunday, February 4, 2018 6:05 PM EST

Tom Agness heard the powerful engines of the commercial news drones overhead, followed by what might have been a helicopter zipping towards the main stage. It was on. The Media Industrial Complex had caught wind of the story and with the proper algorithms activated, was turning the *Some Will Die* premier into an international media happening. The time to activate the troops was right now. *Right this second.* The stage was becoming a fuzzy glow in his center of vision indicating his sight was slowly returning. Maybe the vertigo that kept him clinging to the tree branch would start to go away. Then he heard a voice under him.

"*Agness!* Agness! Where are you?"

Could that be Drab? Drab of all people looking for him out here?

"Roger?"

"Keep your mouth shut, idiot! Where's the radio?"

"I'm in the tree, Roger!"

"Right. Where's the fucking radio?"

"Get me down, Roger." Agness squinted, able to make out Drab's weaving flashlight hunting around the base of the tree. He saw the beam stop.

"How do you use this damn thing?"

"I'll have to show you. Get me out of this tree!"

"Get yourself out."

"I can't see yet."

Drab looked at the main stage, the lights were down again indicating another commercial break.

"Then we wait. Looks like we've got time."

CHAPTER THIRTY EIGHT
While Rome Burns

Georgia Dome North Club Lounge: Atlanta, GA
Sunday, February 4, 2018 6:15 PM EST

Vance was having an atypically hard time removing himself from a conversation with one of the MVN shows' "stars," and her entourage of male hangers-on. It was part of his deal with Brill: play nice with the hired help while at the party.

"So you will be promoting '*Letta's New Life*' as well Mr. Vance?"

"We're doing the whole network, Letta, so I guess that means yes." Letta Levitz was a former ABC soap opera star who was killed off then elevated to online stardom through an aggressive YouPorn personal branding campaign. Now she was going to be an MVN soap opera star.

"But I want the *Some Will Die* treatment, darling."

One of her companions, an aging dandy named Gregory who described himself as a musician and temporarily broke international jet setter, spoke up for his patron.

"You work for the network and Letta's part of the network so you technically work for Letta, right? So if she wants some promotion, she should get it." Gregory tightened his silk scarf around his neck and straightened the lapels on his velvet lizard print sports jacket. Vance was coming down fast and had no capacity left to play nice. Brill could fuck himself. He had delivered the dollars. This act was beyond the limits of any retainer or payout.

"Here's my card, Gregory. When your inheritance comes through we'll give you a quote on promoting Letta. In the meantime, maybe mommy here will up your Grecian formula allowance. You gotta start hitting those eyebrows if you want all your painted parts to match." Vance turned and left the area, he didn't want to get run over in Gregory's mad rush for the nearest mirror.

Vance was done with partying with the vapid movie and television stars that had been chum in the water for the pre-show press. He headed back to his little control center in the Green Room to check in on his launch. Brill was busy body surfing through the crowd, working the room as if he didn't have a care in the world, or a network to run. Watching him cavort about was just a buzz kill. The Escobar fuel had done its job, lasted him through the launch. Now it was time to fight off the alcohol in his system long enough to finish the moment, then go back to having some fun. Not here and certainly not with any of these bees, wannbees and has beens.

Naomi Stiles wasn't speaking to Vance anymore. He knew that to get any kind of response out of her he'd have to ask specific questions, kind of like working with a primitive calculator. He sat down opposite her and she buttoned the top button of her blouse.

"How do the sales look?"

"According to Peggy Bump we've sold over $100 million in advertising. She also says that she'd actually like to see the money."

"And the numbers?"

"The Super Bowl has a 32% global share and *Some Will Die* has a 19% global share."

"We need to push this over the edge."

"So phase two, or is it phase three?"

"Forget the number, Naomi. On my mark. Hold on, I want to see this." He walked to the window overlooking the field.

"Do it."

Stiles sent a special invitation to all the registered MVN subscribers located within the area of the field:

> *You're invited to the North or South Club Lounge to party with the A listers: free lobster, wings, champagne, beer, and alcohol on MVN. Join the biggest party in the world right now! Your subscription is your pass.*

Within 15 seconds at least half the attendees in the full stadium stands were staring up at the lounges. Several of the players on and off the field checked their devices as well. 30 seconds later, as reality began to hit, waves of fans left their seats and headed towards the nearest upper exit. There were two Club Lounges in the stadium, and Vance had rented both of them. Now he was throwing open the doors and inviting the world to mingle with the stars. Each super suite could accommodate 1000 people. In less than two minutes he had created a stampeding riot of people and players leaving the field. He hoped that some of the precious celebs in the room would sustain physical damage. The on field referees, confused and enraged, called a delay on the game, suspending play.

"Okay. That's it," Vance observed, pleased.

"They're calling a halt to the game until they can find out what's happening."

"How's our share?"

"Up two points."

Vance looked over at his producer.

"Cut into *Some Will Die* and run a live feed from the suites. I want two minutes of nothing but celebrities and people with the following crawl: *Super Bowl fans abandon game to party with the stars at MVN launch!*"

Stiles pointed at the monitor on the table receiving the NBC feed. The image cut from the field delay to Grecos in a news helicopter, hovering over the *Some Will Die* stage. Vance's crawl appeared almost word for word at the bottom of the screen. He shook his head.

"*Fucking news people.* Can't even think of their own headlines anymore."

CHAPTER THIRTY NINE
Death Breath

**Main Stage of the Encore Park Amphitheatre: Alpharetta, GA
Sunday, February 4, 2018 6:30 PM EST**

Ben Bigelow heard his name and saw the smoke and flames and the platform and knew it was time. He felt his body lumber out from the line and move towards center stage to stand by Vlad Berber. He was there but he wasn't. He closed his eyes and for a moment heard nothing, then opened them and looked out at the crowd. He was back in the moment, feeling pain as he attempted to lift his massive chest with nothing heavier than the weight of the air in his lungs, lungs that would soon stop filling.

His vision faded in and out. He could feel his poor heart, choked with fat, attempting to push triglyceride-laden blood through arteries that had narrowed to the radius of an aspirating needle. God, he had lived like this so long he couldn't remember anything else... *the merciful end was near.* But was it so merciful? Was life so awful? He felt Berber pat him on the shoulder and direct him to do his "trick," a push up.

Bigelow slowly descended to one knee, then another, nearly blacking out as he knelt to all fours. He attempted to straighten into the plank position but couldn't, then felt Berber's strong boot collapse into his fleshy buttocks, pushing him firmly to the stage. Bigelow was on his stomach, face to the floor, arms splayed out like a chicken carcass waiting for Jacques Pepin's fillet knife. He pressed his palms flat, straightened his feet, closed his eyes, grimaced and put on his war face, like Vlad had trained him. He pushed and felt himself actually rise up off the floor. Suddenly he was alive and awake. The pulse pounding in his ears diminished and he heard the crowd screaming. He turned, feeling a smile twitch on his face as Vlad barked in his ear,

"Go, boy, go!!!!" And then his heart stopped, and he slumped to the floor dead.

George Grecos, hovering over the stage in the NBC Bell 407 helicopter screamed at his cameraman.

"Zoom in on that! Fucker's gotta be dead! Holy shit! *Am I live?*" Grecos pulled himself together and positioned himself by the helicopter's port window, the stage suddenly out of focus behind him.

"George Grecos reporting live from the MVN *Some Will Die* premier at the Alphretta Georgia Amphitheatre and ladies and gentlemen we may have just witnessed history. We're the first major network to cover a live death on television. It doesn't get any more real than this folks. Welcome to Grecos vision!"

Every one of the thousands of buzzing amateur drones flying around the field attempted to zoom in on Bigelow's face, his tongue lapping out of his mouth and a stream of vomit slowly leeching from his throat. Several large professional news drones, each bearing a network logo, blew in from where they had been hovering, just over the field's berm, knocking the smaller drones out of the way as they tore towards the stage.

Jimmy Welles watched from stage right as Bigelow's mother started screaming. *Where the fuck were his security guards!* His satellite phone rang. It was Vance, of course.

"We just cleared over $200 million in ad sales, boy. *You done good!*"

"We global?"

"Every fucking network's running us, baby! Clean up your mess and pack your bags. You got a medical emergency. Show's over!"

Above the stage the words "Some Will Die" appeared on the smoke screen and a chant, prerecorded by James Charles Bones, was fed into the auditorium's sound system. The crowd picked it up and joined in: "*Some Will Die... Some Will Die... Some Will Die!*"

Offstage the show's paramedics, handpicked for their documented incompetence, fumbled with the gear that Jimmy Welles had carefully unpacked while they were on one of their many scheduled cigarette and beer breaks. Welles calculated it would take them at least five minutes to respond to any emergency and another ten to figure out a course of action once they were on scene. He wanted to make sure that Ben Bigelow stayed dead.

It had been eight seconds since Ben Bigelow collapsed onto the stage and it didn't look like he was coming out of it under his own power. Death was something that Vlad Berber had had his fill of. He was trained for these medical emergencies and there was no more room for any more blood on his hands. Suddenly all he cared about was one thing: bringing this jiggly blob of a man back to life.

Berber tilted Bigelow's head back, pinched his nose and blew air into the prone man's lungs, tuning out the *"Some Will Die"* chant that reflected the crowd's sympathy. Nothing happened. *Where were the damned paramedics?* Berber grabbed at the corded microphone that dangled above him on stage and tore it from its wire. He stuffed the powered cable into Bigelow's mouth and punched the man in his chest as the electricity from the cord coursed through his body. Bigelow jerked, opened his eyes and bolted up. The crowd went silent except for one person: Bigelow's mother. Her screaming increased as Welles' two handpicked security guards finally made their way to her side to quiet her.

"Benny...Benny...Help me!" She blared as the larger of the two security guards attempted to place a muzzle over her mouth. She bit him and he responded by punching her in the kidneys from behind.

"Benny! Help!" She screamed again as the second guard grabbed one of her arms to zip tie her.

Berber tugged Ben Bigelow to his feet and the crowd started cheering. But the two men were fixated on one thing: Bigelow's mother being assaulted just ten feet in front of them.

"Help her..." Bigelow managed to wheeze, looking at Vlad.

Berber, seeing that his immediate mission was completed, moved into action. He bounded across the short distance to the stage's edge like a hungry cat after a clipped wing canary. He didn't bother walking off the stage but leapt, grabbing the two guard's heads with his giant, paw-like hands, to stop his trajectory. Mrs. Bigelow wriggled loose and the crowd made room for the fracas. Berber kept his hand on the smaller of the two men, bringing his head to his knee, then following with a right uppercut that sent the man reeling into the crowd. That left the bigger of the two.

The two men circled each other, sizing up the situation. As the security guard reached for his taser Vlad crossed the distance between them. He had been taught not to rely on weapons in a fight: *he was a weapon.* He deflected a wayward attempt at a right cross and used the man's momentum to spin him around. Berber crushed the man beneath him, knee to his back, and ground his face into the dirt. Berber felt in control. He wasn't going to kill this man, just make him regret living for the rest of his life. He slapped him hard across the right ear, knowing he just ruptured an ear drum.

It happened as Berber was deciding how much of a cripple he wanted to make his squirming victim. First he became aware of several other blue shirted security types rushing towards him, then the entire field filled with smoke and the chant *"Fat is beautiful!"*

overwhelmed every other sound in the area. He felt a wall of pro-testors pushing him over, then back towards the stage and looked up to see the guard that he had just been fighting trampled under a moving mountain of obese people holding signs. *The HOP protest had begun!* Berber picked himself up and bounded back towards the stage where he encountered the swollen purple hand of Ben Bigelow extended to help him onto the stage.

CHAPTER FORTY
I See Pulitzer

Main Stage of the Encore Park Amphitheatre: Alpharetta, GA
Sunday, February 4, 2018 6:40 PM EST

George Grecos had missed Vietnam, Desert Shield, Desert Storm and all the media-worthy fighting in Afghanistan and Iraq, but today destiny had placed him in the center of a real story. A death and a protest was happening right below him and he was the only live reporter in the entire world at the eye of this storm. Those fools back at network wanted to waste his time covering another declawed Super Bowl. This was going to be his vindication, *his fucking Pulitzer, baby!*

"Get all the cameras on this. I want the whole thing captured before the cops show up!" Grecos screamed at anyone any one and no one. The rented Bell Jet Ranger helicopter was outfitted with multiple cameras in an enclosed pod underneath the cabin. At just 50 feet over the stage the oily smoke was obscuring the system's lenses. Grecos' team had filled the aircraft with additional mobile transmitting gear and drones, including infra red equipment which could be deployed in case of a blackout. The weight of the gear, three passengers and smoke being sucked into the air intake system was slowly suffocating the craft. It lumbered through the sky like a wheezy old salmon struggling upstream to its spawning grounds.

"We can't see at this altitude! We have to climb to get a shot or drop some infra drones," Grecos cameraman, busy controlling the multiple video feeds yelled out.

"*Well neither can anyone else!* Drop me onstage with a hovercam!"

"I can't land there – it's an FAA violation." Grecos pilot responded to the exuberant, 67 year old sports reporter.

"Then get high and get the shot and I'll tell you what to do!"

The helicopter ascended to 300 feet. From their vantage point they could see that the hysteria was confined to an area extending roughly ¼ mile around the front of the stage. The front lines were a smoky melee with a clearly demarcated wall of protesters and a cluster of guards holding them back. The rest of the thousands of people in the SRO area saw some smoke, heard some chanting and were probably wondering why the show's cloud monitor was offline. Grecos narrated while his cameraman tracked the action. He called his producer and was able to get his live coverage inserted into the holes left by vacating advertisers, then directed his crew to release two large camera drones.

"Head over behind the stage, set down there. Keep the motors running."

"Motor!" The pilot yelled back. "We've only got one and it needs a rest!"

The pilot maneuvered his machine to a helipad located behind the stage, clearing the smoke as he touched down. Grecos and his cameraman exited and headed for the stage's rear entrance. They found it unlocked, opened it, and were almost overrun by a stream of confused and trapped contestants, choking and gagging their way off the stage and into the fresh air of the field. Grecos and his cameraman made their way up the short stairwell and found themselves entering on stage left. Smoke was everywhere and the stage was beginning to burn from a Molotov cocktail that someone had thrown. Grecos narrated as he made his way towards the two figures that he was seeking.

"This is George (cough) Grecos...reporting live from the riot at the *Some Will Die* premier in Alphretta, Georgia. From here on the actual stage I can see a massive group of protestors...they appear to be from the Human Obesity Party and they are fighting with clusters of security men."

Grecos picked his way towards the two figures standing in the middle of the stage. A large man lay on the floor between them.

"There's mass pandemonium here and I expect the rioters to breach the stage at any minute. The police are probably on their way..."

At that moment a Molotov cocktail went sputtering across the stage and broke into a leeching flame in front of Grecos. He turned to his cameraman and yelled.

"Cut it! We need to get Berber off the stage and get out of here!"

Grecos reached stage center at the same time the befuddled paramedics arrived with a gurney. He looked up at Vlad Berber, over at Mrs. Bigelow, down at Ben Bigelow and extended his hand to Berber.

"George Grecos, NBC, come-on, I've got your ride out of here! Let's go! Vlad, have those paramedics load Bigelow on their gurney, my chopper's in back!"

Berber responded without saying a word. He helped the paramedics place Bigelow on the gurney and took charge of steering the operation out the back as a third Molotov cocktail hit the stage. His programming kicked in. He was evacuated by a friendly. He moved into action.

"Let's go, let's go!" Grecos screamed as they exited the rear of the stage, Berber clearing the way for them. The rioters had fought their way to the stage and were moving the battle up the front stairs. Professional and amateur drones crashed into the stage walls, their internal guidance systems running off balance in the smoke and the heat from the creeping fire. Within fifteen seconds Grecos' group had cleared the building and was heading towards the waiting NBC helicopter. Grecos' cameraman opened the fuselage door and helped the paramedics load Ben Bigelow into the aircraft. The pilot looked over at his new cargo, then down at Grecos and Berber.

"I can't lift off with all this weight, we're over limit already!"

Grecos looked at Vlad.

"Get in there and toss whatever's not bolted down."

Berber jumped on board, he knew this drill. Behind them the flames could be seen lapping the top of the stage. The turbine whine of police helicopters was becoming loud.

"Fucking move! We gotta get out of here!" Grecos yelled.

Berber heaved three large equipment cases out the door then helped Mrs. Bigelow into the cockpit. Grecos scurried in then slammed the door on his cameraman and barked at the pilot.

"Get us gone!"

They rose slowly, the bird turning away from the stage. The pilot couldn't clear 25 feet. The Bell was speced to cruise at 150 knots with four passengers and 240 pounds of baggage. The addition of Berber, Bigelow and his mother left the aircraft dangerously overweighed. Its turbine engine wheezed as they slowly crept towards the tree line. The pilot spoke to Grecos through his headset mike.

"Our best bet is to crest the tree line and then call for a ride. We blow this engine and we're shit outta' luck. I ain't writing no one a three million dollar check to replace this thing!"

Jimmy Welles had retreated to the relative safety of the Green Room when he saw the first Molotov arc towards the stage. With all the smoke and confusion in the area there really wasn't much he could do except call the police and wait to be rescued. He heard the police helicopters and knew that he didn't have much time to get a call out. He dialed Vance on his satellite phone.

"What the fuck is happening there?"

"Some kind of HOP riot, the cops are here, they'll EMP the place in a few seconds."

"Where's Vlad and Bigelow?"

"No idea boss, they were on stage, but the monitors are smoked. Can't see shit."

"What happened?"

"HOP...I said it was HOP. Fucking Fatass Potlatch in his wheelchair."

"They fucked with our show. Doesn't matter, we're already golden. Make nice with the cops. Don't tell them shit until you hear from me or Gould. I'm sending Giletti in to get you."

"Got it."

Three Sikorsky H-92 medium duty helicopters operated by the Georgia State Patrol took position over the stage and the protestors. Their first order of business, while announcing their presence and advising all agitated parties to calm down, was to capture as many identities as possible. They did this by intercepting and processing all the cellular signals emanating from the area and using their infra red technology to instantly match the signals with the location and identity of heat signatures.

Within two minutes they had recorded, processed, tagged and catalogued over 2000 people who, through their location and movement, were presumably going to be found guilty of something. Disorderly disturbance citations and arrest warrants were automatically being issued for everyone under suspicion, as well as tow orders for their cars. The State Patrol was burning through a lot of avgas to keep these birds in the air and somebody had to pay for it.

Stage two involved shutting down all communications with a local EMP. That meant no drones in the air and a communications
blackout. Once the crowd was muzzled the aircrafts did a slow cir-
cular pass over the action, spraying sticky white foam that would
not only put out the flames, but lock everyone in position for at
least seven hours. Several protesters, familiar with the passive
crowd restraining technology, attempted to bolt at the edge of the
field, but were glued into position like frozen statues covered with
molten marshmallow. One of the helicopters landed on the back
stage helipad and disgorged a dozen SWAT team members.

The team spread out around the stage, picking their way
through the sticky field. Their gear was impregnated with a highly
frictionless nano-coating that allowed them to glide through the
foam. Two of the team members reached the open back stage door
and checked out the stairway. Finding it clear they moved up the
stairs towards the now blackened rear of the stage, dripping with
wet foam. The smoke was replaced with steam from the charred
middle of the stage where the three Molotov's had hit. As the team
approached the once green door of the Green Room, it swung open
and Jimmy Welles emerged. He was probably the only clean person in a mile radius of the area. He straightened his tie, put out his
hands and walked out to confront the officers.

"I'm Jimmy Welles, with the show. Can I help you, gentlemen?"

Grecos' Bell JetRanger touched down just over the tree line behind the field as the State Patrol's EMP hit. Their communications
were knocked out. Berber regarded the old sportscaster for a moment before speaking.

"What you intention, Mr. Grecos?"

"I want your story, Mr. Berber. The story of *Some Will Die.*"

"My story? My story is all public, Mr. Grecos. There is little to
tell. Just watch the videos."

Grecos shook his head. All this work for this?

"There has to be something, Mr. Berber. What were the plans? What's next? Didn't MVN tell you anything? What about Jack Vance?"

Mrs. Bigelow, who had just experienced the trauma of watching her only son die then live again, stretched her short, thick legs. She needed a smoke.

"I unnerstan the news people pays for stories. Dat right, Mr... Greckos?"

Grecos paused for a moment. There was something here, he *fucking* knew it.

"That's right, Mrs..."

"Bigelow. Ben's mom. You recognize Ben of course. He's been on TV. I might gots sometin fer you. You got money, we kin talk."

CHAPTER FORTY ONE
Castling

Motel Six: Alpharetta, GA
Sunday, February 4, 2018 7:30 PM EST

Potlatch had a bottle of champagne waiting when Drab and Agness arrived back to the room. The two men entered as they had left, bickering and whispering curses, both covered in mud and scratches.

"You look like a couple of good ol' mountain boys! 'Cept for them Italian shoes, of course. Nice work!" Potlatch roared. It almost seemed as if he was about to stand. He pointed at the large television monitor with his cane. An overhead shot of the smoky, foam covered Amphitheatre field filled the screen with the crawl: *MVN's Some Will Die flames out...Who's paying for this mess?"*

"You got your wish. The show is over, HOP made its reappearance on the national stage and everyone's going to be looking to blame someone real soon. I'd call this a cause célèbre, gentlemen," Potlatch continued.

Drab walked over to the table and had a sip of the champagne then spit it back into his glass.

"Warm. Jesus. We're not celebrating yet. The work's just started. Any injuries reported?"

Agness scrolled through the news on his phone.

"We got some heads smacked in. Some HOP people messed up, nothing severe. Security guards reported to be out of control."

"Good." Drab pulled a burner phone out of his pocket and handed it to Agness.

"Time for Mr. Vance to make one last call." Agness took the phone and hit redial for the one number the device had called. Someone on the other end answered.

"Yeah, it's Vance. I told you I wanted people in the hospital, re- member? I don't care about the smoke and I don't care about the police. I wanted the fat people targeted and I wanted them put down. Like dead, was I unclear? What the fuck are a couple of nicks and scratches! A fucking Girl Scout could do damage like that. I wanted people dead, you hear me? *Dead!* Yeah, that's right I'm fucking disappointed. So disappointed that you pussies aren't getting another dime out of me. Really? I don't care who you tell. Go fuck yourself...*bitch.*" He hung up the phone and pulled its SIM card.

Drab smiled. Now they were getting somewhere.

"We have a little more work to do before we leave Atlanta, gen- tlemen. It's going to be a long night," he said.

CHAPTER FORTY TWO
Just Spell My Name Right

Georgia Dome North Club Lounge: Atlanta, Georgia
Sunday, February 4, 2018 8:10 PM EST

Jack Vance and Naomi Stiles were glued to the small monitor on the table of the Club Lounge Green Room. The fact that the Super Bowl down below was stalled and about to be cancelled didn't seem to bother the 1000 plus people partying on the other side of the two way glass in the adjacent room. Nor did the *Some Will Die* riot. It didn't bother the advertisers either, or Sidney Brill, who was busy lapping champagne off the breasts of as many willing young MVN starlets as he could coerce into pulling down their tube tops. The only people who seemed troubled were Vance and Stiles and they both knew that they were about to become the center of attention for the press corps in the room.

A satellite phone lying on the table rang. Vance nodded for Stiles to pick it up.

"How we doing, Peggy? Really? Nobody cared about it? So we've peaked? Calls are coming through? OK, I'll tell him." She placed the phone down. "You can stop buying drinks now."

"What did we hit?"

"$440 million. Peggy figures that's about it."

"Anybody mention the mess at the Amphitheatre?"

"Yeah, they said any network that could deliver a show like that was a sure winner. We were the number one story in the world Mr. Vance. *In the world.*"

"You're right, I can stop buying drinks."

"And the press are calling for comment, from Brill."

"Of course. Tell the facility the party's over, bar is closed, put away the cheese chunks and get Gould on the phone with Welles and the cops and the Amphitheatre. Make sure we don't have any insurance issues."

"We won't."

"How do you know?"

"Because I bought the insurance. If anyone's getting a dime out of you for a lawsuit it's gonna be me."

"Clear this place out for the press. I'll get Brill teed up."

Vance pushed his way out of the Green Room and onto the crowded floor of the Club Lounge. He moved past celebrities and locals, getting sloshed on booze that was costing him at least $10 a glass. Every minute this party continued pulled another $1000 out of his pocket.

It wasn't hard to find Brill, he was the only man sitting between two naked women in one of the private VIP alcoves. Brill was starting a champagne cocktail toast when Vance parted the curtain and sat down in a deep chair across the table from him and his new friends.

"To the man who made me rich! The biggest brain in marketing. Girls meet Jack Vance, a geniuses' genius!" Brill raised his glass and promptly dropped it.

"This might not look so good on camera, Sidney. Need you to pull it together. Press is going to want a statement about *Some Will Die*. And they're already in the room, we invited them to the party, remember?"

"Really? Wha happen?"

"The riot, Sidney. I've got a few messaging points for..."

"Fuck the messaging. I want a massage. You handle it, Vance, that's what I'm paying you for. Just get me out of here. Me and the girls."

Vance stood up. Fucking prick. He was defiantly resigning this asshole before the week was over. He turned and shut the curtains behind him. For the moment his fortunes were still tied to Brill. Vance found Stanley Best where he was supposed to be, parked by the bar, at the ready for trouble.

"Brill's over there. He's a mess. Get him out of here quietly, take him wherever he wants to go then see if Jimmy needs any help, Giletti's already over at the Amphitheatre. I want all your asses back to the city ASAP. I'll meet you there tomorrow." Vance returned to the Green Room where Naomi Stiles was already fending off multiple press inquiries from a cluster of reporters at the door. The party was over, the booze was cut off and they were pissed. It was time for them to make someone pay. Vance watched as Stanley Best hustled Brill and company out a side entrance and raised his hands.

"Okay, press conference time. Let's get this done." Within ten minutes Vance was facing about 75 reporters representing all the networks and multiple independent news outlets, blogs, portals and forums. He had Stiles set up a direct news feed with the equipment brought in for the launch. Most of the civilian partygoers were exiting, indicating the utter unimportance of the "news" in relation to the next party of the evening. Vance was ready to go.

"I'm Jack Vance of Blowfish Communications representing MVN this evening. I want to thank you all, the NFL and the rest of the world for tuning in and making MVN the biggest network launch in history. We had a little disturbance over at the *Some Will Die* premier tonight, but I understand from our contacts working with the Georgia State Patrol that there were no significant injuries, so all seems to be in their capable hands. We should know more tomorrow and I'm sure you'll all find out whatever it is you think your viewers want to know. Any questions?"

A reporter from NBC spoke up.

"Any news on the damage done at the Amphitheatre?"

"By the crowd or by your NBC helicopter that I understand was buzzing the field?"

A reporter from CNN waved his hand and began talking.

"Who started the riot?"

"HOP as I understand, but I'm sure the police will have their own statement by the morning." Another voice from the back of the room,

"We heard your guards were beating people down, any comment?"

"One man's beat is another man's defense. They're a local security company, call them up." The next question came from a CBS reporter.

"It looks like some Super Bowl ads appeared on MVN and not on NBC. How much money did they lose over this?"

"Ask the guy from NBC, he's standing right over there."

The questioning went on for another seven minutes before Vance and the reporters grew tired of playing cat and mouse on live streaming media. Vance closed out the session with a promise to issue an official statement of some kind within the next 12 hours. He reiterated the statement that the open bar was now closed. If any of them wanted to continue to drink they'd have to do so on their own dimes. He knew that would clear out *any* roomful of reporters.

Vance loosened his tie and walked back to the Green Room, the lights in the main room being dimmed, bank by bank behind him. He slumped down in a chair across from Naomi Stiles, who was still busy doing something important for some aspect of the day that Vance really didn't care about anymore. He looked at her until she stopped and looked back.

"What?"

"Hell of a day."

"Month."

Vance's satellite phone rang.

"Executive?"

"*Where the hell are you?* All Okay?" It was Vald Berber calling from an unlisted number.

"Fuck you, Executive. I quit." The phone went dead.

"That was short," said Stiles, still watching Vance.

"He just quit."

"Who?"

"Berber."

"You bring out the best in everyone, Mr. Vance."

"Probably got a better offer after his big coming out numbers."

"You were dumping the whole account anyway, remember?"

"*But not tonight.* Press will love this. I'm sure he'll do the circuit."

"That's what you trained him for."

"Great seeing my children turn on me." He paused and looked around the now quiet, darkened space, suddenly feeling alone and empty. Maybe he just needed a drink.

"Looks like I'm out of friends down here."

"You got money, go buy some."

Vance exhaled loudly and placed his elbows on his knees.

"I know I've been an asshole..."

"Little late for this, Jack."

"Not Mr. Vance?"

"Okay, little late for this, Mr. Vance."

"I know the shit's going south between us and you're going to quit and sue me for sexual harassment and I'm going to let you win and give you all the money you want. Then you can go on with your life and forget any of this happened."

"You're a mind reader Mr. Vance."

"In five or ten years you'll be a mom with a couple of kids and a nice guy who doesn't question why you have so much money in the bank and aren't really working."

"Got my life figured out? Maybe I'll open my own firm with the cash. Or a coffee shop. No, a tea shop. You think all this leaves a great taste?"

"Tonight it does. You know it does. How about we just go out and have a drink and celebrate what we did here, together. Can we put down the guns and have a simple, pure moment? How about that, Naomi? Because frankly, I *am* out of friends."

She looked at him for a moment, then waved her Smart Phone off, slid her flexible tablet and scattered papers into her limited edition Coach leather valise and stood up.

"Okay, Mr. Jack Vance. One drink."

CHAPTER FORTY THREE
Rude Awakening

W Hotel, Extreme Wow Suite: Downtown Atlanta, GA
Monday, February 5, 2018 7:15 AM EST

The air conditioner in the Atlanta W's $2000 a night Extreme Wow Suite wasn't supposed to rattle, the beds weren't supposed to creak and the blackout windows should have kept every inch of the 1750 square foot space in a soothing nocturnal blanket. So why the hell was the sun blazing a path into Vance's coddling darkness? The black was the only thing that was even remotely capable of mitigating the painful damage he had inflicted on himself during last night's celebratory binge.

Little pieces came screaming back. Partying with rock and movie stars at every place in Atlanta that could command $50 for a glass of single malt; hiring a limo off the street and drinking champagne through the sunroof. Then there was her, wasn't there always a her in nights measured by the ounce? He was buying of course, newbie millionaires always picked up the bill. Now he was left with the pain and sun and...her. God, what happened to Naomi and Vlad and Best and Giletti and Welles and the rest of his crew *and* that ingrate asshole Brill? Vance was temporarily, blissfully amnesiac.

A naked female form silhouetted in gold at the window sidetracked his memory train before it veered into a replay of the *Some*

Will Die riot and press conference and everything else that did or didn't happen. He tried to speak, but there was not enough fluid left in his body to lubricate his throat and let words slip out. The figure turned, giving Vance a slippery profile of a pointed breast, and approached him, bent down and whispered in his ear.

"Brill called."

"Ms. Stiles!" Vance was very suddenly awake, nervously pulling his sheet up to cover his body. He had never felt awkward with his nudity in front of employees before, but this was uncharted territory. Naomi Stiles folded her arms and shook her head. She was in no rush to hide herself.

"Now you're modest? It's almost... cute... Jack."

Vance had enough trouble reorienting himself after last night. It was an evening that had clinically shortened his life by at least three weeks. Now the employee he had lusted over for years who was about to quit and sue him for sexual harassment, was standing in front of him, in his hotel room, naked.

"It's time to get back to work, Jack, don't you think?"

"How did we..."

"You mean why did I? You paid me!" She slithered over to a desk that was submerged in one of the room's dark pockets and emerged wearing one of his newly stained Charles Trywhitt shirts. Naomi produced a crispy new check and danced it in front of her beaming smile.

"100,000 clams, or is it smackers? Whatever you gamblers say, it's 100,000 of them. Thank you, Mr. Vance, it's enough for me to officially quit."

Vance ran his eyes from hers to the check she held out. Reality was coming back.

"You quit last night. I remember, before we did anything. So seduction is off the table."

"Don't worry, Jack, I won't sue you for harassment. This settlement was a hell of a lot easier and I'm not losing money on attorney's fees. We're square."

She was the most expensive memory that he had ever lost.

Vance touched the bedside, activating the plasma wall. He slid his hand across the table, skipping from news station to portal. Last night's *Some Will Die* episode was trending hard, with coverage split between the MVN launch, Super Bowl cancellation and show riot. Stiles slid next to him and pointed at the NBC feed in the corner of the large split screen.

"There."

Vance enlarged the screen. NBC's George Grecos filled the wall.

"Tonight on NBC's Special Reports I'll be conducting an exclusive interview with Vlad Berber, former host of the ill fated *Some Will Die* MVN reality competition show. What Berber has to say will open your eyes about how non-networks are run. Don't miss my exclusive interview with Vlad Berber, the former host of Some Will Die, and a special surprise guest this evening. Only on NBC."

Vance leaned back into his big pillow, wishing he could go to sleep.

"We have a problem here, Naomi?"

"Not as long as his graft is still in place. He won't remember a thing about our thing. Would take a doctor to find it and I doubt NBC is giving their guests medical exams before appearing on a show. Can you see Berber submitting to that?"

"No. Another disgruntled whistle blower. Fuck him. Let MVN deal with it. NBC is pissed. They'll do whatever they can to strike back for the shortfall of Super Bowl revenue. What's that?" Vance caught another crawl on one of the reduced screens and enlarged a feed from CNN. Veteran newsman Harry Queen filled the screen, an image of Gekko Potlatch behind him.

"And don't miss tonight on the Harry Queen Live program when we'll talk with none other than former Georgia Congressman and head of the Human Obesity Party, Gekko Potlatch. Gekko will discuss their successful protest during the *Some Will Die* premier last night. We'll find out what this means for their organized protests across the United States and for you. *Only on Harry Queen live.*" Vance thumbed off the screens.

"And who really cares, Harry? Talk about piling on. What a bunch of assholes. Where's the thanks? We just gave that fat crybaby an excuse to rekindle his career."

Naomi Stiles pulled herself out of bed and began dressing. Vance's satellite phone rang.

"Mr. Vance? It's Peggy Bump. We received some of the money this morning from MVN, any idea when we can expect the rest?"

"Some? How much?"

"About seven million. Leaves us $11.75 million in the hole thanks to that great interest rate you negotiated. Not to mention the hundreds of millions we're expecting, you know, the revenue part of the equation, the part that gets us out of debt."

"We have until midnight. Maybe there was a hiccup. I'll find out. Jimmy there? Let me talk to him." Vance waited on hold for 30 seconds.

"Coming back today?" Welles asked.

"Where are all the contestants, Jimmy, what happened with the cops?"

"Giletti and Best are still down there working with them to sort it all out. They are going through the surveillance feeds and the insurance docs. We have a few people in the hospital, rough security team you hired Jack."

"I didn't hire any security team."

"That's not what they said. Couple of them are talking with the cops now. I don't know anything yet."

"What about Bigelow and the contestants?"

"They're debriefing all the contestants. Bigelow I haven't seen. Best will run interference but I'd get up here. Stuff's busting loose. And Gould's sending you a local number to call."

"For what?"

"Atlanta criminal attorney. Just in case."

"Just in case what?"

"In case the cops want to talk to you. Like I said, you better get up here Jack, shit's happening. We can't have you stuck down there."

"Get me the earliest flight back. Today."

While Vance was speaking a text came through, probably the number of the attorney. Vance would deal with it later. He had a more pressing problem at the moment. After a couple of tries his call to Sidney Brill was answered.

"Sidney? I can hardly hear you! Still celebrating? We need to talk. You're where? I'll find it. See you in 30. Sidney, we only got part of the money. *Sidney*? Sidney!"

Vance dropped the phone and moved across the room to his closet. Naomi Stiles was already fully dressed and going through the "I'm about to leave now motions." He selected a medium blue Brioni suit and paired with them Alden wingtips and a creme shirt that had been handmade to his measurements in Hong Kong. He grabbed a bossy Brooks Brothers navy and red striped tie, thick enough for a proper double Windsor knot. Looking sharply conservative would give him an edge, especially when dealing with guys who had been drinking all night long. He splashed some Bay Rum after shave on his unshaven face and spritzed himself with a few blasts of a limited edition Tom Ford cologne. Whore bath. Stiles was as packed up as she could be and started moving towards the door.

"I'll walk out with you."

"And into a cab. You're coming with me."

"I'm sorry Jack, I quit, remember. I don't work with you any-more."

"Since we're officially lovers I'm asking you as a personal favor. You're coming along to see Brill."

Naomi Stiles shook her head and couldn't resist smiling. "They really broke the mold when you crawled out of the amniotic fluid. Okay...lover. I'll see how this ends. But that's it. You're on your own."

"So booty calls are out of the question?"

"Depends how often you want to write out $100,000 checks. Everything's negotiable."

CHAPTER FORTY FOUR
Cat Scratched

The Cheetah Club: NW Atlanta, GA
Monday, February 5, 2018 8:15 AM EST

Twenty minutes later Vance and Stiles arrived at the address that Brill had given them, the Cheetah Gentlemen's Club. It was a windowless, painted cinderblock building with a gold door and red velvet rope. The owners probably felt it looked classy at night. During the day it was hard to distinguish it from any other storage building in the area. This wasn't a Sidney Brill kind of place, at least not the Sidney Brill that Vance knew. If Brill and company were still here at 8:00 the next morning, chances were he wasn't a Sidney Brill anyone would recognize.

It wasn't hard to find their quarry. MVN had clearly paid to keep the club on, and with the ruckus they were causing, may have even bought the place. Vance followed a river of spilled champagne, empty bottles dotting his way to the main stage where Brill, shirtless, was being body massaged by the oiled behinds of no less than three dancers. The rest of his board and executive staff were either staggering around drunk, passed out or being similarly attended to by other naked women. This wasn't the B team either. The club's "talented" crew was taking care of the executives. Stiles clung to Vance. This was not her environment. She whispered in his ear.

"And I thought you were bad."

He looked around the room and pointed to the MVN PR guy, asleep in a pillow of vomit. "I am, but in a good kind of bad way."

Vance jumped on the oily stage, almost losing his footing on the slippery polished surface and shouted to attract Brill's attention. He felt like the dismissive headmaster catching a student in the middle of a self-hazing gone wrong.

"Sidney!" He pinched the dancer blocking his view hard enough to make her jump off his client.

"Sidney!" Brill saw him and shoved the women aside, embracing Vance in a greasy bear hug. Vance grimaced at the new stains on his $1975 suit.

"How the fuck is the man who made me rich? Vance, you genius, I'm gonna fucking kiss you, anything you want baby, whip it out I'm yours!"

"Listen Sidney, we need to talk about the account. How about we get off the stage and go over to a booth or get some air or something."

Sidney looked around at his girls, then back at Vance.

"What account, Jack?"

"Enough, Sidney. The money's not in our bank from the ads."

"You don't have the account anymore Jack...*I sold MVN.* You made me a millionaire you beautiful marketing man. Unzip your pants, these girls will take care of you. You earned it."

"Sold? When?"

"15 minutes after the game started. NBC saw how much money they were losing. They made me an offer and I sold them the whole thing. The whole thing, man. All of it! Done! Took my bonus out of the deal and I am fucking retired! That's what a startup's all about. Why do you think they weren't so pissed about the Super Bowl? Shit boy, it's marketing 101. Own your own competition! Maybe they'll hire you to write the press release. S'okay, I'll put in a good word."

Vance felt the air leaving the room around him, little pin pricks tickling every square centimeter of his body.

"15 minutes? What about my cut... our deal?"

"You got your cut for as long as I owned MVN. No one can say Sidney Brill ain't a man of his word!" Brill slapped him on the back, sending oil spraying into the air.

"How 'bout a lap dance... I'm buying!"

Vance felt the room spinning. He staggered off the stage and propped himself against one of the poles on the floor where Stiles stood waiting for him.

"Didn't go well? He wanted to keep you on? What happened?"

Vance grabbed her by the hand and pulled her out of the club, collapsing on all fours as soon as he felt fresh air. He began vomiting. Stiles looked down at him, shaking her head.

"And you told me you were a good, bad Jack."

But Vance was in no mood for gallows humor, especially when it was at his expense. He wiped his mouth with the $50 Dunhill handkerchief that he had tucked up his sleeve and barked at her.

"He sold the fucking company 15 minutes after the game started. Fucking bullshit rat. Let's get outta here."

Vance's satellite phone rang.

"It's Peggy, Mr. Vance. How are we looking on freeing up those funds?"

"Not good at the moment, Peggy. What's our house fund look like?"

"About $60,000."

"Make sure everyone gets their paycheck. Today."

"Payroll's not for another week."

"Just do it."

"A Mr. Ferriola has been calling the office for you."

"Message?"

"None. Said you'd know what it was about."

"When he calls back get his transfer information, send him the seven million we received."

"So we're still negative nearly $12."

"Yeah, but I made payroll. See you in a few hours." Vance hung up.

"You didn't get the money in there?"

"Brill hosed us out of $207 million bucks. We took the money from NBC and gave it right back to them. The joke's on us!"

The cab Naomi Stiles had called pulled up to the pair. They entered.

"The W," Vance ordered, sliding in before her. There was silence in the car for the first 60 seconds of the ride.

"Where's that check I gave you?"

Naomi Stiles produced the now worthless $100,000 check drawn on the Blowfish account. Vance immediately snatched it from her hand and tore it up, handing her a $100 bill in exchange. She yelled to the driver. "Stop the god damned car," then turned hard to look at Vance for a full two seconds before speaking.

"You would have been ahead of the game offering me nothing, or better yet trying to kiss me. I know the numbers asshole. You didn't have to do that. And yes, if there's anything left of your pathetic company to sue by the time I can find a lawyer to take my case you can bet your ass I'll go after it." As the cab slowed she opened the door.

"Hey, I'm sorry..."

"Fuck you, Jack. You were right last night. You are an asshole and you'll always be an asshole. I don't think you can help it. I really, really don't. And I was actually feeling sort of sorry for you back there."

She left the car, the $100 and Vance behind. The driver turned and shook his head at Vance.

"Dames, huh?"

"Mind your mess and drive."

Vance gave up trying to brush the dirt and vomit off his suit as they approached the W. He saw several police cars outside the hotel.

"Take me to the airport. I've had it with this town."

The cabbie eyed Vance in his rear view mirror.

"You one of those TV guys, right? I knew I seen you before. That sure was some looker you let git away. Guys like you probably got 'em stashed all over the place no problem, right?"

"Somethin' like that."

Vance looked at the reflection of his face in the cab's window. God, he was really looking old. He read the text on his satellite phone then pulled one of the burners out of his pocket and dialed a number, conducting his call in a hushed voice.

"Mr. Spring? Danny Spring?"

"How y'all doin? Who's this?"

"Jack Vance. Stu Gould told me to give you a call."

"And good timing you got, boy. Tol' me you might be callin'. Been talking with my buddies down at the State Patrol office and seems like there's gonna be some issues with the guards you hired."

"I didn't hire any guards, Mr. Spring."

"Well that's not what they think. Matter of fact they might even want to talk with you. These Patrol boys down here get's up on somethin', they just wanna put it down."

"And how long would all that take?"

"Well depends. I know they busy. All the muss and fuss about last night. Might get around to you by Wednesday."

"And if I have legal representation."

"Then I can handle it for you. *For now.*"

"I'll transfer $10,000 to your account. That cover us?"

"Let you know when it don't. Where you going to be, in case we need to talk all of a sudden?"

"I'll be on this number. In case we need to *talk.*"

"Okay, Mr. Vance. You got yoself a Southern lawyer."

"Southern? Gould told me you were from Cincinnati and graduated from Northwestern with him."

"I did, but *well spoken* Yankees don't get any slack down here when the police go out looking for their clients. Go do your job, Mr. Vance. Make some money. *Y'all might need it.*"

CHAPTER FORTY FIVE
Strange Revelation

Jack Vance's Condo: Chicago, IL
Monday, February 5, 2018 2:30 PM CST

It felt like a decade in line at the post office since Vance had been back at his North Lake Shore Drive condo. He walked through the immaculate and spare chunk of the property that he had purchased with his first big retainer check. Or at least someone named Jack Vance had purchased it, not the pissed off, scared, self doubting stranger walking through it now. He ran his hand across the smooth, dustless vintage mahogany Herman Miller dinner table in the dining room, looked across the walls at a collection of original Man Ray photos and Robert Longo oils and felt like an intruder. The man who had so successfully used his slippery tongue, drugs and alcohol to have his way with women on everything from his Eames chaise to the suede wrapped walls of his bedroom didn't live here anymore. The beat up, deflated, lizard skin that was now Jack Vance didn't even feel like having a drink, even if it was already 2:30 in the afternoon.

His message wall was full of business hour names. He ran his eyes up and down looking for anything from anyone who wasn't a client, reporter, employee or lawyer. Nothing. Vance slowly unpeeled his suit and stuffed it into the incinerator. It was as vomit and dirt soaked as his life had been. And what were the results?

An empty wallet, a run in with the law, a blown opportunity with the woman of his dreams, the loss of his entire business; maybe something worse if and when his creditors were unsatisfied come midnight. There wasn't a single person he could call who wasn't being paid to listen to him. And right now he didn't have the spare cash to purchase a shoulder to cry on.

A steam shower and a shave infused a little bounce into Vance's muscles, but did nothing to relieve the dread and jaundice that set into his brain. The original Jack Vance would have hemmed and hawed over which Hugo Boss suit to wear with what cordovan brogues. This version didn't think twice about pulling a brown North Face Kevlar turtleneck over a pair of Belstaff Black Prince trousers and donning handmade White's Traveler's boots. He slipped on a 1¾" thick bull hide money belt with $1000 neatly hidden in its zippered recesses. These were clothes that were designed to protect, not impress and at this stage of the game, he needed all the armor he could find.

Vance turned over his platinum Ulysse Nardin Marine Chronometer Anniversary 160 automatic watch and read the inscription: *To JV with all my love: MD.* He strapped it on, knowing he'd be able to hock it for decent cash anywhere in the world. It was worth $30 grand and would fetch seven in a heartbeat. Found money, he hadn't paid for the damn thing. He opened his wall safe and extracted a passport, $20,000 in mixed currencies and the prized Microtech automatic knife given to him by Scooter Munderbund, who had used it in an episode of the Fox spy thriller series "48. He reached for his generation six Glock 30 biometric.40 caliber carbon fiber semi automatic handgun, checked the magazine, chambered a round and slid the weapon into the rear of his waistband. In the back of the safe, in the Cohiba box, lay his father's heavy Soviet OTs-33 Pernach automatic pistol. It was a felony just to own the thing. He tossed it on the bed.

He donned a competition grade Vanson Enfield Firenze leather jacket, shoved three burner phones in his pocket and placed a pair of Oliver Peoples data glasses on his face. He pulled a small Scheyden flight case out of his closet and dumped his satellite phone, passport, small Dopp kit, Blancpain 50 Fathoms Watch, Chloe's lighter, a pair of regular Revo sunglasses, spare magazine for the Pernach, vial of Percoset, handful of B vitamins, a stick of morning after pills and four condoms into the bag's tough 1000 denier cordura recesses. He threw in the automatic Soviet pistol, leaving the box on the bed. He placed $1000 in cash and his Amex Black credit chip into his Blowfish custom slim black Dunhill wallet. Vance closed the door of his condo wondering if he'd ever hear its reassuring vacuum seal again. It felt like it was all slipping away.

Vance's 2017 Bentley Continental GT Speed Convertible always put a smile on his face, and today was no exception. The Brits realized that only a body designer from Ferrari could move their streamlined brick from bulldog to greyhound and had tossed their egos out the window for last year's model. It worked. The car was faster, sexier and more muscular than anything on the road. Vance had placed discrete little stars, the same midnight blue as his vehicle, along its leading fender, representing all the women that he felt it had helped him bed. The tally had not escaped Naomi, Vance mused, who would probably use it in her pending sexual harassment suit. It was all in fun, he explained on more than one occasion, sort of fooling himself and sort of not. It would be coarse to add a star for her, and in respect he decided against it, for now.

He exited his garage, pointed the Bentley south on Lake Shore Drive, and veered off when he made the Michigan Avenue exit. He wanted the car close at hand, but not in his building, and left it with the valet at the Drake Hotel down the street from his office. Vance buttoned his case into the retinal sealed compartment in the trunk and threw on the car's jammer, effectively blocking any signals that its onboard communications systems sent out. It was designed by the same lab that had provided his personal jammer, which he suddenly realized that he had forgotten at his condo. He slapped himself in the forehead with the palm of his hand. *Fucking moron!* Maybe he wouldn't need it today. The car, at least, was temporarily Off The Grid. He took the valet's number and left him with $200 and instructions to keep it in front and ready to go should he suddenly need it.

CHAPTER FORTY SIX
From the Ashes

Hancock Building, Blowfish Offices: Chicago, IL
Monday, February 5, 2018 4:00 PM CST

"Mr. Vance! You're back! Welcome and congratulations!" When it came to employees like his receptionist Missy Slats, some things would never change. But that's why she had been hired. The job description was simple: ever effusive, never moody, always helpful. For the first time Vance actually appreciated the service she was providing. Maybe in her next job she'd learn to file, answer the phone and recognize clients by name.

"Why Missy...thank you." It felt good to respond, even though Vance knew that given their current financials and the situation at hand he'd be firing her in about fifteen minutes. As he walked beyond her Missy slid down into her chair and thought *"finally a compliment."* That could only mean one thing: a raise was coming!

Vance heard Jimmy Welles' voice from the direction of the War Room.

"He's here!"

Then something very strange happened. Someone began piping music through the office. Not just any music, but "Hail to the Chief." Vance could take a joke, but this one was either the sickest or the most naively planned he had encountered in years. He entered the War Room and found his executive staff had dwindled to

Jason Mayhew, Peggy Bump and Jimmy Welles. Stanley Best was presumably still in Atlanta, probably working with Giletti and the cops on the mess they left behind. *Some Will Die* had cost him his top dogs and separated him from his two heavies. What could happen to him in his own house?

"Please stop this it's...inappropriate." Vance walked past his desk, the staff emanating an odd collective liveliness for 4:00 in the afternoon. He took his chair at the head of the War Room table.

"I'm afraid that I have some bad news, news that will impact each and every one of you and for once I'd like to say three words that won't even come close to expressing what happened in Atlanta. *I fucked up.*"

"Shouldn't we wait for Naomi?" Mayhew asked.

"I fucked up there too. She quit. I trusted a client. My mistake. Within 15 minutes of the network launch Sidney Brill, our former client, sold the company and any of our profits to NBC. I didn't read the tea leaves. Didn't watch the money. Didn't do... my job. I'll make this as direct as possible. We're broke and I'm going to ask you to..."

Jimmy Welles had heard enough. Boss or no boss he had to rain on Vance's pity parade. He stood up and motioned at the cloud.

"You're wrong Vance, if anything we're going to be rich and I want some stock options this time."

"Jimmy, I barely made payroll and we're 12 million in the hole after paying for that launch, just ask Peggy. I'm through here. I got nothing left."

"Maybe not, Mr. Vance. If we can stall your creditors, we might stay in the game," Peggy spoke, motioning to the cloud.

The cloud filled with streams of messages coming in too quickly to process. Welles slowed them down and they became legible. Vance's mouth moved as he read them to himself. He felt the fatigue of self doubt seep from his body. The words above the conference table were reinvigorating him. He slid back a recessed panel in his chair's armrest and withdrew his emergency flask. He had no idea what it contained, but took a long pull and continued to read across the nearly 100 new client inquiries that had come in overnight. Welles couldn't contain himself.

"GM, United, Fox, Pfizer, fucking *Mellos* caramel corn! They all want proposals...they all want to be the next MVN! If we land a tenth of this we'll be millionaires!" It was true. By some utter miracle word of the MVN sale had already spread through the global marketing community. Overnight it seemed that Blowfish had become the hottest communications agency in the country and everyone wanted a piece of the mojo. Vance felt very aware of his surroundings and trappings, *why the hell wasn't he wearing a suit!*

"Have you started processing?" He looked over at Jason Mayhew, knowing that his chief research man would at least have answered a few letters.

"God, yes. Since 8:00 AM. We'll be here all day and all night going through this stuff."

"We need to get commitments. If we're this hot we can collect some upfront money. It's the only way anyone's getting our time. No one gets anything without paying in advance." He paused, twisted a little thought around in his head and then spat it out before he could talk himself out of it.

"As of now you each own a 5% share of this company. I'll have Gould draw up the documents. You've all stuck around for the ride. It's time for the payoff." Vance looked over at Welles.

"Let's get some Dom flowing...no sense wading through all this money without some lubrication!"

The cloud was tuned to follow the growing tidal wave of content concerning the MVN sale to NBC, which effectively flushed the negative post-game fallout from the news cycle. It buoyed up the sales climate and provided a welcome backdrop to their community effort.

By 8:00 PM Vance's team had spoken with over 20 potential new clients and secured verbal retainers for nearly five million dollars. The burner phone number Vance had given to his creditors rang. He answered it.

"Mr. Ferriola. You received the first payout, correct? The balance? Maybe tonight, maybe in the morning. I know you don't like that word, but have you seen the news? We're kingmakers. Yeah people pay for that. We've got five mil committed right now. No, not the cash yet, but that's coming. Look, we're halfway there. The Harry Queen Show and the Grecos Special? Why should I be worried? We're past that now. Come if you want to. Sure, you can hang out until we collect the money. The sofa in the lobby is comfortable. Okay. See you round 9:30." Vance returned to his sales list and document review. The show, the network, the Super Bowl, the police, Atlanta, his past doubts seemed like they happened another life ago.

"We have anything to worry about with those programs, Mr. Vance?" Peggy Bump asked, taking a moment away from her spreadsheets.

"Like what?"

"Like anything that could hurt us."

"Pissed off ex employee and an ex congressman looking to rekindle his career? We were hired guns, that's all. Anything else the insurance company can deal with."

"We should watch."

"I'd rather make money and drink."

"We need to know if there's anything there, Jack."

" Buzzkill."

"Grecos is coming on at 8:30, so is Queen. Dueling old cocksuckers." Vance stood up and clapped his hands.

"Okay. Peggy wants a TV break. Everybody can officially put the phones down, we're all going to watch George Grecos together and see what our old friend Vlad has to say. Who wants a drink?

I'm buying." Vance opened another bottle from his Dom Perignon collection and refilled glasses while his little staff relaxed and leaned back in their chairs to watch the special programs. It was a welcome break from the success they were enjoying. Vance felt like he was licking fingers dipped in chocolate and covered in gold dust.

CHAPTER FORTY SEVEN
Special Guests

Hancock Building, Blowfish Offices: Chicago, IL
Monday, February 5, 2018 8:30 PM CST

The George Grecos Special opened with the full NBC graphic and video treatment, making it appear that the host had spent his career analyzing news, not sports. After a self congratulatory introduction, Grecos quickly laid claim to being the only reporter at the *Some Will Die* premier to brave smoke and fire for the story. The studio camera pulled away from his face to reveal not only Vlad Berber, but Ben Bigelow and his mother, the "surprise guests."

Vance and Welles put down their glasses simultaneously. The party was over.

"Wasn't that your contestant, the one who died?" Mayhew asked. Vance shot Welles a look. The level of his mood just dropped from the clouds to the sewers.

Grecos moved slightly in his studio chair, making sure the camera had the best of his best side, then launched into his show.

"We all know my special guest Vlad Berber from his exposure on such shows as *Survivor: Chernobyl* and most recently as the host of MVN's *Some Will Die*. Vlad and I have had some time to talk and he's been gracious enough to appear on this special edition of NBC Reports to tell us about his experience with MVN and in particular working with Ben Bigelow, one of the contestants.

Mr. Bigelow and his mother are also joining us in the studio today."
The producer cut to a captioned shot of Ben Bigelow and his
mother.

"Mr. Bigelow was the contestant who died on *Some Will Die*, and
was brought back to life by Vlad Berber just in time to witness his
mother being almost killed by the show's security detail. Quite,
quite a story. Looks like you saved the whole family, right after
NBC purchased the entire franchise, almost like kismet. Vlad, how
did you come to be the host of the show?" Grecos asked.

The studio producer cued a medium shot of Berber. It was the
first time most of the world had ever seen him in a suit. He was
clean, shaven, his hair neat and gleaming. He looked like he
smelled good. *Guess this is how the big boys play it,* Vance thought
to himself. His former star smiled at Grecos then started.

"I was first kidnapped from jail in Mexico, then drugged and
brainwashed."

The producer cut back to Grecos.

"Our network sports physician actually found a small psy-
chotropic drug patch implanted on Mr. Berber, presumably by
whoever wanted him to be the host of the program. At his request
we removed it. As you were saying Mr. Berber, who kidnapped
you?"

"A man called Jack Vance and his team. He runs a company
Blowfish in Chicago, where they brought me." Upon hearing the
name Mrs. Bigelow cut Berber off.

"They got a skinny black guy over dere Vlad?" Berber turned to
her.

"He had woman, and a Mr. Welles at events."

"Dats gotta be him! Damn I knew he wasn't from no fatty organization!"

Grecos was eating this up. He saw a Pulitzer getting closer with
every word that came out of their mouths. He leaned in, wanting
more of the salacious details he knew these guests were about to

give up from their pre-show briefing. It was all going according to script, the surprises and the revelations. Grecos already knew what was going to happen next.

"So what happened to you, Mr. Bigelow? How did you become the contestant that died on *Some Will Die?*"

Bigelow pulled the oxygen mask off his face and attempted to speak but didn't have the strength. His mother patted him on the arm and spoke for him.

"Benny, he was recruited by this skinny black fella, like I said. He had a different face when I saw him, one of them projectors I think. Clever. Said he was from the HOP organization. Knew right off the bat they wasn't gonna send out a skinny black guy into Kansas to meet wit folks like us, I mean, come on, right?" Berber laughed.

"They very clever those peoples." Berber said.

Mrs. Bigelow touched Berber's arm.

"But this man...this man he saved us both. Oh God. Me and Benny." She started crying. Grecos goosed the conversation along. He wasn't much for dramatic pauses.

"So then what? How did Ben come to be on the program?"

"I presumes that Jack Vance fellow tol his skinny black man to offer us money."

"Before the show, to *compete* for money? They offered you money in advance?" Grecos asked.

"Not really compete, no sir. To *die* on their show, Mister. They found us and knew that Benny couldn't take much activity. If he did he would die. So they done paid him to die at a certain time. Ain't no way that was for anytin' but ratings. We needed the money, Mister, and he did die and then he came back to life...and they never paid us the rest! Welchers!"

"So you would say this would be like an assisted suicide, for the sake of generating interest, Mrs. Bigelow?"

"Don't know no law, Mr. Grecos. They jus wanted him dead. You think that ain't legal in Kansas?"

"That's up to the authorities, Mrs. Bigelow, and as this is the first public disclosure of these facts, I'm sure they're watching. Would you be willing to speak with the authorities, Mrs. Bigelow or you Vlad, concerning the kidnapping and the drugging?"

"Any coppers wanna come down n' talk about this deal and what's their names...them Blowfish guys, me an Ben are ready. Maybe sue em for not paying out."

Vance was unaware of the drool running down the side of his face until a burner phone rang, jarring him out of a nightmarish trance. His hand shook as he picked it up.

"Yeah?"

"Vance, it's Gould. You got problems boy. I just got a call from my buddy at the Chicago Avenue cop shop. The State of Illinois is issuing a warrant for your arrest. They're probably on their way now. You home?"

"For what?"

"Try kidnapping, brainwashing, and that thing about paying for Fatso to die? *What the fuck, Jack!* Thank God you didn't do that here. My advice? If you got any hard evidence on any of this stuff, get rid of it. You been watching the Queen show?"

"Hang on!" Vance put the phone down and swiped the channels to the Harry Queen program. Queen, every 87 years of him, was conducting a video conversation with the same security guard that Agness had spoken with in the Florida car rental lot earlier in January. The text under the man's image read: *Chris Zales, CEO, BlackNight Security.* Congressman Potlatch sat next to Queen watching the monitor with his host. Vance turned up the volume as Queen peppered Zales with questions.

"So you're saying that this Mr. Vance ordered you not only to beat up members of Mr. Potlatch's party, but to kill them?" Zales fidgeted in his chair.

"We're in the business of keeping the peace, Mr. Queen. Protecting folks. This Mr. Vance, he asked us to get some of them fat people killed."

"And Congressman Potlatch, you've secured some evidence to this effect, correct?"

"Indeed I have, Mr. Queen. Using my sources and working with Mr. Zales we have actually gotten a hold of physical evidence putting Mr. Vance at the scene of the meeting where he intended to hire hit people."

"And you'll testify to this, Mr. Zales?"

"Damn right I will, Mr. Queen. BlackNight is in the protection business, that's all we do. We're willing to work with Mr. Potlatch and the police on anything they want. And my apologies Congressman, we was just followin' orders."

"Well, let's see what you have, Congressman."

Another of Vance's burner phones rang. He pulled it out while he watched a video of himself in a Florida parking lot, apparently talking to Mr. Zales, whom he encountered by a black Hummer. It looked like a standard parking lot pole camera mounted video. *This was utterly impossible!* He answered the phone.

"Vance."

"Mr. Vance? This is attorney Spring, down in Georgia. Listen, the Georgia State Patrol's probably issuing a warrant for your arrest for hiring them goons to beat up the HOP party at yer little shindig. Now my sources tell me that our boys is fightin with the Florida boys and the Kansas boys over who gets you first."

Vance could barely speak. Gould was still on hold on his desk, but he couldn't pull himself away from the call with Spring.

"Seems that this whole thing with Bigelow violates the Assisted Suicide law. Now, it originated in Kansas, so they want a piece, but it was transacted in Georgia, so my guys think it's theirs. Now the Florida thing, that's a whole separate issue. See, placing a contract for murder, well, that's a bad news felony any way you slice it.

With all your travelling around it's probably Federal and they always want first dibs. I think everyone's gonna want to speak with you. Vance? You there?"

Vance put the phone down and looked around his room. No one had to speak, the sweat running through their clothes told the whole story. Mayhew's phone rang, intruding on the silence. He answered it with a shaky voice.

"Yes, yes we were watching. Yes, same Blowfish. Oh. I see. Should I call you tomorrow? Oh. Okay. You have my number." He placed it down.

"That was UPS. They want to think about engaging us now. No retainer tonight." Messages started filling the cloud with short fast texts that read "hold," and "cancel" and "thinking about it." The sales drive was collapsing. Vance swiped the transmissions off. If it was going to get any worse, he didn't want to hear about it. He activated the speakers on both phones while shouting.

"Everybody go home. Get out of here before the police pull you out! NOW!" His staff moved immediately, Jimmy Welles turning for a second before hitting the door.

"Jack... I..."

"Get out of here. Gould will back you up. It's all on me, Jimmy. Remember that."

Within thirty seconds Vance was alone in his War Room.

"Gould, Spring?" Vance spoke to both the phones that he had left on speaker mode.

"You on an open line Jack? I think attorney Spring would agree with me that..."

The lines went dead. The cloud above him went black. Was he being jammed by the police? He slid open a recessed white panel on his desk and placed his face in front of a lens for a retinal scan. This was the control panel for the physical SSD drives hidden in his office walls. He felt it was safer to have his files here, not on some server on some ranch somewhere. It would take two minutes to initiate the process that would erase the drives and eliminate the evidence of the plotting and planning surrounding Berber and Bigelow. Maybe he could reduce the situation to their word against his. Of course there was Welles and the strange video and who knows what else might come slithering out of the information swamp to hang him. His server contained credit card receipts, booked flights, calls, campaign notes, and incriminating plans. He hadn't anticipated having to cover all his tracks on this project. He was supposed to be rich and retired now, a spiked drink in hand and Naomi Stiles rubbing herself all over his chest.

Vance heard the distinctive swoosh of the War Room's door and looked up to see Missy Slats standing between two dapper men wearing dark overcoats and hats.

"Mr. Ferriola and company are here, Mr. Vance!" The two men entered the room, leaving Slats in the corridor behind them. Vance could see the back of her large white calves peeping out through her skirt with every brisk step that carried her towards the exit.

"You left the door open!" Vance yelled. But she was gone and the office was now empty save for three men who had a little business to conduct.

CHAPTER FORTY EIGHT
Payday

Hancock Building, Blowfish Offices: Chicago, IL
Monday, February 5, 2018 8:47 PM CST

Sal Farriola, 69 years old with a strong posture that could have belonged to a UFC fighter in an earlier part of his life, unbuttoned his heavy wool overcoat, removed his hat and sat down in a chair at the War Room table across from Vance. His companion, a six foot tall Motorola Brick Phone of a man stood behind him. His face was hidden by his fedora and his bulk by a brown leather trench coat. Farriola pulled out a small black box with three antennas pro-truding from its top deck and placed it on the table in front of him.

"Sure a guy like you has seen one of these before, right? Jammer. Cuts off radios, cell phones, even cameras. Lovely thing. No one has us coming into this place, or leaving. Let's talk money. You said you'd have it tonight. Tonight is now." Vance stabbed numbers into the hard drive access panel while they continued to word salad the room.

"Those things are illegal, Sal. Got your phone on? Tonight's not over. I said we got money coming in. *Blowfish is hot now.*"

"After those TV shows? Only thing hot in this room is you Jack. You're practically public enemy number one. So we don't have much time. I need the twelve million."

"Our receivables aren't in yet. Give me a couple of days."

"You'll be in jail in a couple of days Jack."

"Then take the fucking agency. It's my collateral anyway."

"This? I don't even know what this is all about Jack. Show me trucking, show me construction and I'll take home some trucks and machines. What you got here? Words? *Computers worth 25 cents on the dollar if I'm lucky?* Your reputation? Who am I gonna sell this place to? Feds'll take all this before the week's out any-way. You either have a buyer now or yer outta collateral."

Vance's access code wasn't working. He stabbed at it again, leaning forward in his chair.

"Know anything about actuarial tables, Jack?" While Farriola talked his companion moved into the light emanating from the War Room's shiny white surface. He pulled a velvet bag out of his pocket and slipped it off revealing a five pound ball peen hammer with a glistening gold head.

"Insurance companies pay out for body parts. Arm's worth, say, 30 grand. Leg, maybe 40. Depends on the circumstances. Surgeon's hand could go for a couple of million. You make your money with your head, with your mouth. Whatta think they're worth? Say four million, and I'm being generous."

Vance stood, fuck the servers.

"The cops are on their way now, Sal. I wouldn't try anything. You'll get your cash, just settle down."

"Chicago cops? They're going to your house first, Jack. People aren't usually at their offices this time of night. Protocol. You ain't there, then they looks for you here. You ain't here then they sends out an APD. We got a little time to finish our business."

"Which is?"

"You're distraught over the collapse of your empire, as it is. So you leapt off the roof. Course we get to extract a little payback out of your head and jaw first. No one will know, there won't be enough pieces left of you to tell. Let's go."

Vance whipped his Glock out from his waistband and leveled it at Farriola.

"I'm going, but alone." He grabbed his jacket with his left hand and started moving towards the door. Farriola sniggering and nodded at his associate.

"For that break his hands first." The large man moved around the table towards his prey. Vance looked from Farriola to the thug.

"I don't want to shoot him."

Farriola started laughing.

"That's a safe gun with an electronic trigger, Jack. Needs a radio connection to fire. That's so's the cops know where you are every time it goes bang. Only you can't shoot." He picked up his jammer and continued. "No signals here remember?" Maybe go old school next time, like a 1911, like the pros carry.

The monologue was interrupted by the fast sound of two pops, like a baby farting underwater. Farriola's thug dropped his hammer and grabbed at his arm.

"That toy's not working on my gun pal." Stanley Best entered the room, a suppressed Beretta 92S in his hand. He walked over to Farriola and slapped him savagely across the face with his heavy black firearm, then baby farted the other man again in the leg. He punched Farriola in the stomach, knocking him to the floor.

"Sorry I'm late. Help me with these assholes." Vance stood still, his Glock hanging in space.

"Stan... I..."

"Pull it together Jack, check this guy. We got no time." Vance walked over to the bleeding hood, now collapsed to one knee and in considerable pain.

"Check him!" Vance didn't know what to do. Best placed his Beretta against Farriola's right palm and squeezed a shot then moved over and did the same to the thug.

"Why the palms?" Vance asked.

304 · Steve Lundin

"So they don't shoot us Jack. Most guys don't do well lefty. You better get outta here. I been listening to cop radio, you got cops from four states arguing about who gets you first. There are so many charges against you you'll spend a month going from cell to cell before they can even agree on bail. You're a couple of hours from a national manhunt. Fed's will take you first, bastards always get the good stuff."

Vance walked to the back of the room and tried accessing the servers again.

"How long?"

"I dunno, just go underground. Get rid of that car, get rid of those phones and get that damn chip out of your head. Leave the country."

"The head phone's not registered. Where's Giletti?"

"Covering your ass in Atlanta or at least trying to. Just get lost Jack. Get lost."

Vance couldn't get into the server. Something was fucked. Best saw what he was working on.

"Do that remotely." He grabbed Vance and shook him.

"Listen to me. You have a ten minute window here, in this office, then maybe an hour or two on the road. Leave town, get out of the country. Let your lawyers figure it out, if they can."

"What about... these guys?"

"I'll take care of them. I deal with bad guys remember? Their friends will be after you too. They're maybe worse than the cops."

Farriola, crumpled on the ground, spat at Vance.

"We are worse than the cops you fuck."

Best kicked Farriola in the face then yanked his thick overcoat up over his head. He placed the silenced pistol against the man's head and squeezed the trigger. Vance jumped back.

"What the fuck?"

"Gangland slaying. Only one cares is this guy's wife and she only wants about his money." Best looked over at the thug.

"On your feet. You're helping me. Get lost Jack, it's been a hoot." Best held out his hand. "Give me the Glock." Vance handed him the pistol. Best pulled a Walther PPS out of his waistband and handed it to Vance.

".40 cal. Fleming would have given this to James Bond if it was around then. No radio wave bullshit. Gimmee your Smart Phone and some tape."

"Tape?"

"Cord?"

Vance handed his flexible Smart Phone to Best then rummaged through his personal drawer in the War Room table. He pulled out a pair of nylons. Best cut the CPU out of the Smart Phone, wrapped it around the thug's mouth and knotted the nylon around his face.

"He gonna need his wallet?"

"Not for 48 hours."

"He's gonna live?"

"Someone's gotta take back a message."

"What message?"

"Don't fuck with the marketing budget."

Vance pulled the thick wallet out of the thug's coat and removed it. He opened the compartment in his chair arm, extracted a vial, selected two pills, crushed them with his gun butt on the table, swept them into his hand, threw them down his mouth then took a long pull from his flask. He closed his eyes for a second and felt the rush of Adderall and high octane spiked vodka shake the slink out of his body. He refilled his flask with the last of a bottle of Belvedere, threw on his jacket and headed for the door. Best and the sweating, crying, bleeding thug were mopping up the room around the recently deceased Farriola.

"What about this?"

"Hancock's got an incinerator, remember?"

"Do I need to worry about these guys as well?"

"You'll be long gone by the time they invest $500,000 in a hit man to dig you up. That's about a day or so...right?"

"500? That's it?"

"They're already down 12 mil, Jack. How much you spend on collections?"

"What's Farriola worth to them?"

"You just saved them another pension to pay. Does it look like he earned a paycheck tonight? He's a has been, look who he's loansharking to. No offense, but this guy's well past his day."

Vance took the thug's hat on the way out the door and tipped it at Best.

"Why you doing this for me, Stan?"

"Who says I did it for you? Maybe I just miss blasting bad guys."

CHAPTER FORTY NINE
Squirrel in a Monkey House

Hancock Building: Chicago, IL
Monday, February 5, 2018 9:40 PM CST

Vance took the garbage room exit at street level and crept along the East side of the Hancock Building. With his Smart Phone gone he was officially Off The Grid which was already a red flag on an alert screen. Three black Dodge cruisers pulled up in front of the 175 East Delaware entrance as he moved from the alley to the sidewalk. Vance walked straight past them, hat pulled down, as a half dozen Chicago cops and State Troopers hustled into the lobby. He walked quickly to the Drake, flagged his valet and was behind the wheel of his Bentley within 45 seconds. He headed west, mind racing for the next move. He needed counsel and time to think.

He drove the car to the 800 block of Rush Street and parked it in front of the Gold Coast

Bentley dealership. This was the only place in the city where a car like his wouldn't attract any suspicion. With the jammers activated in his car he was unable to send or receive calls. He exited the vehicle, pulled one of the burner phones out of his pocket and called Stu Gould.

"The cops came."

"You got out."

"Any idea where I stand?"

"You got multiple state warrants online now. I think the FBI will be involved by the morning. Maybe sooner"

"Jesus. So I'm federal."

"And a fugitive."

"Just give it to me."

"Well, conspiracy to commit murder is probably 25 years, intercontinental kidnapping, brainwashing, violation of the Assisted Suicide law, conspiracy to incite a riot, assault, and here's a new one: conspiracy to incite hatred through programming. The list goes on."

"Where did that last one come from?"

"Potlatch. Listen to the news. He's pressuring the FCC. You think the administration is happy that the show was so popular? What does that say about the U.S. to the rest of the world? They need a scapegoat Jack, a twisted Svengali. Remember Aaron Swartz? You're the guy they can hang it on."

"And Brill?"

"Middle aged family guy manipulated by crazy, drunk, marketing man who was kicked out of New York by the mayor. You write headlines Jack, this one writes itself. He's got plenty of money to go OJ. He'll walk with a hand slap and stay rich. You fucked yourself on this one."

"That murder thing. I didn't hire anybody to kill anybody."

"You want to tell that to the cops? That's just one charge Jack, you got another fistful to deal with after that."

"About 50 grand left in your retainer slush fund, right?

"Yeah."

"Take care of the staff."

"And Jack Vance?"

"Just look something up for me?"

"Sure. Might be the last thing I can do."

"Find me a vehicle storage facility with late hours, near Midway."

"I'll send it to your phone pal. Good times, huh?"

"What Stu?"

"We had some kicks on this one."

"Not sure the fun was worth the hangover."

"Stay safe pal, maybe we'll be laughing about all this someday."

"Sure Pollyanna, when you're licensed to practice in Mexico." Vance hung up and attempted to access his server again via the burner phone. He was still unable to get past the login screen. He shut it down, yanked out its battery and its sim card and stomped on it. If Gould's phone records were seized the burner's number could be pinged and its location discovered. Each phone was a one call proposition at this point. He took stock of his vital gear: three burner phones, a satellite phone, a little over $21,000 in cash, a hoodlum's identity and credit cards, enough booze and pills for 36 hours, a .40 Walther PPS and the bare bones of an escape plan.

It took about 30 minutes for Vance to make it to the Cube Stor‑ age Facility on Cicero Avenue. They closed at 11:00. He could count on whoever was running the show to want to get a last minute customer out the door as soon as possible. Vance parked his Bentley down the street and entered the building, his fedora pulled down to conceal his face from the security cameras. The counter was empty. He tapped a bell and a young black man with neon tattoos running up and down his arms emerged from a wall door, a commercial tablet in his hand. He was very clearly closing the facility.

"Like to rent an indoor car space."

"Our rate sheet's there." The man went back to his tablet. It was obvious that his mind wasn't on a transaction happening this evening. Vance had no time for playing kick the tire games. He pulled the thug's wallet from his jacket and extracted an Amex card and a driver's license. The man's name was Anthony Scaglianni. Vance looked at the sheet.

"The 15 X 25 inside unit. I'll take it."

"Now?"

"Yeah. How late is access?"

"Close at 11:00."

"Then we better get moving." Vance leaned in as the kid started grudgingly going through the system to enter a new customer.

"Got things to do tonight, huh?"

"Yea, and this takes about a half hour."

"You still got paper forms here?"

"Yeah."

"I gotta get home to the wife. What say I just fill out the paperwork and you can enter it all tomorrow? I'm just gonna throw some boxes in storage tonight anyway." Vance pulled out two hundred dollar bills and slid them across the counter. "For your trouble. You get a commission right? I'll pay the first two years in advance."

Suddenly he was the facility's favorite new customer and filling out his own forms. He used a derivation of Scaglianni's name that looked close enough at a fast glance when it came time to flash the ID.

Vance walked out of the facility at 10:50 PM with a new access card and key to an indoor car storage space in his pocket. He drove the Bentley through the gates and parked it in its temporary home, where it would live peacefully for at least the next two years. He flipped a switch deactivating the battery and the car's transponder, grabbed the title and registration and pulled his case out of the trunk. He unsnapped the license plate and closed the gate on his car. Vance couldn't afford to leave the car where it would be found, its built-in black box contained a compete record of every conversation, text, data transmission and every place the vehicle had traveled since he purchased it. That left him with two options: destroy it or hide it. It would be like asking an old lady to throw her pet cat in front is a freight train. No, the beloved Bentley would live.

In three minutes Vance was in a cab heading towards Midway airport. He found what he was looking for and had the driver pull over, exiting the vehicle down the street from the shabbiest looking car rental agency on the block. He looked over their fleet. Most of the cars were a good decade old, and didn't contain any tracking technology. A place with an assortment like this wouldn't invest in anything fancy like that anyway. Their clientele just put down big deposits and found themselves gouged with damage charges when they returned the vehicles. It was time to get out of the city.

He entered the lot's tiny office and woke a skinny, shabby middle aged man who could have been the desk attendant at any $29 a night trucker motel off the Interstate.

"Help you?"

"Need a car, nothing fancy."

"How long?"

"Three days."

The man tapped an old, unresponsive tablet on the counter several times before giving up.

"How about we go outside and just take a look?"

"That works."

30 minutes later Vance was nosing back into expressway traffic in a 2007 Acura with 130,000 miles on the clock. It was rented for three days to Anthony Scaglianni, who had declined the fuel option. Vance didn't like using the card to complete the transaction, but knew that as long as Best kept its owner on ice he was fine. That gave him 36 hours to skate on Scaglianni's identity and make his play, provided the man wasn't being tracked himself. It was nearly 11:00. Vance had to move fast, anyone that could enable him to leave the country was already closing shop.

He headed North on Cicero Avenue, past Midway Airport, towards I-55. He found a trucker gas station a couple of blocks off the Expressway, parked around the side and headed in through the truck driver's entrance. Past the game room, showers and TV room he found an Internet lounge. He pulled out Scaglianni's wallet and extracted the items that would be of use to him: an Illinois driver's license, a platinum Amex card, a couple of Master Cards and a Detective's License. Figures a thug would have one. He swiped one of the Master Cards into the pay bar affixed to the side of the old Dell computer monitor and was online.

He waited impatiently while downloading a Tor browser so that he could be online anonymously. When it was installed he checked the BBC for the current headlines, looking for his name. He found the UK coverage of American events far less varnished than anything originating in the U.S. The top story was devoted to Potlatch and his just-announced 100 million pound march on Washington to protest hate programming. Below that he found a piece on concerns over the fugitive marketing Svengali Jack Vance. *Concerns?* He was practically Public Enemy Number One and the best the fucking Limey twats could come up with was *concerns?* He wasn't going to miss the news business for a single second. He checked the CNN site where his face was now the lead story under the caption: *Rogue marketing mayhem and murder maker missing.* That was, unfortunately, more like it. He had to be underground by daybreak before this overnight story was read by the waking public.

Vance dumped the site and conducted a search for charter operations at local airports. Within 60 seconds he found several candidates that looked promising. His closest bet was DuPage, about an hour away. He could make it there by 12:15 or so. He pulled one of his last two burners out and called the SkyMasters Jet Charter. A service answered and gave him an after-hours emergency number.

"Skymasters."

"This is Detective Anthony Scaglianni, to whom am I speaking?"

"Vince Puglisi. Captain Vince Puglisi. You need a charter, Detective?"

"Yes."

"Call the same number in the morning. This is the emergency number."

"I need a flight tonight, Captain."

"Okay. Emergency flight, we charge 30% more."

"I can do that."

"Where you going?"

"Midland International."

"Get you a rate." Pause. "Looking at about 2400 miles round trip. Get you from DPA to MAF in a Citation Eagle in around three hours. Runs $1500 an hour, so call it $9000 with a $3000 surcharge. That's $12,000."

"Okay."

"I'll need $3000 now to hold it and we'll start filing the flight plan."

"Here's an Amex card, see you in an hour."

Vance found a car rental service in Midland and reserved an SUV online. He'd arrive in Texas at 4:00 AM, pick up the car and head towards Big Bend National Park. He'd blend in with the 8:00 in the morning tourists and make his way for the border to Mexico, on foot. His father had told him about the unguarded crossings on the banks of the Rio Grande, mentioning that it was one of the only ways to get out of the country without a passport. He'd need to gear up in Texas, find some 24 hour WalMart, and plan on getting dirty and wet. He had a small window, but could make it if he was on the road in the Lone Star state before daybreak.

Vance attempted to get into his servers again and again found himself locked out. He pulled the SIM out of the burner he had just used then bent the phone in half. As he exited the facility he tossed Scaglianni's wallet and the phone into a stinky trash can and headed to his car, placing the man's ID's and cards into his own Dunhill. He couldn't risk the wallet containing a hidden embedded theft chip. He then headed west on 55 toward DuPage Airport in the rental. If Scaglianni was paying his bills on time he'd be able to put the entire trip onto the man's Amex card. If not, his third world cash stash was going to be severely depleted.

Vance had just taken the 355 ramp by Bolingbook, IL when his ear chirped. *Shit*, he should have picked up Farriola's jammer. This bug in his head made him vulnerable, as did the sat phone in his bag. He tugged at his ear lobe.

"Yeah."

"Stan."

"Is this *important Stan?!* We might have a party line soon."

"Your office is cordoned off. The feds'll have a search warrant by morning. Whatever you got on your servers better be gone."

"I'm working on it."

"They're also gearing up for an APD, probably have your photo to all border crossings by tomorrow afternoon. If you're using that mug's ID it ain't gonna pass the smell test real soon."

"How about Park Rangers?"

"If they work for the government they get the picture. I been sweating our friend here, says that they got guys all over the jail and with the cops. If their hit man don't get you they don't care, you wouldn't last a night in jail anyway. Saves them money that way, no travel expenses."

"This is where we say goodbye, Stan."

"Oh one more thing."

"What?"

"You're famous."

"Don't remind me."

"I think you're gonna make *America's Most Wanted*. They're doing a special edition tomorrow night, all about you. Audience share's supposed to be huge."

"Looks like I saved everyone's career but my own."

CHAPTER FIFTY
Channeling Corrigan

DuPage Airport: Aurora, IL
Tuesday, February 6 2018 12:30 AM CST

Vance pulled in to the DuPage airport and found the SkyMaster's Jet Charter sign on a one story FBO building. He parked and looked through his case, pulling out all the connected technology including his sat phone and HUD glasses. It all had to be rendered inoperable. He yanked out their batteries and sims, placed them on the ground by the car and pissed all over them. Liquids were still the best way to destroy electronics. He left the scene with two unregistered pre-ban burner phones, his nearly travel bag and the Walther in his jacket pocket. He was almost an analogue man. He buzzed the front door, was let into the corporate suite, and followed the signs to the only lit office in the place. He knocked, entered and was greeted by a short, stocky, late 50's man wearing a white Captain's shirt and black tie. The man didn't look up.

"Plane's gassed. Any luggage?"

"Captain Puglisi?"

"Yeah. How do you want to pay for this? Your balance is $9000."

"Put it on the Amex."

Puglisi tapped on the keyboard embedded in his office desk then looked up at Vance.

"Declined."

"Try six and put the balance on this MC." Vance pulled Scaglianni's Master Card out of his wallet and slid the large, old style card to Puglisi, then flashed the man's driver's license and Detective card.

"That went. Don't see many of those big cards anymore. Grab your bag, we're in back."

Vance looked over his shoulder as he entered the small turbojet. This was it. By tomorrow night he'd be in Mexico and hoofing his way to a new life in God knew ultimately where. No more private jets, cushy beds, 70's tough guy movies, national TV shows, client expensed binges, bespoke suits, pocketful of burner phones, media manipulation or meetings at the Four Seasons. He was too tired and beat down to reflect on everything that happened in the past twelve hours, who might be responsible for his current situation and what he could reasonably do besides run. Maybe in six months or a year of laying low and eating grubs and forging peyote buttons he'd come up with a plan B. At this moment, all he wanted to do was stay out of jail and out of the gun sights of the crime families.

The rented Cessna Citation thundered off the runway and into the dead calm night.

'Per FAA regulations your cell phone must remain on at all times during the flight." Puglisi announced. The NSA didn't want anyone going OTG, even when they were airborne.

Vance leaned back in his nicely padded leather chair and closed his eyes. Bits and pieces of his night with Naomi came back. Her legs in the air, the smell of her neck, the salty, yeasty taste of the bottom of her foot. Then his cochlear device rang. *Not again!* Without the HUD on his Smart Glasses or the screen of a Smart Phone he had no idea who was calling. It could only be Best, Gould, Naomi, Welles or Peggy Bump. All of whom he trusted. He tugged his ear lobe.

"Well, Jack fucking Vance! Hell-fucking-lo!"

Vance sat up in his seat. How was he hearing this voice in his head?

"Agness?"

"You're probably wondering how I have this number."

"No. I'm wondering why you're using it."

"You gave it to me, back when we was partners. Drinking partners. Said it was for emergencies."

"If you need a job reference send your request to MissySlats@blowfishPR.com."

"We both know the Blowfish staff is offline by now. Last I heard the federales had the place on lockdown. You in jail Jack? Nah, not you, you're not one to go down with the ship. According to CNN you're on the lam. Can't wait to see what they say about you on America's Most Wanted. You're a famous guy Jack."

"What do you want Agness?"

"I want you and I want Blowfish."

"You can have it. The key's under the front mat."

"Oh I know where the keys are Jack. *Tried to get into the servers lately?* I'm going through them right now. What a treasure trove. Can't imagine why you didn't erase all this. But oh, wait! You couldn't get in could you? I left a back door Jack and I locked you out."

"Where we going here Agness?"

"Simple Jack, you give me the title to everything you own including Blowfish and I'll erase these servers and keep your staff out of jail. The feds will impound everything anyway. It all needs a new home where it can be safe and sound."

"And how am I supposed to do all this?"

"Sign papers. Easy. Just come to me."

"Where?"

"Louisville."

"Give me a couple of hours."

"I don't think so. *I'll give you until right now!* Sound familiar? If the answer's not what I want I'll send the feds a little present, the number to that neat little cochlear phone in your head. Ought to make pinging and finding you pretty damn easy, dontacha think? You're lucky I'm not asking you to hand over that little piece you been keeping to yourself all these years."

"I always knew you had a thing for Mayhew, Agness."

"Naomi, dickface. Everyone knows you've been poking her. Why else would you shower her with perks while the rest of us got gift cards?"

"She did something you never did Agness."

"What's that Jack?"

"Her job."

"I'll take this as a yes Jack. Am I right?

"Yeah. It's a yes."

"I'm taking everything Jack. Condo, car, bank accounts, fuck, I even want all your suits. And those watches. And that art. You got a lot of stuff, Jack."

"Where we meeting, Agness?"

"Galt House, in Louisville. Give you five hours to make it here. Room 714. See you soon Jack. Remember, that phone is your ticket to jail. I'll be waiting. One more thing, Jack."

"What?"

"Keep your phones on, *Bitch.*"

Vance's mind was racing. This explained things. Agness was no little opportunist showing up out of the blue. He knew too much. He was tracking, monitoring, waiting for the moment to leverage the situation. This wasn't some random extortion but the payoff moment for a...campaign. Vance slid another Adderall under his tongue and let it dissolve, washing it down with a sip of Belvedere from his flask.

His plans were suddenly changed. There was no way he could make Mexico through his intended route now. This also narrowed the window on his assumed identity. Best was good, but who knows what might happen. If Scaglianni somehow got away he'd have cops and hoods all over him. His own organization would report him missing if they felt it would lead to Vance. The hood was already used goods, another employee who didn't do the job. He unbuckled and moved towards the cockpit.

"Permission to take the co-pilot seat, Captain?"

Puglisi nodded and Vance slid in beside him. He looked over the advanced glass display and up to the deck. There was a bobbing hula girl, of course. Can't these pilots ever come up with something original to "personalize" their workspaces? It was like Harley drivers who managed to delude themselves that they were individuals when they went so far out of their way to look the same.

"You own a Harley?"

"That why you came up here?"

"Just asking. We need to make a course change."

"Had a '72 Norton Commando since '03. Keeps my hands dirty."

"Love those rubber motor mounts. I had a Vincent for awhile."

"Black Shadow?"

"What else!"

"So where you want to course change to?"

"SDF."

"Fee'll change. You won't get your funds back for three or four days."

"S'fine."

"We'll be there in a little over an hour. Save you some money."

"Maybe not. We're not staying."

"What's our final destination, Mr. Scaglianni?" Puglisi turned from his instruments and gave Vance a sideways look.

"I'll tell you after Louisville."

"Mind my asking what you do, Mr. Scaglianni?

"I'm a Detective. You saw the permit."

"So you're on a case?"

"Missing person."

"Scaglianni...Scaglianni...your family's from Sicily too."

"Uh...of course. With a name like Scaglianni, where else?"

"Forse siamo parenti, ha ha."

"Si, La dolce vita."

"Guess you're more of an Italian in name only."

"Brother, you don't know the half of it."

CHAPTER FIFTY ONE
Survival Supplies

Louisville International Airport SDF: Louisville, KY
Tuesday, February 6 2018 3:00 AM CST

Zip Cars were a new experience and a welcome find at the Louisville Airport. Vance couldn't rely on taxis for his plans and didn't want to go through the entire process of renting and returning a car. He needed to be back in the air before dawn. As he steered into the blinking lights of the city he called up a list of 24 hour Walmarts on the car's nav system. This would be a night of firsts.

He found the Walmart Supercenter in Louisville's Outer Loop delightfully busy in the middle of the night. This would provide good cover in a store that expected a high rate of theft and monitored every square inch of floor space. He kept his hat down and his collar up, grabbed a cart, bent slightly and affected a limp. Vance selected a coyote brown Carhartt trucker's jacket, a green Caterpillar cap, a small nylon travel bag, a medium sized rolling bag and a pair of thick, horn rimmed reading glasses with the mildest correction he could find. He meandered down the electronics aisle and found an old style microcassette recorder and grabbed a roll of duct tape then took his place in line and paid in cash. He made a two sided color Xerox of his Bentley title. As he left the store he placed a three minute call on his second to last burner phone then destroyed it.

PT's Show Club was only one place drawing any activity in downtown Louisville. It was a strip joint located a few blocks down the street from the Galt House Hotel. If he left the area as planned he'd fit right in with the other late nighters trying to get home before their wives or girlfriends or dogs knew they were missing. He parked in the lot across from the Club, placed his new clothes and bag in his roller and walked to the Hotel.

He entered the Galt wearing his horn rims and his fedora brim snapped low, walked over to the small office/vending area off the main lobby floor and found a FedEx box. He filled out an air bill and slipped it into a FedEx envelope. He moved to an ATM, pulled out his wallet and took the maximum cash advances against two of his own credit cards. This gave him another $1000 in cash. If his cards were being tracked he just sent up a nice big flare. He stuffed the money in his jacket and walked to the front desk. His palms felt clammy. Vance looked around at the three people staffing the night desk and the two bellhops at the ready by the lobby's glass doors. He picked the youngest of the bunch, a man who was probably no more than a few months out of college.

"Can I help you, sir?"

"Room for the night."

"Very good, sir. How many beds?"

"Just one."

"Okay. I have something on five tonight. River view."

"Non smoking?"

"That's correct, sir. I can give you a rate of $290 for the night."

"That'll work."

"ID and credit card please Mr..."

"Vance. Jack Vance."

Vance didn't know if his hands were shaking or if the brim of the hat was keeping the sweat off his face. He felt like an underage kid using his father's card to check into a hotel with a prostitute. It could all end now.

"Heard that name before...Jack Vance."

Vance's heart stopped beating while the night clerk puzzled over the thought.

"*You're famous, Mister!*"

Vance looked around. He couldn't bolt now. Shit.

"Ever heard of the book *The Star King*?"

"Uh, no."

"Jack Vance. Science fiction writer. Died a few years back. Here, I'll google it for you."

"No please, I believe you. I'm in a hurry, late for a meeting."

"Sorry. Mr. Vance...like I said, *you're famous!*"

The clerk handed Vance his key.

"Listen, I need you to send up two bottles of your best Brut champagne to room 714 in about 30 minutes. I'll be there to sign for it. You can put it on my bill now."

Vance exited the lobby and took the elevator up to the sixth floor, leaving his rolling luggage in the stairwell. He took the stairs up to seven and entered the hallway. He moved carefully down the hall to room 714. Light leeched out from under the door. He bent down and heard talking. Maybe Agness was on the phone. He turned on the microcassette recorder and taped it to the lower part of the door, close to the frame. You'd have to be looking for it to see it and Vance was planning on being the center of attention at this party. It was 4:40 in the morning, which gave him an hour and twenty minute element of surprise. He knocked.

Chapter Fifty Two
Showdown

Galt House Hotel, Room 714: Louisville, KY
Tuesday, February 6 2018 4:40 AM CST

It took a full sixty seconds between the time Vance knocked and Tom Agness opened the door. Agness wasn't expecting his guest to arrive so quickly. The two men locked eyes and Agness smiled and extended his hand. Vance pushed past him and entered the room.

"Let's get this over with. I need those servers unlocked."

"You're a fast driver, Jack. Gonna miss that Bentley I'll bet."

"What do you have for me Agness?"

Vance looked around. He was in one of the Galt's multi-bedroom suites. It had probably been the site of hundreds of massive bourbon and fried food orgies during every Kentucky Derby since the 70's. The only illumination in the room came from a low hanging light situated over an eight person dining room table on which were arrayed three neat stacks of paper. Vance thumbed through the documents. Agness had done his homework. A light came on in the lounge section of the suite and another figure stood and walked slowly through the darkness towards the table. That explained the talking. The gait was unmistakable. Vance knew who it was well before the dated French Shriner loafers and floppy, pleated pants came into view.

"First things first. Take your clothes off Mr. Vance."

Drab! It all came together now. Agness had the wits but not the resources. He knew the moves, but needed a backer and a fellow hater. Agness found the one man who would enable his revenge. They probably leveraged Potlatch as well.

"Take off your clothes." Drab commanded again.

"What?"

"We're not taking a chance that you're wired or have any cameras or anything tricky." He picked a small device off the corner of the table.

"Jammer, in case that fancy little cochlear device Mr. Agness told me about is connected somewhere else. Our business is private. You signed the documents of your own free will, without coercion."

Vance looked over to the cluster of chairs where Drab had been sitting. He saw Agness' jacket lying over one of them and walked into the semi-darkened area, praying that his former employee was a creature of habit. Vance palmed his own Dunhill wallet as he took off his jacket and casually tossed it next to Agness's. The two men both stood watching him disrobe. He took off his shirt and laid it on the chair but he needed some privacy to make his moves.

"You mind?"

"We don't trust you," Agness said.

This wouldn't work. Vance stared at Agness but concentrated on his night with Naomi while he slowly slid his pants down. He began to get an erection and smiled at both men. Drab turned away first, then Agness.

"Jesus, Vance, you freak," Agness reacted. Vance counted on them both knee jerk turning away. In that moment he leaned over the chair feeling for Agness' wallet in the pocket of his jacket. He found it and switched Agness' wallet with his own identical Dunhill. He straightened and walked over to the table, naked. His erection had subsided. Vance left his watch on. Drab sniggered at the

man he had waited 15 years to see reduced to nothing, now standing in front of him.

"She still hates your guts Vance, just like many, many people
who are willing to do almost anything to see you fail." Drab said.

"Sorry Roger, I didn't really want any prematurely bald kids
anyway."

Agness walked to the table, realizing that Vance's history with
Drab was a little deeper than he knew.

"You worked together?" Agness said.

"Yeah. Where do you think I learned to hire assholes like you?
Let's wrap this up," Vance responded. He looked down at the stack
of papers on the table that covered everything that he could possibly give away. He picked up the pen that was laid out for him and
signed the first of several documents assigning his Corporation to
Drab and Associates.

"Okay. Open up those servers now Agness." Vance said.

"You're just getting started Jack," Agness answered back.

"I don't have time. Open the servers or we're done." Vance
looked at his watch.

"Go ahead Mr. Agness. We've got the number in his head anyway. We're men of honor Mr. Vance, we don't want to see your
poor innocent employees go down, matter of fact, we're going to
need them," Drab said.

Agness brought a thin convertible laptop tethered to an Ethernet
cable to the table and opened it. He typed for a moment then slid it
over to Vance. The servers were still online, which meant they
were still intact and still in the wall. He entered the codes and
started the reformatting process, then logged out and shut the case.

"Let's finish this."

Vance read the second document, the one that assigned all of
Blowfish's assets to Drab and Associates, including office equipment and all intellectual properties.

"Think of all that business you're leaving on the table. That's the really galling part of this whole mess, eh Vance. That and being a fugitive from justice." Drab chided.

Vance looked at him as he signed the documents. "What business, Roger? Blowfish is worthless."

"I don't think so. We've been conducting a targeted new business campaign for the past 36 hours. We sent out letters, took out ads aimed at getting Blowfish new clients. Where do you think the sudden influx of business came from this morning? Blowfish was set to reap the rewards of your labors, Jack. And it still will. We're going to feed the story of our takeover of Blowfish to Ad Age this morning and then we'll pick up all the pieces you left on the table. Blowfish will go on. We're just cutting out the cancer to save the patient. Can't let all that brand equity go to waste. It's just *good business*, Jack." Drab drummed his fingers, pleased that he could finally have his victor's moment.

Vance finished signing the second stack of papers and turned to the third.

"The Potlatch play was nice. I assume that was Tom's move. But he doesn't have the style to come up with the hit man concept, how'd you pull that off, Roger? It was...inspired." Vance said.

Drab puffed up as Vance had expected.

"Timing. You couldn't resist a new business call or a first class ticket or a Mercedes rental. Someone as important as you deserves the best, doesn't he? You walked into the lot as we were taking off." Drab smiled while he spoke.

Vance nodded while he signed away the title to his condo and all his possessions.

"Very *Bobby Fisher*, Roger. You haven't lost a step."

"Mr. Agness' natural gift and your vanity were all I needed. You're twin sons of different mothers. But you're right, hiring them was genius."

"Nothing for Tom here?" Vance nodded.

"Oh, he gets your office, Jack, and your condo as a bonus, if his first year's numbers hit what I think they will."

"Still settling for promises, Tom?" Vance stared at Agness. It was time to leave. He placed the pen down. Agness looked at Vance's wrist.

"The watch. My Christmas bonus."

"Fuck that."

"Give me the watch and we'll give you an hour before we call in your number to the cops."

Vance unbuckled his $30,000 watch and held it by its strap, ready to slam it against the edge of the table.

"Three hours, or you can bring the pieces to a jeweler."

"I got the time Jack. Ha ha, get it? *Sure.*"

"I can get dressed now right?" Vance walked over to his clothes and started to put them on then returned to the table with his jacket over his arm, than laid it over the small jammer on the table. He needed that device.

"Three hours, remember."

"The title Vance, Drab promised me the Bentley." Agness held out his hand.

Vance had to sell this. He slowly pulled the folded Xerox of the title out of his back pocket and flipped it on the table, then pocketed the jammer as he picked up his jacket. He then unfolded the title, signed it and tossed it on the pile. Vance put his jacket on and walked towards the door, then turned before exiting the room.

"She always was a lesbian Roger," Vance said, then left the room. When the door closed behind him he bent down and pulled off the small microcassette recorder. He couldn't thank those two bastards enough for the signal jammer, what a going away present! He moved quickly to the stairwell and bounded down to the sixth floor. He unzipped the rolling luggage bag he had stowed, removed the Carhartt jacket, Caterpillar hat, small black tote bag and FedEx pouch. He placed his Vanson jacket and the FedEx pouch in the tote, donned the new ensemble and walked briskly to the elevator.

When he hit the lobby Vance walked directly to one of the other night clerks, a middle aged woman thumbing through an early morning copy of the Louisville paper.

"Mr. Agness, room 714 checking out." He announced, loud enough for the other clerks to hear. She tapped away at her desk then looked up at him.

"We thank you for staying at the Galt, Mr. Agness. Do you want to leave the room on your card?"

"No, let's put it on another one." Vance pulled out Agness' custom Blowfish Dunhill wallet, slipped a Master Card chip out of a sleeve and slid it across.

"I'll need to see an ID with this."

Perfect. He flipped open the wallet and displayed Agness' Illinois license, signed the electronic hotel receipt and walked out the Lobby's front door. He felt for the jammer in his pocket and turned it off. He pulled his last burner phone out of his pocket and dialed *67, then 911 while walking towards his car.

"This is the Hotel Galt. We had a man check in here, a Mr. Vance, Jack Vance, that man the police have been talking about. He's in room 714. That's right, 714. Is he dangerous?" He slipped the SIM and battery out of the phone and deposited it in the first garbage can he passed, then turned the jammer back on.

Three squad cars with flashing lights blazed by him as he pulled his car out of the strip club lot. He took 20 seconds to place the microcassette recorder and Agness' ID into the FedEx pouch labeled for Stu Gould's office. He added a note stating that the voices on the cassette implicated Drab and Agness in a conspiracy to hire a hit man and frame him for it. He dropped the pouch in a FedEx box on the way to the airport.

Agness was just placing the room phone back in the cradle when he heard the sirens down below in the street and looked over at Drab, gloating over the stacks of signed papers.

"That was fast."

"You earned your keep, boy. I've been looking forward to this day for years."

Agness walked over to the table and picked up the folded Bentley title, realizing that in all the excitement he forgot to ask Vance for the key and the location of the car he presumed was parked by the hotel. Not a problem, he'd just have the dealership send him down a new one.

"What did he do to you, Roger?"

"He quit. Took three significant accounts and had the audacity to become successful."

"That's how everybody starts an agency."

"*And* he was engaged to my daughter, who he dumped right after he left."

"And?"

"And she became a lesbian. He turned my own daughter into a fucking lesbian and had the audacity to get successful with my business. That's what he did, Mr. Agness. Embarrassed me, personally and professionally. I don't want to discuss it." Drab picked up the Ulysse Nardin watch Vance had left. "And this is technically mine."

"No, it's mine."

"I gave my daughter the money to buy it for him as an engagement present. Now I'm taking it back. The engagement's been over for 15 years."

The paper in Agness' hands felt funny.

"This is a goddamned Xerox!" He exclaimed.

A knock on the door interrupted the banter. Agness opened it. Eight officers in SWAT uniforms entered the room with guns pointed at Drab and Agness. Someone yelled, "U.S. Marshall Service! Hands in the air!"

In seconds Agness and Drab were face down on the table, their hands zip tied behind their backs. They straightened and were confronted by lead Marshall William Vickers, wearing a black suit and a Kevlar vest with a shiny gold badge prominently pinned to his chest. He held an older, Toughbook Smart Phone up to Agness' face and compared Vance's image on its screen to the man he was arresting.

"I have a warrant for your arrest, Jack Vance."

Agness shook his head, "I'm Tom Agness. Vance was here. We called you, ask Mr. Drab."

"Shut up until we get lawyers idiot," Drab said.

"Got ID?" Vickers asked.

Agness nodded at his jacket and one of the SWAT team retrieved it from the chair and brought it over. He handed it to the man in charge.

"Here, Marshall."

Vickers riffled through the jacket pocket and produced the thin, black Dunhill wallet.

"This yours?"

Agness nodded. There was another knock on the semi-opened door.

"Room service."

"Stay there!" Vickers threw a response as a Galt Hotel porter stopped in the middle of the doorway with a rolling table. It bore two bottles of Dom Perignon champagne chilling in separate buckets. The porter looked around the room, not prepared to deal with eight armed men.

"Who ordered this?" Vickers asked, still holding the Dunhill wallet. The porter looked down at the slip in his hand.

"Mr. Jack Vance."

Vickers opened the wallet, looked down at it, then up at Agness again.

"This is your wallet, right?"

Agness nodded. Vickers slid the license out. "Then this is your license."

Agness nodded again.

"Then you're going to jail, Mr. Vance."

Agness rolled his eyes. "This is a mistake. I'm Tom Agness. *Tom Agness*, I just look like Vance!"

"Call down to the desk. This room is registered to Agness," Drab said, sweating. He needed this situation sorted out and didn't like all the suspicious looking documents laying out on the table. Anyone who could read would be able to tell that they had just done some business with a fugitive and that could mean aiding and abetting.

Vickers believed in evidence. What he was seeing added up to what he suspected, and it was almost too ludicrous to believe. A couple of dead to rights Yankee crooks attempting to talk their way out of a national manhunt! He'd humor them, making mental notes on the situation for his inevitable interview on Fox News. He was about to be famous. Vickers picked up the hotel room phone.

"This is Marshall Vickers in room 714. I'm looking for a Mr. Tom Agness. Anyone by that name registered in this hotel? I see." He placed the phone down. "Mr. Agness checked out earlier this morning, Mr. Drab. Let's go."

Drab squirmed as the he was shoved against Agness. "You can't take me!"

"This room's vacated. You're both here room illegally and you're both under arrest. Vance is a fugitive and you're aiding and abetting." Vickers yelled, fed up with the bullshit.

As the SWAT team began systematically picking up all the evidence in the room Agent Vickers read Drab and Agness their Miranda Rights.

"Vance is getting away. You can ping him. Agness has the number!" Drab shrieked.

"It's 212-68..." Agness started before Vickers cut him off. He didn't like anyone talking when he was reading Miranda. He'd seen perps get off because the arresting cop had forgotten to finish the citation after an interruption.

"What now?"

"Vance has a phone. You can track him." Drab spit desperately, feeling he could still straighten this out.

"Really? And why wouldn't he dump this trackable phone?"

"Because it's in his head...we were jamming it."

"In his head, huh? And what you jamming this high tech phone with?"

"With that...jammer." Drab and Agness looked down at the table where the jammer was supposed to be. Vickers rolled his arm in the air indicating that it was time to wrap up the scene and move the party elsewhere.

"Cellular signal jammer? Your device, Mr. Drab?"

Drab remained motionless.

"Possession of a cellular signal jammer is a felony misdemeanor in this state. Good thing you don't have one. And where are your phones? If they're off that's another charge."

One of the SWAT officers picked the Ulysse Nardin watch up off the table. He had two evidence bags, one for each of the perpetrators.

"Whose watch?" He held it up.

"Mine!" Drab and Agness spoke simultaneously. Vickers took the watch from the officer, looked at it, then flipped it over and read the inscription.

"*To JV with all my love: MD.* OK, I know who JV is, who's MD?"

Drab rolled his eyes. "My daughter. Marilyn."

Vickers shoved the watch in a zip locked evidence bag and twirled his hand over his head.

"This roundup's over. We'll sort it out at the station. You boys just earned me a promotion on national TV. I should be thanking you."

Agness looked over at Drab and whispered, "When we're out of this we'll send him a bill for the publicity services."

CHAPTER FIFTY THREE
Many Happy Returns

Air Space over the Florida Keys
Tuesday, February 6 2018 11:00 AM EST

Vance opened his eyes and recognized the white ceiling. He had been in this room before, but not from this angle. He looked down at his body. It was hidden under a coarse white sheet. His arms were pierced with multiple tubes trickling liquids. He heard a monitor behind him and tried to raise himself. A stinging pain ran through his stomach. He was in a hospital room. *What the fuck?* Had the plane crashed? Was he caught and shot? Two figures walked from dark edge of the room into the bluish fluorescent light shining over his bed. *Must be the cops.* He focused...

"Dad!" Vance said, with as much strength as his weakened self could muster.

Benjamin Vance, looking robust and healthy for a dead man, stopped at the foot of the bed and smiled.

"Glad to see you pulled out of it, son."

He was joined by another familiar figure who sidled up to him and put her arm around his waist.

"Gunshots look better on your father, Jack," Naomi Stiles cooed.

"You were shot, Dad... not me... this is your bed."

"It's yours now, son. You put yourself in it. You fought for the wrong people."

"He fought for anybody with a budget," Stiles said.

"I wasn't around to teach you right from wrong. I guess it's all my fault, right?"

"And what were you? Some kind of spook, mercenary? Killer?" Vance asked.

"A mercenary, yes. But for the right people. For the people who needed protecting."

Stiles squeezed into Ben Vance. "Principles, Jack. He said *no* to the scumbags. He made a difference."

"I made a difference." Vance defended.

"You sold fancy soap, son. You were a *Marketing whore.* That's about it." Bloody bullet holes started to appear on Ben Vance's body. Stiles dabbed at them.

"People pay for principles," she said.

"Like taking you away from me? That's principled?" Vance strained up. This was too much.

"You bought me, Jack. Men like your father earn me."

A warm blast of Key West air woke Jack Vance. He blinked up at the hot white light streaming into the Cessna's small cabin. Captain Puglisi looked down at him, a rugged Smart Phone in his hand.

"This our final destination, Mr. Scaglianni? If so we need to settle up. I don't leave the continental United States without more paperwork and your passport and ID."

"No, we're here." Vance said, pulling himself up and creaking towards the cockpit door. He maxed out whatever was left on Scaglianni's MasterCard and exited the plane, checking that the jammer was still on. He had no phones to tell him the time and rummaged through his flight bag for his Blanpain 50 Fathoms. It read 10:00 CST, making it 11:00 AM Florida time. The flight had taken nearly four hours. Whatever was happening in Louisville would be unfucked as soon as they ran prints on Agness and started tracing flights into and out of SDF. Key West wasn't the biggest place in the world for a fugitive seeking shelter.

Vance left the terminal and flagged a cab for the one mile ride to the Hilton Grand Key Resort. In three minutes he was in the hotel lobby. He checked his watch again, walked to the rear of the building and found the poolside Gumbo Limbo Tiki Bar. There wasn't enough booze left in the world to bring his confidence back at this moment.

The place was turning a brisk business in Mai Tai's and Pina Coladas, keeping the thirty or so pastel-clad vacationers well lubricated. He squeezed his way between an elderly gay couple who were renewing their vows and raised his hand to order. He felt a tap on his shoulder. Vance turned to see a man he almost didn't recognize. The man's close cropped hair, proper straw fedora and breezy linen suit threw off his memory.

"Commandant Regus! Thank God you made it!" Vance hugged the former Mexican prison official. Regus returned the hug and whispered in Vance's ear.

"Shsss...it's Mr. Rodguiez."

"That name's like Smith up here for Mexicans, Carlos."

"Then it works. I'm blending in. You don't have time for a drink, Jack."

Vance followed Regus out of the bar and back through the lobby.

"The boat's down the road at the Coconut Mallory Marina." Regus said.

"How long?"

"Five minutes to the dock."

"To Mexico?"

"It's almost 400 miles to Cancun. Should be there by tomorrow afternoon if you don't have any problems." Regus signaled a cab.

"Like what?"

"Engines, chop. Problems Mr. Vance, boats can have problems."

"Can't believe you pulled this together, Carlos."

"We didn't land your jet in Kansas by accident, Jack. Ten years it took to set up my U.S. network and get out of Mexico. My man will meet you in Cancun, get you started, but from there you may be on your own."

A cab pulled up and Regus slid into it. As Vance was about to enter the vehicle its door was slammed shut by a thick man in a khaki suit who appeared from nowhere.

"We've got your trip covered, Jack," purred the last voice Vance expected to hear on this little island at this particular moment in his life.

"You?"

Chloe Battista stood in a dark business suit, apparently immune to the swampy heat of the Island, arms folded. She effusing a light exotic fragrance that wasn't sold in traditional retail stores.

"*You remembered!* Flattered, Jack. Been so long since you called. Busy with other women... or just busy?"

"I've gotta go, Chloe. Text me sometime."

She nodded at the man who had just closed the door on Vance's cab. He extracted a small silver device with a conical antenna out of his jacket and pressed a button on its side. Vance felt something getting hot in his pocket very quickly. He pulled Drab's jammer out and dropped it on the ground. It began smoking then fizzed. The air filled the distinctive smell of melted wires.

"We call it a *Jammer Whammer.* Cute, huh? Figured you had something tricky going on when we lost your signal in Louisville. Looks like you're all out in the open now. Won't get too far on...let me guess, a boat?" She bent down and waved at Regus in the cab. Regus was making the universal "*let's get the fuck out of here*" sign. They didn't have much time.

"Hell of a start for a second date, Chloe."

"Who said anything about a date, Jack? This is about business. *It's always been about business.*"

Regus exited the other side of the cab.

"You done? We need to go Jack."

Chloe Battista gave him a stern, but understanding look.

"He's got a lift Mr..."

"Rodriguez."

"Of course it is."

"Do you Jack? You Okay? Who is she?"Asked Regus.

Vance looked hard from the woman to her well dressed companion.

"Do I? What the hell are you doing here, Chloe? ...how did you find me?"

"We've got a plane full of answers, Jack. And you don't need a passport. Way I see it, with that chip in your head you don't have a lot of options. Death boat or plane...hmmm...you choose. I bet the Coast Guard gets you within twenty minutes, if the sharks don't."

Vance walked around the cab to Carlos Regus and shook his hand.

"If I'm not at the marina in 30 minutes take off."

"That's our window, Jack. Good luck."

Vance entered the vehicle, this time with Chloe and her companion, leaving Regus behind at the hotel's cab stand.

The cab pulled up to a waiting Embraer Phenon 300 at the Key West International Airport. Battista and her companion exited and started walking towards the mid-sized jet. Vance looked it over, catching some obscure military markings on the tail adjacent to the flag of Switzerland. Battista stepped inside the plane and Vance followed. No impromptu TSA on this flight. The cabin sported a lot of red and white, looking and smelling like someone's government toy. Chloe Battista sat down in one of the well-padded club seats. A large bottle of champagne and two glasses were arrayed on the table in front of her. Vance took the opposite chair as she filled the glasses and offered him one.

"A real toast?" He haltingly picked up his glass and allowed her to clink against his. Vance let the comfortable familiar bubbles tickle his upper lip for a second before taking a sip and placing his glass down.

"So where do you want to take me?"

Battista took a long pull off her glass and placed it down. The cabin sealed shut and the man in the Khaki suit took a seat in the far end of the cabin, placed his sunglasses over his eyes and reclined fully.

"Someplace safe."

"Switzerland?"

"Oh this? *It's borrowed.* Swiss ambassador likes me. Diplomatic badge comes in handy, no?"

"Battista's not very Swiss sounding."

She removed a file folder from her seat and slid it across to him. Vance opened it and looked at a new passport bearing his photo, journalist credentials and a travel visa. He held the visa up and scrutinized it.

"John Vince?"

"Easier for you to remember."

"And a visa for...Cuba?"

"No extradition to the U.S., should your identity become known." Vance placed the documents down as the pilot shut the cockpit door and prepared for takeoff.

"And why would Cuba welcome me?"

"Because, Mr. Vance, you're a guest."

"What's the Cuban government want with a busted down marketing guy on the lam from the U.S.?"

"Not the government per se, just a powerful faction that's interested in changing American perceptions."

"What perceptions?"

"Perceptions about Cuba. Imagine us as a...commonwealth, enjoying all the fruits of an association with the United States, like

Puerto Rico." As she refilled their glasses the captain turned down the cabin lights and spoke through the intercom.

"Please strap yourselves in, we're taxiing."

"Hold on captain. We're not leaving just yet." Battista spoke into an intercom in her armrest.

"That's one hell of a campaign. You talking about an anti-revolution revolution? Your people want it?"

"We know what they don't want...what they have."

"Why didn't you ask me to do this the normal way? Make a call, set up a meeting, come to the office..."

"Seems like that's what I was trying to do Jack. I made the calls, set up meetings. You're the one that threw up curve balls like the police and the media and Lord knows who else might be after you. Creditors maybe?"

"This work, it'll cost you."

"More than your freedom? What do you think finding you and arranging to get you out of this country is costing us? Believe me Jack, I'd rather be handing you a retainer than a passport with a fake name. You gave us no choice. You're the man for this job."

Vance settled back into his chair, letting the business mission start to heal him. He was a shaper of opinions. A man whose career was devoted to just one thing: being paid to manipulate. He could never wash it out of his skin or run away from it. It could be for good or bad. It really didn't matter. His father was right. His next business card should bear two words: marketing whore. And as uncomfortable as he wanted the suit to feel, it still fit better than anything else on the rack.

Chloe Battista bent down and pulled an old brown holster out of her bag and placed it on the clean white table top between them. A Cuban National Police crest was tacked to its grimy oiled leather surface.

"I think you might have something that fits in this holster," she said.

Vance pulled his father's Soviet OTs-33 Pernach automatic pistol out of his bag and slid it into the holster.

"Like a hand in a glove." Battista turned the holster over. It was inscribed with the initials B.V.

"Keep it. They go together. Your father would have wanted it."

"You knew him?"

"Oh, many of us knew him, and you. We've got files on you from the hospital where you got that nasty inconvenient cochlear implant to the numbers of all those pre-ban burner phones you had. You were easy to track, all over the country and right down here."

"What was my father doing in Cuba?"

"Not drinking and whoring and messing around with illegal technology, like his son. Let's say this might be an opportunity to pick up where he left off, and learn something about your heritage along the way. A mission of atonement for you, I'd think. Now, are you strapping in or are we leaving you with your boat, Mr. Vance... Jack?"

Vance picked up the holstered gun and looked it over carefully before placing it back in his flight case. He extracted a stout padlock key and a storage receipt from the case and placed them on the table in front of Battista.

"On one condition...get me my car."

Jack Vance will return in
The Manipulator: Book Two

www.ingramcontent.com/pod-product-compliance
Lightning Source LLC
Chambersburg PA
CBHW070803180626
46818CB00001B/80